CONQUER THE DARK SERIES BOOK THREE

CARNAGE

T.L. PAYNE

A POST-APOCALYPTIC EMP SURVIVAL THRILLER

Carnage
Conquer the Dark Series, Book Three

Don't forget to sign up for my spam-free newsletter at www.tlpayne.com to be among the first to know of new releases, giveaways, and special offers.

Created with Vellum

Contents

Preface v

Prologue 1
1. Ayden Miller 11
2. Mia Christiansen 20
3. Ayden 25
4. Tyson Mueller 32
5. Ayden 40
6. Ayden 46
7. Ayden 52
8. Mueller 58
9. Ayden 63
10. Ayden 67
11. Ayden 76
12. Mia 81
13. Mueller 85
14. Ayden 89
15. Ayden 95
16. Mueller 102
17. Ayden 105
18. Ayden 113
19. Mueller 122
20. Ayden 131
21. Ayden 136
22. Ayden 144
23. Ayden 155
24. Ayden 162
25. Mueller 169
26. Ayden 173
27. Mia 179
28. Ayden 183
29. Ayden 190
30. Ayden 195
31. Ayden 200
32. Ayden 205

33. Mueller 209
34. Mia 217
35. Mueller 221
36. Ayden 226
37. Ayden 232
38. Mueller 237
39. Ayden 245
40. Mia 251
41. Mueller 255
42. Ayden 265
43. Ayden 271

Sample of Endure the Dark 283
Also by T L. Payne 301
Acknowledgments 305
About the Author 307

Preface

Real real towns, cities, and institutions are used in this novel. However, the author has taken occasional liberties for the story's sake, and versions within these pages are purely fictional.

Thank you in advance for understanding an author's creative license.

Prologue

Sagebrush Prairie Wind Farm
Fremont County, Wyoming
Day Five

A pine-scented breeze wafted in through the open door as security team leader Daniel Dixon stood in the shadowy interior of their makeshift command center, a repurposed construction company trailer at the edge of the wind farm that the team now used as their tactical operations center (TOC), as Sergeant First Class Shane Demiski assembled his special operations team.

Demiski's hulking figure was imposing, with broad shoulders that filled the narrow space. His rugged, weathered features spoke of countless missions and the scars on his face and hands of hard-won battles. His short-cropped hair was flecked with gray, hinting at the experience and wisdom that came with age.

"All right, team," Demiski began, his voice a steady, low rumble. "We've got a critical mission ahead of us. We're going to take control of the underground bunker. This is a high-stakes operation, and failure is not an option." Demiski's gaze scanned the room, his piercing blue eyes sharp and alert, missing nothing.

Dixon searched the faces of the team Demiski had gathered. They were an intense group, and each one appeared confident in their skills and duty. Dixon felt so unqualified for this mission. Dixon was just a security guard with a bit of tactical training. These guys were the real deal.

Demiski ran his hand over his chiseled jaw, framed by a few days' worth of stubble. "Winters, you'll be handling the breaching charges."

Paul Winters, the team's demolitions expert, nodded.

Dixon hoped he had some special explosive that could break a bomb-proof door because otherwise, this mission would fail right out of the gate.

"We need that door open but intact enough for us to get through quickly," Demiski said.

He pivoted toward Jennifer Ross, the intelligence analyst with a piercing gaze that seemed to read minds. "Ross, once we're inside, you're on point for gathering intel and extracting information." Quickly breaking eye contact with her, Demiski shifted his focus to Jay Knebel, one of the two muscle-bound weapons sergeants.

"Knebel and Osgood, you'll neutralize any immediate threats and secure the area."

Rodney Osgood was the second weapons sergeant. Dixon wouldn't want to be one of the ones to meet him in one of the bunker's dark corridors. He could break a man in half with just his massive biceps.

"Copy that," Osgood said.

Demiski gestured to Terrance Hoehn, the communication guy. "Hoehn will ensure we stay connected with our external support."

The geeky-looking guy appeared even more out of place on the team than Dixon, with his wire-rimmed glasses and skinny build. Hoehn was in charge of communications. From what Dixon had been told, he was requested by the FBI for the wind farm mission. Obviously, he had some special skill for them to ask the US Army to send him specifically. Dixon had asked about it but had been told that it was above his pay grade. Everything had been above his pay grade—until now.

"What about me?" Dixon said. "What's my role?"

"You stay behind me and don't do anything that might get yourself killed," Demiski said. He turned his back to Dixon and addressed the rest of the team. "Our first phase is reconnaissance. Even though we know the layout and security protocols, we need current intel. Four days have passed since the doors were sealed, and a lot could have changed since then."

"Especially if the Spetsnaz team was somehow able to alert their Russian counterparts inside," Ross said, tucking a stray strand of red hair behind her ear.

"We have to proceed as if they did," Hoehn said.

Everyone nodded.

"Okay, then. Let's move out," Demiski said.

By the time the team set out, the sky had darkened to deep indigo. The half-lit moon cast a silver sheen over the rugged terrain. The night air was cool and carried the earthy smell of the surrounding forest. Gravel crunched softly beneath Dixon's boots as he closely followed Demiski. They trailed Knebel and Osgood, approaching the perimeter of the bunker. The green glow of Dixon's night vision goggles cast eerie shadows on the tall chain-link fence surrounding the area.

The team stopped behind, and Knebel and Osgood moved closer, using thermal imaging binoculars to scan the area for any changes in guard rotations, new security measures, or unusual activity.

Osgood's voice came through Dixon's earpiece in a whisper.

"Looks like they've reinforced the patrols. There are more guards than last time, and they seem more alert."

"Try to get closer and see if they've added any new surveillance systems," Demiski said into his mic.

Meanwhile, Osgood and Knebel approached the bunker's back side to check the ventilation and emergency exit shafts they had marked earlier.

"The cover is still in place," Osgood whispered into his radio. "But it looks like they've added some kind of sensor."

Demiski keyed his mic. "We'll need to disable this without triggering an alarm. Mark it and keep moving."

Using a small drone, Ross flew it over the bunker to get a top-down view of the area, focused on the main entry points. The drone's camera transmitted live footage to a tablet Ross held.

"They've fortified the entrance." Ross pointed at the screen. "There seem to be more guards and new sandbags and barricades just outside the door.

Winters examined the feed, the blue glow of the tablet screen reflecting on his face. "We can still breach it, but we'll need a distraction to draw the guards away so I can place the charges."

Demiski nodded, laying out the next steps. "Good work, everyone. Pull back and meet us at the TOC."

Dixon followed Demiski back to the tactical operations center, where the leader laid out the plan to take control of the bunker. "Here's the plan: we'll synchronize our entry through the main entrance and the emergency exit shaft. Dixon and I will create a diversion and then blind the cameras while Winters sets the charges on the main door. Osgood and Knebel, you'll disable the sensor on the emergency exit and proceed down the shaft. Ross and Hoehn, you'll handle communications and intel extraction once we're in." He looked around at his team. "We move in one hour. Gear up and be ready. This is our shot to take control of the bunker and get the information we need. Let's make it count."

The team dispersed to prepare. Each member focused on their

task. Dixon took a moment to steady himself, knowing that the next few hours could determine the success of their mission and the safety of countless lives. The fate of the bunker, and potentially the country, hung in the balance.

The hour had passed swiftly, and the twilight had deepened into the full darkness of night. The team gathered at their designated positions.

As they set out for the bunker, Dixon and Demiski took point, crouching behind a cluster of rocks, waiting for the guards who patrolled the perimeter to approach. Dixon waited next to Demiski, hunkered down in their hiding spots, heart pounding in sync with the rhythmic crunch of gravel under the guards' boots. Days before, he'd eaten lunch with them, speaking of their families and concerns about the fate of the nation. Now, he found himself on the opposite side, ready to eliminate them in order to gain access to the bunker and those inside who might have answers to Demiski and his teams' questions about what the enemy was up to in hopes of stopping them.

Dixon held his breath as the guards approached. When they reached the rock outcropping, he and Demiski sprang into action, striking swiftly and silently. The faint thud of bodies hitting the ground was the only sound as Demiski neutralized the threat with practiced precision. Dixon's hand-to-hand combat training paid off as he dispatched his target, ensuring the guard was unconscious before he hit the ground.

With the guards out of the way, the path to the main entrance was clear. Ahead, the main entrance was illuminated by a single floodlight, and Dixon could see the faint red glow of surveillance cameras sweeping the area.

Demiski removed his flashlight from his tactical belt and pointed it at the surveillance cameras to blind them temporarily.

"This should give us enough time for Winters to move in without being seen," he whispered.

Demiski signaled to Winters, who approached with the charges. "Let's get that door open," Demiski said.

Winters placed the charges with meticulous care, ensuring they were positioned to breach the door without causing a cave-in. His whispered voice came through Dixon's earpiece. "Charges set."

Demiski glanced at his watch, counting down the final seconds. "Three… two… one…"

A muted thud followed by a controlled explosion shattered the stillness of the night. The door blew inward, creating a ragged opening just large enough for the team to slip through. Dust and debris hung in the air and the acrid smell of explosives mingled with the cool night breeze.

"Move, move, move!" Demiski ordered, gesturing for Ross and Hoehn to follow him inside.

Dixon followed close on their heels.

As they entered, the narrow corridor was immediately filled with the sounds of alarms blaring and red emergency lights flashing. The interior was stark, metallic, and clinical—a labyrinth of hallways designed to disorient any intruder. The scent from the explosion lingered, mixing with the sterile smell of the bunker.

"Eyes open. Watch your sectors," Demiski commanded, sweeping his weapon from side to side.

Suddenly, a door burst open ahead of them, and a group of armed guards, clearly alerted by the breach, poured into the corridor. Gunfire erupted, echoing off the metal walls and the air with the thick black cloud from a smoke grenade.

"Contact front!" Demiski shouted, ducking into an open doorway and returning fire with precise, controlled bursts.

An instant later, Osgood radioed that they were inside, having used the emergency exit they had identified earlier. "Two guards down!" came through Dixon's earpiece.

With the way cleared, Dixon, Demiski, and the others began to advance.

"Go, go, go!" Demiski said, chopping the air with his hand, pushing forward while Winters and Dixon suppressed the remaining guards.

Osgood and Knebel suddenly appeared at the end of the corridor, advancing quickly. "This way is clear," Knebel said, gesturing sharply back the way they'd come.

With the immediate threat neutralized, the team pressed deeper into the bunker. They encountered sporadic resistance, each engagement brief but intense. Osgood took point, checking corners and ensuring their path remained clear.

"We need to find Ferrick," Demiski reminded them, his voice tense. "He's our best shot at getting the intel on Gadwell and his folks."

As they approached Ferrick's office, another group of guards ambushed them from a side corridor. Bullets ricocheted off the walls, forcing the team to dive down a side corridor for cover.

"Covering fire!" Knebel yelled, squeezing off shots and taking down a guard. The firefight was fierce, but the team's superior training and tactics quickly overwhelmed the defenders as they pushed deeper down the hallway.

Breaching the door to Ferrick's office, they found him huddled behind his desk, his eyes wide with fear. The office was filled with the scent of expensive leather and cigar smoke. Knebel and Dixon secured Ferrick while moving in Ross to interrogate him.

"Where's Gadwell?" Ross demanded, her voice cold.

"I don't know!" Ferrick stammered, sweat pouring down his face. "He… He's in his quarters."

"Where?" Ross asked, pressing her weapon to his temple.

Demiski slapped a schematic of the bunker down on Ferrick's desk.

"Where is he?" Ross asked.

Before Ferrick could answer, a loud crash echoed down the

hall. "That's the secondary security team," Osgood warned. "We need to move now."

Following Ferrick's reluctant directions, the team made their way to Gadwell's quarters. They found the door locked and fortified, but Winters quickly set another charge, blowing it open.

Inside, they found Gadwell standing defiantly. As they rushed him, he smirked and popped a cyanide pill into his mouth, collapsing instantly.

"Damn it!" Demiski cursed. "Secure the room and search for any intel. We can't leave empty-handed."

In a nearby room, they found the remaining Chinese operative cowering and injured. Knebel and Osgood dragged him to a chair, and Ross began the interrogation.

"Talk," Ross commanded. "What's the plan for this bunker?"

Hours passed as the two special forces soldiers took turns using their skills in persuasion to brutally convince the operative to give up what he knew about China and Russia's plans in the United States.

When the operative finally spoke, he didn't have all that much information to offer. "The bunker… is a control center. Russia and China plan to use it to establish dominance over the Western US. They need the resources—food, energy, and communication hubs. The EMPs were just the first phase."

"What is the second phase?"

"The command team's survival of the initial ground invasion. We anticipate heavy resistance from your remaining military forces and civilians. We are prepared for heavy casualties—maybe up to fifty percent of our forces. It is predicted that due to the lack of communication, coordination of meaningful resistance will be hindered. In the coming weeks, the US population will be weakened from starvation, disease, and violence enough that our offers of resources will be welcomed, and the remaining population will become easily subdued and controlled using food and security."

"Why? Why not just kill everyone if you're here for the resources?"

"We need workers. If we are able to keep twenty percent of your citizens alive, we have all the workforce we need."

"What's the purpose of the bunker?" Ross asked.

"The bunker was to insulate our command and control center from air or nuclear attacks from US or allied forces. It was supposed to be impenetrable. We were guaranteed of that."

"That would be our fault," a short, stocky woman said, entering the room. "We sabotaged as much of the infrastructure as possible, did the inspections, and submitted false reports."

"And you are?" Ross asked.

"FBI Special Agent Mary Sheldon," she said, glaring down at the Chinese operative.

Dixon absorbed the information, the weight of the revelation sinking in.

"The feds knew and did nothing to stop this?" Dixon said.

"My team and I did everything we could with the information we had."

Dixon shook his head.

"What? Should we have lobbed a nuke at China and Russia without fully knowing what they were doing here?"

"Stop!" Demiski said. "This doesn't help us now." He turned to Ross. "We need to get this intel to our military."

"I need comms," Ross said. "Just get me comms, and I will know who to contact."

"Hoehn, we need those comms. What's it going to take to get them up and running?"

"You'll first need to get to the towers before the Spetsnaz seize control of them," Agent Sheldon said.

ONE

Ayden Miller

St. Peter's Roman Catholic Church
Harpers Ferry, West Virginia
Day Five

An hour after Joyce McMillen's tearful reunion with her grandson in Harpers Ferry, West Virginia, Ayden Miller navigated her behemoth motorhome, heading north toward Pennsylvania along a narrow, tree-lined road that paralleled the Potomac River canal path. In the passenger seat, a road atlas lay across the lap of Joyce's nineteen-year-old grandson, Dominic. He was still wearing his sweat-stained bro tank shirt and dirty shorts. His dark brown hair was pulled back into a man bun.

"Sharpsburg looks to be about ten miles from here," he said. "We'll cross the Maryland state line into Pennsylvania at Hagerstown in like…"

There was a long pause as Dominic calculated the distance.

While Ayden waited, his ears picked up on the conversation in the back of the motorhome between Clara, Joyce, and the Appalachian Trail thru-hikers: the two young females, Tina

Turner and Laney Mueller; and the kid they all called Lunch Box—a man in his late twenties with shoulder-length, bushy, untamed hair, and a goatee. Ayden couldn't recall the young man's real name. The young adults all still referred to one another by their trail names.

"How did your father even know to build a survival compound?" Clara asked Laney. "Did he have some kind of inside knowledge?"

Ayden recalled their conversation with Clara's neighbor the day the lights went out. The guy told them his uncle had received a call from a former intelligence officer to get out of the city. He'd mentioned something about "apocalypse insurance."

"I don't know. He's just been into that sort of thing all my life." Laney chuckled. "I remember going camping with people who thought like him when I was a little girl. In my world, everyone played army when they camped."

"Was he in the military?" Clara asked.

"No. He wanted to join, I think. He injured his back playing college football, but that didn't stop him from taking all sorts of tactical training courses. He traveled all over the United States to learn how to defend the compound he was building."

Dominic glanced over at Ayden and raised an eyebrow. "I feel better knowing someone with training is there after hearing what happened to you all on the way to Harpers Ferry."

Ayden stiffened at the memory. They'd barely survived the air assault on the convoy they'd been forced to join by the US military. Supposedly, the armed forces had been evacuating people away from the fighting but failed to reveal that embedded within the convoy of refugees was the presidential motorcade—a primary enemy target.

"Anyway," Dominic continued, "we'll be crossing into Pennsylvania in about twenty-five minutes and reaching our first stop at Greencastle in forty minutes."

"Plenty of time before dark," Ayden said, smiling. "I really hate maneuvering this beast at night. There's just too much debris on the roadways to navigate efficiently."

Dominic nodded. "And the last thing we need is to have to change a tire on this old machine." He sighed heavily. "The last time I camped with Grandpa and Granny, we had to change one in the pouring rain outside Virginia Beach. It sucked."

"I bet."

The mention of Virginia Beach brought back a memory of something he'd overheard the soldiers at Frederick, Maryland, talking about. At the time, Ayden had been focused on trying to come to terms with the idea of enemy forces on American soil. It had been such an inconceivable concept to him. Even after the EMP attack that had left the country crippled and in the dark, Ayden hadn't thought the foreign actors who'd instigated the attack would or could physically inflict more damage on the US. It was still hard to wrap his head around, but he'd seen it firsthand less than twenty-five miles from their current location.

As they continued north, he imagined China's People's Liberation Army would avoid the Appalachian Mountains and choose major routes across Tennessee or Pennsylvania, perhaps the very same route he'd intended to take across the country to Wyoming and…

Ayden couldn't help but think of his girlfriend, Mia, and her boys. Reaching western Wyoming, where Mia lived, seemed all but impossible in the face of the current circumstances. The enemy, with their planes and drones, made the highways dangerous options for travel, and soon, the weather would render even the back roads impassable with snow. They lacked clothing for travel on foot, and with Clara's leg injury, inflicted in their gun battle back in Harlem, walking to Wyoming was out of the question.

Slowing, Ayden steered the motorhome into a sharp turn. Lunch Box gestured to a sign on their left. "Camp Evergreen up ahead."

Ayden thought nothing of it until they climbed the next hill and rounded the bend. Ahead, there was a pileup of vehicles, tires, and debris blocking both lanes of the road. "Roadblock!" he yelled, stomping on the brakes. Immediately, he put the motorhome into Reverse and checked his side mirror for a place to turn around.

"Get down! He's got a gun!" Dominic shouted.

Ayden did his best to keep the old beast between the ditches as he accelerated backward. Suddenly, two men stepped out of the trees behind them, rifles directed at the motorhome, and Ayden stomped on the brakes.

"Everyone out!" one of the two men shouted. "Get out of the vehicle."

"Ayden!" Clara cried. "What do we do?"

"We have to comply," Joyce said. "We don't have guns to fight back."

Clara winced as she pushed herself up into a seated position. "But they'll take the motorhome!"

"Nothing we can do about it," Joyce said, moving to the back door.

Ayden twisted in his seat, ready to move to assist Clara, when his door was suddenly yanked open.

"Driver! Out of the vehicle!" the man at the door shouted.

Ayden's gaze shifted to him as the man backed away, his rifle trained on Ayden's chest.

"We're complying, but my sister is injured. I need to—"

"You need to shut up and get out down on the ground before I shoot your ass," the man spat.

"Language, Mark! Watch the language," a woman's voice chastised.

"Get your *butt* on the ground," Mark said, overemphasizing the word.

Ayden threw his hands in the air. "Okay! Okay! I'm getting out."

Dominic's door opened, and he was pulled from the passenger seat. "Granny!"

"I'm okay, Nicky," Joyce called out.

Ayden could hear Laney arguing fiercely with a woman at the back of the motorhome. "You put one finger on me, and you better be prepared to pull that trigger 'cause I'm going to rip your guts out and stuff them down your throat!" Laney spat.

"Whoa there, little girl," Mark said.

"Little girl? Why don't you put that rifle down, big man, and I'll show you a little girl," she was saying as Ayden was thrown to the ground.

"Laney, chill the hell—" Lunch Box said. He let out a grunt as if the wind had been knocked out of him.

As Mark searched Ayden for weapons, Laney continued to antagonize their captors.

"Shut the hell up and get on the ground!" the woman demanded.

She sounded older, maybe in her forties or fifties.

"Make me!" Laney gritted.

"Sammie, put her butt on the ground," the woman ordered.

Ayden heard the shuffling of feet and then the obvious sound of a punch. The man grunted and then fell backward, landing face up with his head within Ayden's view. He was holding his throat and gasping for air.

"Anyone else want to try that?" Laney asked.

"How about I just shoot you in the face?" the woman spat.

"Laney!" Joyce cried out. "Laney, dear. Please just do as they ask—for the rest of us."

"For us, Laney," her companion Tina pleaded.

There was a long pause.

"Fine," Laney growled.

A second later, boots slapped the pavement at the rear of the motorhome. Casting a surreptitious look beneath the vehicle, Ayden could see two sets of boots. The smaller of the boots moved toward the back.

"You enjoyed that, didn't you?" Laney asked as the woman stepped back.

Mark finished frisking Ayden and then grabbed him by the arm. "Get up and move to the back."

Gravel dug into Ayden's left knee as he was forced to stand. Mark gave him a shove, and Ayden limped around the back bumper past Sammie, who Laney had struck in the throat. He was red-faced and still struggling for breath on the ground.

Joyce, Tina, and Laney were prone on the pavement on the other side of the motorhome. Clara was still inside the vehicle, bracing herself against the doorjamb. Their eyes met. A slight smile played on her lips.

"What do you want?" Joyce asked.

"We wanna know what you're doing out here and what you have inside that RV," the woman snapped.

Laney lifted her head from the pavement and glared up at the woman. "None of your business!"

"We're making it our business!"

"Back off, Kim," Sammie rasped, pushing himself up on his elbow. You're not helping."

"Why the need for such rough treatment?" Joyce asked.

"We don't get much traffic out here. Never have," Mark said, forcing Ayden back onto the ground next to Laney and Tina. "And with everything going on, strangers just kind of make us nervous. We'll check out your motorhome and if everything's okay, we'll send you on your way."

"We don't have anything to steal," Joyce said.

"We're not thieves," Kim said, grabbing Clara's hand and assisting her from the motorhome. She gestured to the ground and Clara slowly dropped to her knees.

"What are you looking for?" Clara asked as she lowered herself to the ground.

"We just want to make sure you're not transporting PLA soldiers or aid for the enemy."

Joyce rolled onto her side and stared up at the man, wide-eyed. "What? PLA soldiers?"

Mark climbed into the motorhome.

"How do you know about the Chinese army?" Ayden asked, afraid to hear the answer. The US military convoy they'd encountered at Gettysburg was heading west in a hurry. There could be fighting in the area with more drone attacks like they'd encountered against the refugee convoy.

"Radio," Kim said.

Mark emerged from the RV. "It's clear," he said, exiting.

"What did you hear?" Laney asked, sitting up. "Is there fighting in Pennsylvania?"

Ayden rolled onto his side as he waited for the group's reply.

"It's bad," Kim said. "That's what we heard."

"So our military has been crippled in their response?" Ayden asked.

"Down but not out," Sammie said. He reached a hand out to help Ayden to his feet.

"Thanks," Ayden said, helping his sister stand. He moved her back and lowered her down to sit on the motorhome's back step while Dominic moved around to the back to help Joyce.

Tina ran over and threw her arms around Laney. "I want to go home!"

"Me too," Lunch Box said, brushing sand and gravel from the front of his shirt as he stood.

Laney swept a loose strand of hair from Tina's round, pale face. "Once we get to my place, my dad can figure out how to get you home."

"What if the Chinese are there already?" Tina asked.

"Where is home?" the taller man asked.

Tina wiped tears from her cheeks and glanced up at him. "Indianapolis."

"I haven't heard anything about Indy, but there are rumors that the PLA is really pushing to beat the Russians to the Midwest."

"The Russians?" Ayden's voice pitched. "The Russians are involved too?"

"They hit the West Coast hard. You got Fort Erwin and Camp Pendleton, along with several Naval and Air Force bases in California alone. Washington, Oregon, and California are all huge military targets. The fighting out there is fierce. I'd hate to be anywhere near those bases."

Ayden's mind raced with thoughts of Mia and the boys. Their ranch in Wyoming was less than one thousand miles from Los Angeles.

"I'd hate to be anywhere in those states. Life without electricity and running water is one thing, but having your only shelter blown up around you would make survival impossible," Joyce said.

"Have you heard anything about DC?" Ayden asked, wanting to know if what he feared was true—the motorcade had indeed been carrying the President of the United States.

"Gone—mostly," Mark said.

Kim wore a pained expression. "Nuked is what we heard."

Joyce clung to her grandson. "Oh my God!"

"But we heard that the president got out before the bomb dropped," Kim said.

Ayden glanced over at Clara. She shook her head as a tear slid down her cheek.

"That had to be him," she said, wiping it away with the back of her hand.

Joyce wiped away tears. "He's gone," she said, her voice cracking.

"Who's gone?" Tina asked.

"The president," Joyce said. "We saw his car blow up. It was a drone attack. We were in a convoy of refugees heading to a military safe-zone. The military put the presidential motorcade in the middle of it."

"Yeah," Ayden said. "It wasn't hidden very well. Those black vehicles stood out like a sore thumb even without a presidential seal or flags."

"That would have likely been from a Chinese drone," the tall man said. "Remember the news talking about all those Chinese nationals pouring over our border with Mexico? Well, that enabled China to take a move out of Russia's playbook and infiltrate as a spearhead of a military force, its political operatives, and special forces. When the Chinese Communist Party started its attack against Taiwan and the United States, the Chinese sleeper agents and these special forces guys mobilized to prepare for an eventual ground invasion."

TWO

Mia Christiansen

Christiansen Ranch
Farson, Wyoming
Day 5

Mia Christiansen wrapped her arms around her three sons as they sat on the worn leather sofa in the cozy living room of their family's ranch in Farson, Wyoming. Her body still ached from the ordeal with Kane, her father's former ranch hand, a nightmare that had ended with her narrowly escaping and ultimately killing her captor. She had miraculously made it back to her boys, but her mind remained on Iron Mountain, preoccupied with thoughts of the Russian military landing there.

As the sun set over the ranch, Mia and her family convened around the sturdy wooden kitchen table. The room, usually filled with the comforting sounds of soft jazz music and cheerful chatter, was now heavy with the weight of uncertainty and the looming threat of foreign forces.

"We need to know what we're up against," Neil Christiansen

said, his voice steady but laced with concern. "Information is our first line of defense."

"Dirk," Melody interjected, turning to the ranch manager, "doesn't old Mr. Simmons down the road have a ham radio setup?"

Dirk nodded. "He sure does. If anyone can get us in touch with the outside world and find out what's really happening, it's him."

"Then that's our first step," Neil decided. "Dirk, you and I will head over to Simmons's place. See if we can get any intel on the situation."

As Dirk made preparations to leave, Mia felt a surge of panic, dreading the news he might bring back.

"What could the Russians possibly want in Lander, Wyoming?" Melody asked, voicing the question that had been gnawing at all of them.

"Limestone Mountain," Neil said thoughtfully. "The radio towers and the communication hub up there. If they control the towers, they control a critical line of communication across the region."

Sliding on his cowboy hat, Dirk headed toward the door. "And if they can cut us off, they can operate without interference. We need to protect those towers."

Neil left to inform the wranglers down at the bunkhouse that they needed to be on high alert while Mia and Melody began organizing supplies. They gathered canned food, water, medical supplies, and warm clothing, in preparation for any scenario. Mia's heart ached at the thought of uprooting her children again, but she steeled herself. Their safety was paramount.

"Mom, what can we do to help?" Carter asked, his young face a mask of worry.

"Sweetheart, I need you to pack a bag with your essentials," Mia said softly. "Just in case we have to leave in a hurry. And make sure your brothers do the same."

"Yes, Mom," Carter replied, taking on the role of leader among his siblings.

While the boys packed, Mia and Melody checked the locks on all the doors and windows, ensuring the cabin was as secure as possible. They also took stock of their ammunition and firearms, then prepared a bag for the extra weapons and ammo.

As dusk fell, Dirk returned with news. "Mr. Simmons got through to someone," he said, his expression serious. "US forces are aware of the Russian presence, but it's going to take time to mobilize a response in this remote area."

"What did they say about our immediate safety?" Mia asked, her heart pounding.

"They advised us to stay put and keep a low profile," Dirk said. "But they also warned us to stay vigilant."

Mia's stomach churned. "We need to be ready for anything. We can't just sit and wait for help."

Later, as the family gathered in the dimly lit living room, they devised a plan. They would take turns keeping watch, maintaining a constant lookout for any signs of movement around the ranch. They also mapped out potential escape routes—one heading west into the mountains, seventy miles away, and another north to Pinedale, where they could find a hideout if the situation became dire.

"We'll need all our warm ski clothing," Neil said. "And the teepees."

"And the chow wagon, if we can," Melody added.

Mia thought about survival in the mountains during winter. Although it would be safer from the Russians than the flat area of their ranch, it would be very difficult to survive long in the harsh conditions.

"And leave behind all our cattle?"

"We don't have a choice if we're overrun," Neil said.

The gravity of their situation settled over them like the heavy Wyoming snow. As Mia looked into the eyes of her sons, she knew they had to be prepared for whatever came next. There were still at least three hours of daylight left. Mia sat on the sofa, holding her three sons close, their presence a comfort amidst the chaos. She yawned widely.

"You should go to bed and get some rest, Mia," her mother, Melody, suggested gently. "You've been through so much."

Mia shook her head. "I want to be close to everyone."

"Okay, then lie down there on the sofa and rest at least." Melody brought her a blanket and draped it over her shoulders. The boys gathered around the coffee table, engrossed in drawing and reading books. The familiar scene offered an echo of normalcy that somehow only reminded her of the chaos of the last few days. Mia tousled Xavy's hair. "What are you drawing?"

"Ayden."

"What's he sitting on?" Luke asked.

"A rocket."

Luke laughed. "Why?"

"So he can fly home to us and kill all the bad guys."

Mia's heart broke. How would she explain to him that Ayden wouldn't be coming back to them? It was too much to hope for that he could make it over two thousand miles without transportation—and amid the threat of war.

Leaning back on the sofa, Mia tried to rest, but her sleep was fitful and filled with haunting dreams of Kane and the looming threat of the Russians. The images played out in her mind like a relentless nightmare and prevented her from finding any real peace. After what felt like an eternity of tossing and turning, Mia decided she needed fresh air. She quietly slipped off the sofa and stepped outside onto the front porch. The evening air was cool and refreshing, a stark contrast to the stifling worry inside the house.

One of the wranglers, sitting on the porch with a pair of binoculars, was scanning the driveway. He looked up as she approached.

"What are you doing?" Mia asked, her voice barely above a whisper.

The wrangler lowered the binoculars and nodded toward the

distant horizon. "Just keeping watch. Making sure there's no unexpected company heading our way."

Mia nodded, appreciating his vigilance. "Thank you," she said, her voice filled with gratitude. Knowing that someone was keeping a vigilant eye out brought a small measure of comfort. The two stood in silence for a moment, the wrangler resuming his watch while Mia took a deep breath and tried to steel herself for all the days ahead.

THREE

Ayden

Camp Evergreen
Knoxville, Maryland
Day Five

A hard knot formed in Ayden's gut as he listened to Mark talking about the possibility of foreign fighters on American soil. He hoped the man was just some conspiracy nut. But after seeing the drone attack himself, he had to believe that some parts of what the man was saying could be true.

"These special forces have linked up with Chinese Communist Party (CCP) agents already in place. We're talking up to between five and ten thousand CCP agents who have been here for years gathering intelligence and preparing for this."

Joyce placed a wrinkled hand over her throat. "How did this happen?"

The guy shrugged. "We were warned. Even an idiot could see the writing on the wall. From the moment China was allowed to obtain space dominance, we were doomed. They no doubt used their direct-ascent anti-satellite missiles and directed-energy systems and destroyed our military access to defense satellites."

"But you don't know that for sure, right?" Clara asked, squeezing Ayden's hand.

She was trembling. Ayden placed his arm around her shoulder as he tried to wrap his mind around what the man was saying. Of course, it all made sense. Obviously, someone had been successful in launching an EMP attack. The loss of modern technology was all the evidence one needed to prove that fact. He'd seen the presidential motorcade blown up with his own eyes. Although he had no direct confirmation that China had been the one responsible, they were on the list of enemies of the United States with the capability to carry out these attacks.

"They're using the MARS programs," Mark said.

Kim cleared her throat. "You can't say anything. Remember? You signed a non-disclosure agreement with the feds."

"I know that, but that was before..." He waved his hand in the air. "Besides, who are they gonna tell?"

"What's the MARS program?" Clara asked. "Do we have something on Mars?"

Mark scoffed. "No. The MARS program is the Military Auxiliary Radio System."

Laney rushed toward the man. "You've got a ham?" She placed her hands on her hips and glared at him. "Do! You! Have a radio?" she asked slowly, emphasizing her words as if he were hard of hearing.

"I think you need to calm down, missy," Sammie said.

Laney held her palm out to him but kept her focus on the taller man. "My dad has a radio. I'm supposed to check in with him at a location in Greencastle, Pennsylvania, to let him know I'm all right and headed home."

"Where is home?" Mark asked.

"Washington County, Pennsylvania."

"You have a radio?" Ayden asked the man, wanting clarification on his knowledge of military activity in the area. If this group could help them avoid inadvertently running into either side of the fight again, he wanted to know that.

"Washington County, Pennsylvania," Mark repeated, ignoring Ayden's question. He chewed his bottom lip a moment before answering Laney. He turned to the shorter man. "You heard any traffic out of there?"

Sammie shook his head. "I know a guy up that way. Steve Jackson, I think, is his name. Nice guy. We met at a regional communication skills exercise."

"Steve! Yes! He's a member of my father's group."

"Ham operator's group?" Mark asked.

"His prepper compound group," Lunch Box said. "Right, Laney?"

She shot him a dirty look and nodded. "Yes, he's worked with my dad to build out a ham radio setup at my family's property."

Ayden cleared his throat and moved toward Mark. "Are you in communication with members of our military?" he asked directly.

Mark stared at him for a moment. "That's classified."

Ayden worked his jaw. "Tell me this: Is our military still able to communicate?"

"Yes, but not by satellite. They're communicating through a group of volunteer amateur radio operators using the Military Auxiliary Radio System (MARS) program. There are military station operators at places such as the Pentagon, Fort Huachuca, Andrews Air Force Base, Nellis Air Force Base, and various Navy and Coast Guard locations. Even military aircraft are still equipped with HF radios, and many military aircrews have used MARS phone patches to communicate with the ground commanders."

"Okay," Ayden said, taking another step closer. "Now tell me this: Would it be safe for us to continue north to Greencastle, Pennsylvania?"

Mark responded immediately. "No!"

Ayden rapidly blinked as if he'd been slapped across the face. "Would it be safer for us to head back to Harpers Ferry, cross the Potomac, and travel north on the West Virginia side?"

Mark appeared to think it over before glancing over at Sammie. They both just shrugged.

"You're gonna want to go south," Sammie said. "Not north."

Mark waved a dismissive hand. "Not too far south."

Kim frowned and shook her head. "I'd stay put if I were you."

"That's not an option." Laney flicked her gaze to Dominic and then to Joyce.

Mark gestured west. "You could head back to Harpers Ferry, head southwest to Winchester down in Virginia, and then—"

"That's the opposite direction we need to go," Laney said, interrupting him.

Mark lifted a hand in a stop gesture. "Then you hop on Highway 522 and take that up to Hancock near the West Virginia–Pennsylvania state lines."

"I'd head farther west toward Hancock." Kim furrowed her brow. "Remember?"

"Yeah, but they haven't had time to—"

"But if these folks encounter trouble and get delayed somehow."

Ayden was getting frustrated with them talking all around the issue. "Why can't we cross the border at Hagerstown?"

"Too hot. Lots of activity around there," Kim said.

"Mostly ours right now, though," Sammie said. He tilted his head. "There's a chance they could get through before—"

Mark threw his hands up. "And a chance they get trapped."

"So is there a chance we could still cross at Hagerstown, which is only about an hour away?" Laney asked.

Mark shrugged. "Could, but I wouldn't risk it."

Laney pivoted toward Ayden with a questioning look.

Ayden was torn. He'd spent most of his life taking significant risks and pushing the envelope of safety, but it wasn't just his life on the line now. It was Clara's and the others'. Yes, he was desperate to return to Mia and the boys, but was he willing to risk getting these people trapped in the midst of a war zone? "It's a huge gamble."

"There are also other dangers if we add miles to our trip." Laney nodded toward her companions. "Next time we're stopped, we might cop a bullet and lose the motorhome."

"I think we should stop talking about it and get the heck to Hagerstown before whatever these folks think is going to happen —happens," Dominic said. "What do you think, Granny?"

Joyce raised a trembling hand to her mouth and began to chew on her thumbnail. She stared into her grandson's eyes. "I've already lost your grandfather. I couldn't bear to lose you too."

Dominic took her hands in his. "The sooner we get to Laney's dad, the less likely it will become, Gran." He reached up and wiped a tear from her cheek. "It's your motorhome. You have the final say."

Joyce threw her hands up. "I can't! I can't take that kind of responsibility! What if I choose wrong?"

Tina crossed her arms over her chest. "How about we vote?"

Kim, Mark, and Sammie stepped aside as Ayden and his group gathered outside the motorhome. As he glanced around their tight circle, the tension was palpable. They faced a critical decision: proceed north toward Hagerstown or backtrack to Harpers Ferry and seek an alternative route. Joyce, the elder of the group, her voice steady despite the worry etched on her face, outlined the options.

"If we go north, we're taking a direct path but risking running into military conflicts or worse," she said, her hands trembling slightly. "Going back could mean a longer, possibly safer route through less contested areas."

Dominic leaned against the motorhome, his brow furrowed in thought. "There's no guarantee either way. We might dodge one problem just to run into another."

"Backtracking could cost us time we don't have." Laney's voice was strained, and creases furrowed her brow. "We need to get ahead of any enemy forces. We don't have the resources to get caught behind enemy lines."

Ayden's heart skipped a beat at the image. He knew very well what the enemy could do. He had to agree. Their only hope was to reach Laney's compound and hunker down. "Both options have risks, but moving forward keeps us on target to reach Washington County sooner. That aligns with our mission to get Laney to her family—who might offer us sanctuary."

"I disagree," Clara said, rubbing her chin. "We should play it safe and find another way into Pennsylvania—one that doesn't put us in contact with the PLA."

Tina, usually quiet, spoke up. "I'm scared of running into a war zone, but I'm also scared of running out of food and water if we take too long. I vote we go north. You told us it was less than an hour. We could be at Laney's in—"

"Three hours," Laney said.

The decision seemed to hang in the balance, each person silently weighing their fate. Finally, Joyce looked at each face, her indecision reflected in her tone. "Let's put it to a vote. All in favor of going north, raise your hand."

One by one, hands went up, even Clara's. The vote was unanimous.

As they prepared to leave, Laney approached the group from Camp Evergreen about using their radio. The atmosphere was tense; mistrust hung heavily in the air.

"About your radio," Laney began. "Could I use it…" She paused and smiled. "To talk to—"

"No way!" Kim said, cutting her off. "No one goes into our camp."

"I'm not a threat. I'm just a kid wanting to—"

"You're no kid, and I don't give a crap what you want. My job is to keep my group safe. So NO!"

Mark stepped forward. “I’ll send out a message for you. What should I tell him?”

Laney turned her back to Kim and replied to his offer with a half-smile. “I need to get a message out to the Mad Hatter in Pennsylvania. Give him your location and tell him Cobra is with a group, and we’re on our way to Disneyland.”

He raised an eyebrow, perplexed. “Disneyland?”

“He’ll understand,” she said.

Mad Hatter?

Cobra?

Disneyland?

Were they in some kind of spy novel?

Ayden assisted Clara back into the motorhome, and the others followed as Ayden started the engine. Pulling away from Camp Evergreen, his stomach twisted with apprehension. The decision had been made, but the danger was far from over. As they set off toward Hagerstown, every turn of the road could bring new dangers, and Ayden couldn’t shake the feeling that their troubles were just beginning.

“Disneyland?” Ayden called over his shoulder to Laney.

“The guy at Greencastle’s last name is Disney.”

“Oh, I see! Clever!”

FOUR

Tyson Mueller

New Eden Compound
Somerset Township
Washington County, Pennsylvania
Day Five

The eight members of New Eden's governing council gathered in what used to be a storage barn on the century-old Mueller family farm, which was now surrounded by a four-foot-wide HESCO-styled wall. The meeting room was the nerve center of their fledgling community, its walls lined with repurposed shelves holding maps, documents, and books to help them govern and survive—among them, the Constitution of the United States.

Tyson Mueller stood at the head of the makeshift table, a large wooden slab balanced on crates, surrounded by the New Eden council members seated on an assortment of chairs and benches. The air was heavy with the scent of gun oil and sweat. The room was illuminated only by the faint light seeping through the small, reinforced windows.

Mueller ran a hand through his graying hair, his eyes scanning the room. Each member of the council had their own story, their own reason for being there. Jake, a former police officer, sat to his left, his face stern. He and his wife had been friends with Mueller and his family for over a decade before they each began preparing for worst-case scenarios.

Next to Jack was Linda, a registered nurse, and her expression was one of concern. She was recently divorced and had two small boys. Jack had recruited her before the lights went out.

Frank, a military veteran, sat across from Mueller, his posture rigid. They'd met at a survival training session. Frank had been a weapons instructor.

Mueller's wife, Monica, was beside him, her eyes red-rimmed with dark circles beneath them. She'd barely slept since the EMP attack—filled with worry for their eighteen-year-old daughter, Laney, who had been away hiking the Appalachian Trail when the event happened. Mueller reached out to take her hand, but she pulled away, still angry that he had not yet mounted a rescue mission to find Laney. She opened her copy of *Robert's Rules of Order*.

As the murmur of conversation died down, Mueller cleared his throat. "All right, everyone. Let's call the meeting to order."

Those present turned to face him.

"We're five days in. Most everyone who should be here has arrived. We have some reports coming in about the conditions in the surrounding communities and up at Pittsburgh."

Steve, the emergency communications director for Washington County, had brought the county's communications trailer with him to the compound to establish their ham radio communications. To the right of Steve sat Peggy, an agricultural scientist who had spent years researching sustainable farming practices. Her knowledge was crucial for the group's long-term survival as she was responsible for setting up and maintaining their food production systems. Next to Peggy was David, a civil engineer with experience in infrastructure and construction. His expertise was invaluable for fortifying the compound and planning future expansions.

At the end of the table, completing the council, was Mariah, a former schoolteacher and community organizer. Her skills in education and her ability to bring people together were essential for maintaining morale and ensuring that knowledge and skills were passed on to the next generation.

"Jake, why don't you fill us in on what you know," Mueller said.

"As we speak, East Dentonville is on fire and not just from the trail derailment there. The citizens on the east side are furious with the government there and have set nearly every building on fire."

"No wonder. Craig Hall doesn't have a clue what he's doing," Mariah said. "I spoke with him after one of our state emergency management meetings." She shook her head. "What a piece of work he is."

Jake continued. "Officials in Washington County have instituted martial law to control the flow of refugees out of Pittsburgh."

Mueller knew that would be an issue with having a major metropolitan area twenty-five miles away. It put hordes of refugees within a twelve-hour walk to their city border.

"The gangs in Pittsburgh are fighting one another in the streets for control of the city. The few officers who are still on duty are occupied guarding neighborhoods and setting up roadblocks into them like you would a war zone. They've all but given up hope of maintaining control in the high-crime areas," Jake said.

Steve looked grave. "It's not that much better in the city of Washington. When I left there, business owners were on the roofs of the stores trying to hold back looters."

"Most of them have now been burned to the ground," Frank said. "People are out there burning everything for the fun of it. It's like a scene from the movie *The Purge*. The Washington County sheriff pulled his deputies out of the city and back to the county limits to checkpoints but was quickly overwhelmed by refugees.

They couldn't hold the border. People from Pittsburgh have flooded in and joined the residents in their rampage against any symbol of authority." Frank leaned in. "We need to be even more vigilant in our patrols. We want to address any problems far away from our gates. The wall is strong but only as strong as its weakest link."

Jake cracked his knuckles. "That brings me to the first item on our agenda that we need to address swiftly."

"Okay," Mueller said, interlacing his fingers on the table.

Jake's expression grew serious. "A sentry fell asleep on duty last night."

"That kind of negligence can't be tolerated." Frank leaned forward, his brow furrowed. "If he were in the military, he'd be looking at a court-martial or worse."

Peggy shot him a glare. "But he's not in the military."

"We need to decide how we're going to handle discipline here," Monica said. "Civilian rules or military rules?"

"I move that we adopt civilian rules based upon the Constitution of the United States and that of the state of Pennsylvania," Peggy said, holding up her hand.

"Discussion?" Mueller asked, looking around the table.

Linda looked up from her notepad. "Civilian rules could help keep a sense of normalcy. People might feel more at ease if things don't change too drastically."

Frank shook his head. "Civilian rules? Out there, it's chaos. We need to be strict. A court-martial system might be our best bet."

Mueller listened to the debate, his mind wandering for a moment. Laney, his eighteen-year-old daughter, was out there somewhere, making her way north along the Appalachian Trail. The pre-arranged plan was for her to head toward Pennsylvania, where they'd set up contact points along her route to provide her with supplies. Any day now, he should hear from her. The thought of leaving Monica and the compound to get his little girl was always at the back of his mind. But for now, he had to deal with pressing issues like sentries falling asleep on duty while other members' families complained about the food that was served and being forced to work in the kitchen and on laundry detail.

He brought his attention back to the discussion.

"We need a system that combines the best of both worlds," Jake said. "We can't afford to be lax, but we also can't turn into tyrants."

"Agreed!" Monica said.

Mueller felt a surge of pride at how his wife was handling the situation, especially considering the panic she had felt over Laney in the early days. There had been heated arguments between them, with Monica insisting they abandon their responsibility for the compound and leave immediately to find their little girl. As a mother, her desperation was understandable. Mueller had felt the same urge countless times. But without a way to communicate with Laney and pinpoint her exact location, venturing out blindly would be foolhardy. He knew it was safer to trust in their pre-arranged plan and wait for Laney to contact them.

"How about this," Monica continued. "What if we adopt a civilian-style approach for minor offenses, with warnings and community service? But for major breaches, like endangering the group, we apply a military-style court-martial system."

Jake nodded. "That sounds reasonable. We can set up a tribunal of three council members to handle major offenses. The sentry who fell asleep—what do we consider that?"

"Major breach. Endangering lives," Frank said, throwing his hands in the air. "We've got to make an example of him!"

Linda shifted in her seat to face him. "I agree, but let's ensure the punishment fits the crime. Maybe temporary confinement and extra duty shifts."

Mueller tried to imagine what that might look like. He knew one thing: no one on the guard duty roster would ever trust the guy again. Any job he'd be given would have to be in a position that didn't put the group at risk.

"Do I have a motion?" Mueller asked.

"I move to adopt a civilian-style approach for minor offenses for those not on guard duty. But for those in charge of our defense, we apply a military-style court-martial system with a three-person tribunal," Linda said.

Mueller repeated Linda's motion. "Any discussion?"

Jake raised his hand. "We'll need a committee to come up with the rules."

"Any volunteers?" Mueller asked.

Hands shot up. Monica wrote down their names for the meeting minutes.

"You guys set up your meetings and then report back to the council," Mueller said.

"Can I get a second?" Mueller asked.

Peggy raised her hand. "I'll second the motion."

Mueller glanced over at Monica with a questioning look.

"Now we vote," she whispered.

"All those in favor." Mueller scanned the room for hands.

All hands went up.

"All right, then it's settled. We'll combine civilian and military justice. And we need to make this clear to everyone—law and order will be maintained, but fairness will prevail."

Linda leaned forward. "There are also other factors to consider —mental health, food distribution, and regular communication. This isn't just about punishment; it's about keeping our society together."

Mueller felt a pang of guilt as he thought of Laney again. Getting radio communications up and running had consumed his attention but for a personal reason. He had to believe she was safe, making her way home. He hadn't been able to think past getting everyone into position to secure the compound so he'd be free to leave when the time arrived to go get her. He'd put on the back burner any further governance, leaving issues like food, water, and problems of daily living to the others, but Linda was correct. They needed to maintain order within the walls as well, and communicating expectations and keeping up morale was part of that task. "Linda is right. Let's set up regular town-hall-type meetings to address these issues and keep everyone informed. Unity is our strength now."

As the meeting adjourned, Mueller exchanged a glance with Monica. They both knew the road ahead was fraught with challenges. However, with a balanced approach to justice and a focus on maintaining their humanity, they both believed they could keep their community strong in the face of chaos.

The council members began to disperse, and Mueller allowed himself a moment to look out the small window. The compound was secure for now, but the world outside was a different story. He had to believe Laney would make it back to them. And when she did, he would be there to bring her home. Until then, he had a duty to this community, to keep them safe and unified in this new, harsh reality.

Jake hesitated in the doorway. "Mueller!"

Frank stopped beside him. "Can we get a word with you?"

"What's this about?" Mueller asked, lowering himself back into his chair. He gestured for the two men to take a seat across from him.

"Dentonville mostly," Jake said. "My brother—he's a cop over there. It's a total mess there, as you know."

Mueller nodded. They'd been monitoring nearby communities, wanting to head off any potential spillover of hostilities into their area.

"He says the community leaders have all but decided to bug out. The residents there are in full-blown riot mode now, and they can't restore order."

"Do they have a plan… a place to go… or are you asking—"

"No! I know we agreed—no non-members allowed to join the compound." He shook his head. "No, they have a place."

Mueller's gaze shifted to Frank.

"You remember Cayman?" Frank asked. "He trained with us for a while."

"I recall. I met him at Glasser's Survival School." Mueller recalled how they'd parted ways because Cayman's work ethic was lacking. "I remember that he had some out-there ideas about rebuilding society after the fecal material hit the rotary impeller device."

"He's sort of formed a compound of his own. He and Dentonville's town leaders. They're planning to bug out to this compound soon."

"Where is it located?"

"Holderman Road. Just outside Bowers Township."

"Ten miles? He set up his compound ten miles from us?" Mueller rubbed the back of his neck. "Figures."

"My brother will be with them. We can work together, maybe?"

"With Walt? I doubt that," Frank said.

"I agree. We should assign a team to keep an eye on them," Mueller said.

"Who are we going to assign? We're spread so thin with what's going on in the city of Washington. The whole courthouse square, including the sheriff's office and the jail, has been burned to the ground. The sheriff and his deputies have pulled back to the county limits on the major routes leading from Pittsburgh to deal with the flood of refugees."

"I know!" Mueller clenched his fist. The sheriff's roadblocks were effective at deflecting refugees away from the city of Washington, but it only served to cause them to flood into the rural areas, seeking resources and taking whatever they wanted. Frank was right. At the moment, they couldn't afford to send anyone to monitor Walt until the situation closer to home was under control. "Stay in contact with your brother, Jake. Keep me informed. We'll act whenever it becomes necessary."

FIVE

Ayden

Camp Evergreen
Knoxville, Maryland
Day Five

Ayden steered the motorhome along Harpers Ferry Road, his eyes scanning the horizon for any sign of trouble. The road was quiet, almost eerily so, and the dense forests on either side provided a sense of isolation that was both comforting and unnerving. He tried to keep the atmosphere in the motorhome light, but his mind was on high alert.

Suddenly, a group of National Guard troops appeared around a bend. They were stationed by the roadside, their camouflaged uniforms unmistakable. Ayden slowed the motorhome, pulling to a stop as a soldier approached. He rolled down his window, trying to mask his apprehension with a calm demeanor.

"This road's closed!" The soldier rested his hand near his sidearm, but his posture was relaxed.

"We're just trying to get to Pennsylvania," Ayden said.

The soldier's eyes flicked over the interior of the motorhome in the direction of Clara, Joyce, and the others. He returned his gaze to Ayden. “Sir, you’re going to have to turn back. This area isn’t safe for civilians right now.”

Ayden’s stomach tightened. He thought about pressing for more details but decided against it. “Can you tell us what kind of activity? We really need to get to Pennsylvania.”

Before the soldier could respond, his radio crackled to life, an urgent and commanding voice spitting out coordinates and military jargon that Ayden didn’t fully understand but caught enough to know it wasn’t good. The soldier’s expression tightened, and he turned away, responding quickly to the call.

“I have to go,” the soldier said abruptly, turning back to Ayden. His gaze was stern, all business now. “Find somewhere to hide. Now!” With that, he jogged back to his unit, which was already mobilizing.

Ayden watched them, his heart pounding. The soldier hadn’t needed to say it twice.

Laney’s voice broke the tense silence, her tone sharp with fear and frustration. “What does he mean, ‘hide’? Where in the world does he expect us to go?”

Beside her, Tina clung to her arm, her face pale, barely whispering, “Are we going to be okay?”

“We have to turn around.” Ayden checked his side mirrors. “We can talk about it as we go.” He threw the motorhome into Reverse. His mind raced as he maneuvered the vehicle into a narrow gravel drive and then drove back the way they’d come. The last thing he wanted was to be targeted by drones again.

Joyce let out a deep sigh. “I’ve seen a lot in my years, but nothing like this.”

“We should go back to that camp and ask to stay with them,” Tina said.

“They’re not going to let us in,” Laney said. “You heard Kim. They don’t trust us.”

“We have to go somewhere,” Clara said.

"We have to try," Joyce said. "We'll appeal to their humanity."

"They're going to stop us again when we pass by there to return to Harpers Ferry. Won't hurt to ask them for shelter," Dominic said.

Ayden nodded. "True."

As Ayden steered the motorhome back toward Camp Evergreen, anxiety pulsed through him like a drumbeat. With each passing mile, his anticipation mounted, knowing that their fate rested in the hands of Kim and the other guards at the camp's entrance.

Approaching the roadblock, Ayden's heart clenched with uncertainty. Mark and Kim's wary gazes met his as they recognized the motorhome from their previous encounter. Kim stepped forward, her expression guarded, her posture stiff. She approached the driver's door with the stock of her rifle tight against her shoulder and pointed it straight at Ayden.

"What are you doing back here?" she barked.

"We'd love to tell you, but you need to let us inside the camp."

"Not gonna happen!" Kim shot back.

"Please!" Clara's voice rang out from the back, her desperation evident.

"We're not letting you in," she said, her tone brooking no argument. "We don't take risks anymore."

Ayden glanced up toward the sky.

Kim followed his gaze.

Ayden shifted his focus back to Kim. "You really need to hear what we have to say."

"You can say whatever it is here and then be on your way."

Dominic leaned across the console. "This is important. It regards all of our safety."

Kim pivoted slightly toward the other two guards. She gestured toward the gate, and Sammie took off toward it. Kim returned her focus to Ayden. "You guys need to go. We've told you already, you're not welcome here. Don't make us—"

Before Kim could finish her sentence, a new voice cut through the tension. "Kim!"

All eyes turned to the woman who had emerged from behind the roadblock; her presence commanded attention. Flanked by a man and a woman, she approached the motorhome with purpose.

"What's going on here, Kim?" a woman in her late fifties asked, her voice cool yet authoritative.

Her eyes, sharp and penetrating, bored into Ayden's, assessing him with a shrewd intensity. She stood tall and poised. Physically, she was a formidable figure with wide shoulders and sharp features. Her hair, streaked with silver, was pulled back into a practical bun, framing a face lined with the marks of age and experience. She wore cargo pants, a tactical vest, and combat boots. A holster strapped to her hip held a pistol. Despite her rough exterior, there was kindness in her eyes that belied her stern demeanor.

Kim hesitated, casting a wary glance at Ayden before responding. "These folks want refuge, DaSilva."

"We have information you'll want to hear," Ayden said

"I've already told them—"

DaSilva raised a hand, cutting Kim off. "Let him speak," she commanded.

It was evident that she held the reins of power in this encounter. She was the one Ayden needed to convince. Ayden shifted his attention to the man and woman flanking her.

The rugged-looking man in his mid-thirties eyed Ayden sharply, his hand resting on the holstered pistol, eyeing the motorhome. Ayden wondered if the man had a law enforcement or military background.

The petite woman in her forties, standing to the left of their leader, exuded a formidable presence of her own. Clad entirely in black, she wielded a military-style rifle with a practiced ease that hinted at extensive training. Her icy gaze was fixed unwaveringly on Dominic in the passenger seat.

As the tension mounted at the roadblock, a firm knot formed in

Ayden's stomach. They didn't have time for all this. He knew he had to convince them of the importance of their information. Fast!

"What is this news you have?" DaSilva asked, her tone authoritative yet not unkind like Kim's.

Ayden cleared his throat and sat up straighter. "We encountered US troops. They gave us information you need to know."

The man beside DaSilva's expression shifted, his curiosity piqued. "Where? Where did you run into our soldiers?"

Ayden mustered a smile, hoping to convey sincerity. "We'd really appreciate it if you could just let us inside for the night. We can fill you in on everything we've learned."

"Why would we do that?" DaSilva countered.

Dominic leaned out the window. "Because you need to know what we've learned, and we're desperate for your help."

Joyce moved up between the seats and leaned over him. "We're asking for sanctuary. It's not safe out here right now! Please!"

DaSilva exchanged a glance with the men beside her before turning back to Ayden. "You realize we have to treat you as a threat?"

Ayden shook his head. "You don't have to. You already know we aren't armed. We're just trying to get to Pennsylvania."

Mark stepped forward, offering his insight. "That girl's story checked out, ma'am. She said she was with a group up in Pennsylvania, and I spoke to a guy who knows about them. They've been sending out messages for folks to be looking for her."

"You heard from my dad?" Laney called from the back of the motorhome.

Joyce stepped back, and Laney appeared at Ayden's side. She placed her hand on the steering wheel and leaned over him. "You spoke to my father?"

Mark shook his head. "No, but I spoke to a ham operator in Crystal Springs, Pennsylvania. He told me your group sent out a be-on-the-lookout call, and I gave him your message. He seemed to understand what you meant about heading to Disneyland. He was going to relay the information back to your group the next time he heard them on the radio."

Ayden seized the opportunity to plead their case once more. "Please help us. We're trying to get her home to her parents. We just need somewhere safe for the night. Let us in, and we'll tell you everything we learned from the soldiers."

After a moment of consideration, DaSilva relented. "Fine. We'll give quarter to you just for the night in exchange for all the information you have about the fighting, but know this: if you make even the slightest move to harm us"—DaSilva gestured to the man at her side—"Pasfield here will be forced to take appropriate actions to—"

"Annihilate you forthwith!" Pasfield said, finishing her sentence, his expression hardening.

Ayden nodded. "Deal!"

SIX

Ayden

Camp Evergreen
Knoxville, Maryland
Day Five

Pasfield's words echoed in Ayden's ears as he inched the motorhome toward the gate of Camp Evergreen.

Annihilate them!

Ayden had no doubt Pasfield meant it. He was determined not to do anything to provoke the man into carrying out his threat.

The entrance to the camp boasted a sturdy wooden gate flanked by two towering stone pillars, weathered by time and adorned with creeping vines and ivy. A wooden sign hung above, proudly displaying the camp's name in bold letters. Ayden had never been to a camp as a kid. Instead, each summer, his parents had sent him and Clara on trips to Europe to immerse themselves in culture, supervised by their nanny. As a young boy, he'd found museums and cathedrals to be dull places. He would have had far more fun at a camp where he could have swum, learned archery, and hung out with regular kids. He wondered if Mia ever sent her boys to a camp like this. He sighed wistfully, missing them as the two guards pulled open the chain-linked gate and stepped aside, waving them forward.

Beyond the gate, a winding gravel path beckoned them in, leading deeper into the heart of Camp Evergreen. Lush greenery lined the pathway, creating a serene tunnel of foliage. A female guard gestured for Ayden to park the motorhome at one of the camping spots and then told them to exit the vehicle. From there, they were taken to a large log cabin situated in what appeared to be the center of the property.

Inside, the meeting space was warm and inviting, with wooden beams crisscrossing overhead and a stone fireplace that, in happier times, would have provided a cozy ambiance for the campers who gathered around it. Ayden's thoughts again drifted to Wyoming and Mia. The cabin reminded him of the one she shared with her parents. A slight smile played on his lips as he recalled Xavier, the youngest of Mia's three sons, stretched out before their fireplace with a pad of paper and crayons. Ayden's hand rose to touch the pocket of his shirt, where he kept a drawing Xavy had made of Ayden's dog, Beau Dacious. They all seemed a million miles away, and it was growing harder each day to hold on to the hope of ever making it back to them.

The guard gestured to the seating arranged in a circle near the fireplace where they were to await DaSilva's arrival. Ayden sat at the head of the circle, facing the fireplace, with Clara by his side. Laney took a seat to the left of Ayden. Joyce sat next to her, flanked by Dominic and Tina. As they settled into their seats, Ayden glanced around the room. Sandbags had been placed chest-high in front of all the windows. Beyond them, outside where what would have once been a thick green lawn, trenches were in the process of being dug. In the center of the field stood a tall antenna. Nearby, it looked as if some type of military drills were being conducted in the grassy area of a baseball field. Targets for archery or makeshift obstacles for agility training had been set up around the perimeter of the field. It appeared that these people were already preparing for battle.

Armed guards stood at the entrance to the room, their backs to the wall, staring at Ayden and his party. Surrounded by them, a sense of relief washed over Ayden. He wasn't naivę. He understood that their level of preparedness for war wasn't equal to the power of the Chinese military with its drones and other instruments of modern warfare. Even still, they had weapons and some form of defense. They were certainly better prepared than Ayden and the others with him. But Ayden knew they couldn't remain there long —just until they figured out their next moves.

When DaSilva finally entered the room, she was accompanied by Pasfield, the woman, and a small team of people of different genders and ages. They took seats across from Ayden and his group, and DeSilva wasted no time in getting to the heart of the matter. "You said you encountered US troops. How close are they?"

"Close," Ayden began, trying to keep his voice steady. "We encountered US National Guard soldiers this side of Sharpsburg."

DaSilva was expressionless as if it was something she already knew about, and then her expression tightened as she gestured for Ayden to continue.

"They warned us to 'hide.'" Clara's voice cracked.

Ayden took her hand in his.

"Hide?" Pasfield said, glancing over at DaSilva. "From what?"

"The soldier wouldn't say," Ayden said. He scanned their faces. "The radio transmission mentioned something about the bridge. Hold the bridge or blow the bridge. I can't be sure."

DaSilva rubbed the back of her neck. She glanced over at Pasfield. "That's what happened to our radio signal."

"Damn PLA jammers."

DaSilva nodded. "Confirm this with Russel." She nodded to one of the guards by the door, and he spun and exited the room. She returned her gaze to Ayden and the others. "We believe the

PLA's strategic goal is to advance across the Potomac, possibly at Sharpsburg."

Pasfield shifted in his chair. "Controlling the bridge there would allow the US military to stop the PLA from gaining a foothold in West Virginia and perhaps slow their advancement into the Midwest."

"They wouldn't stop at West Virginia," one of the women on DaSilva's team chimed in. "If reports of Chinese ships at Norfolk are true, they could be aiming to seize control of key transportation routes and strategic points along the East Coast."

Ayden studied DaSilva. "So we're talking Chinese ground forces? Military troops with tanks and such?"

DaSilva exchanged a glance with her team before responding. "We need to consider all possible scenarios," she said, her voice measured. "Yes, troops on the ground. Special forces, from what we've heard. They're trying to secure key routes. The bulk of their forces are still days to weeks away on ships."

"Getting blown out of the water by our Navy and Air Force," Pasfield said.

"They're still operational despite the EMP attack?" Dominic asked.

"Sure," Pasfield said. "The military had hardened planes, ships, and equipment. Those wouldn't have been affected by the electromagnetic pulse. Communications via satellite with command and control were likely interrupted, but they have other means. The military undergoes regular drills to function without relying on satellites."

"You all look like you're well-equipped." Ayden pointed to the field beyond the windows. "And prepared."

Pasfield ignored Ayden's statement. "What else did you hear or observe?" he asked instead.

"That's it, basically," Ayden said.

From DaSilva's expression, Ayden was sure they were about to be thrown out.

"What have you heard?" Laney asked. "About enemy troops in the area. Kim warned us there could be trouble near the Pennsylvania border. Have you heard anything about enemy activity between here and western Pennsylvania?"

Pasfield shook his head. "Nothing."

"Nothing," DaSilva repeated. "But you should plan on going west when you leave here."

Ayden hesitated, weighing his options. "We were planning to head north," he said. "But given the circumstances, we're open to alternative routes."

DaSilva nodded, her expression thoughtful. "There are other safer routes to Pennsylvania," she said, gesturing west. "Avoiding major highways and population centers would be wise."

As they discussed potential routes, Ayden felt relieved to know DaSilva and her team were offering valuable insights and guidance. After much deliberation, they settled on a new route that would take them back through Harpers Ferry and west through less populated areas, minimizing their exposure to potential threats.

DaSilva stood, and so did her team. "You can stay in one of our cabins for the night." She gave them a stern look. "But you will be under guard until you leave. By morning, we might have more information and be able to determine if it is safe for you to continue your journey."

As Ayden and his group were escorted by armed guards to the small cabin, relief flooded through him. They needed this respite, and the hope of receiving more information eased his mind somewhat. The cabin stood amidst the trees, its weathered wooden exterior blending seamlessly with the surrounding wilderness. The door creaked open to reveal a modest interior furnished with four worn bunk beds and basic amenities.

Inside, the cabin was dimly lit by the soft glow of a lantern hanging from the ceiling. The air was thick with the scent of wood smoke and damp earth. The beds were simple but sturdy, each adorned with a threadbare blanket and a pillow that had seen better days. A small table sat in the corner, piled high with books and puzzles.

As the group settled in, one of the guards returned with a bucket of water, a plate of cooked fish, and a basket of fresh veggies. The aroma of the food filled the cabin, stirring Ayden's hunger after a long and exhausting day. Yet, as he sat down to eat with the others, his mind again filled with unease. He'd promised Laney he would see her home, but all he really wanted to do was point the motorhome west and race to Wyoming, putting as much distance between them and the invaders as they could.

After they had finished their meal, Ayden assisted Clara to the bottom bunk of one of the beds. "I'll take the top," he said.

"Here, Grandma." Dominic handed Joyce a pillow. "You take the bottom. I'll make mine up here." He gestured to the top bunk.

Tina and Laney took the other two bottom bunks. Lunch Box occupied one of the top beds.

As they settled in for the night, Laney broached the topic of her father's compound, her voice tinged with both pride and concern. "My dad's compound is well-prepared, too," she said, her words echoing in the quiet cabin. "But I worry that even with all our defenses, we might not stand a chance against a modern army."

Ayden nodded, his thoughts drifting to the challenge of navigating through war zones and making their way west. As they huddled together in the darkness, Ayden couldn't help but feel a glimmer of hopelessness, knowing they were only beginning their struggle.

Night quickly descended upon Camp Evergreen, and Ayden stretched out on this bunk, eager for what he hoped would be a more peaceful rest than he'd had the night before. But that wasn't the case, as their slumber was abruptly shattered by the deafening roar of automatic gunfire echoing through the darkness.

SEVEN

Ayden

Camp Evergreen
Knoxville, Maryland
Day Six

Startled awake by the cacophony of gunfire, Ayden's heart thudded against his rib cage as realization dawned—the camp was under siege. In the dim light, the rest if the cabin's occupants bolted upright, eyes wide with terror. With no weapons at their disposal, escape was their only option.

"We have to move—now!" Ayden shouted.

After clumsily gathering themselves, they scrambled to their feet, following Ayden to the cabin door. Gripping the handle, Ayden inched it open just as another volley of gunfire shattered the night. Through the narrow gap, he saw the silhouette of the camp's armed guards sprinting across the dew-damp grass toward the main cabin, their movements desperate and disjointed in the darkness.

The tall trees flanking the cabin loomed ominously, their branches swaying like specters in the wind, distorting Ayden's sense of depth. Every shadow seemed to stretch farther into the dark, each possibly concealing Chinese insurgents lying in wait. The relentless automatic rifle fire echoed through the night. How many were there? How close? The unknowns multiplied, each adding weight to Ayden's racing thoughts.

"Follow me," DaSilva shouted, appearing at the bottom of the steps. The beam from the light on her helmet and the scope on her military-style rifle lit up the porch. She was dressed all in black like her guards and wearing body armor.

Kim appeared at her side. "They've breached the gate."

"The teams will hold the line," DaSilva said. "We need to get these folks out of the line of fire." She gestured with her hands for Ayden and the others to exit the cabin.

He grabbed his sister, encircling Clara's waist and assisting her in their hasty retreat. He drew a deep breath, trying to calm the pounding in his chest and focus on the sounds around them—the crunch of boots on leaf litter, the distant shouts, the intermittent crack of rifles—all amplified in the deceptive stillness of the night. Each noise seemed closer, more immediate, as if the darkness itself magnified their peril.

It was all so unreal. How could this be happening on American soil? Every muscle in Ayden's body tensed as he anticipated getting shot in the back during their hasty retreat across the grass toward the tree line.

Close behind him were Joyce and Tina, with Laney, Dominic, and Lunch Box on their heels. Together, they followed closely behind DaSilva.

After crossing the grassy area, DaSilva dropped down behind a pickup truck in the parking lot and waved for them to hurry. Kim ran and crouched beside her. Ayden looked back as Pasfield neared them then rushed ahead and dropped down beside DaSilva and Kim. A barrage of automatic gunfire rang out, shattering the windows of the pickup. Pasfield moved in a crouch to the front of a mid-sized sedan parked nearby and began firing over the top of the hood.

Ayden strained his eyes in the darkness, trying to pinpoint the enemy's location, but it was futile. Suddenly, DaSilva's hand sliced through the air decisively. "Move out!" she shouted, her voice cutting through the stillness as she advanced toward Pasfield.

Without warning, the night transformed. Above them, a flare burst into life and flooded the area with blinding light. It hung in the sky like a miniature sun, casting stark, elongated shadows that sliced across the terrain. Ayden blinked against the harsh illumination, his pupils contracting rapidly.

As his vision adjusted, the once-hidden enemy became hauntingly visible. Shadowy figures emerged from the road leading into the camp, their movements sharp and deliberate under the intense light. The sight spiked Ayden's pulse and sent a mix of fear and clarity surging through him.

"Go, go!" DaSilva's command snapped Ayden back to the moment.

He bent low, almost mirroring Clara's hunched form as they followed DaSilva. The rough gravel crunched under their feet. In what felt like an eternity compressed into seconds, they reached the classic Volkswagen bus. Ayden held on to Clara's arm as she leaned against the fender, her chest heaving in and out. His own breath came in ragged gasps—he realized he had held it the entire dash, a tight band of panic and exertion clenching his chest.

It hadn't been a long run, but the world seemed to pivot around that frantic, illuminated moment. The flare continued to burn overhead, a relentless beacon that stripped away the comfort of darkness.

"Where are they?" Clara asked, craning her neck above the rear bumper to see.

Pasfield grabbed her arm and pulled her backward. "Keep your head down!"

Her brow knit tight, and her jaw clenched as hunched over. "What are we going to do? We don't even have weapons."

"And you don't know how to use them," Kim said sarcastically.

Clara huffed.

"I do," Laney said. "I know how to shoot. Give me a rifle. I'm ready to kick some Chinese butts."

"Not gonna happen," Pasfield said.

"We're powerless to defend ourselves without them," Joyce said.

"Yeah!" Dominic said. "At least give us a pistol or something."

"Not happening!" Kim said.

As the gunfire slowed to just a few shots here and there, Ayden resisted moving to get a look, not wanting to risk taking a bullet. A moment later, he heard footfalls crunch on gravel and stiffened until he saw a barrel-chested guard he recognized from the roadblock earlier drop down next to them.

"Flanagan, where's Sawden?" DaSilva asked.

"Right behind me. Be ready to move," the barrel-chested guard said.

Then the night erupted again. Shots ripped through the air once more, piercing the brief silence that had settled over the camp. As the echo dwindled, a guard rounded the back of the VW bus, joining the group huddled in the harsh circle of light cast by the flare overhead.

"Two tangos eliminated. Let's move out," he barked as he dropped his rifle's magazine and snapped a fresh one into place. He gave Ayden a brief nod, then surveyed the rest of the group.

The flare's brilliant light washed over DaSilva's face, highlighting the creases of worry etched deeply around her eyes and mouth. "How many have infiltrated?"

"Too many, ma'am," Sawden replied, his face grim. "Jeanine's team is holding the line at the hill while we get these civilians to the boats."

"Boats?" Joyce's voice trembled with panic.

Sawden shot her a quick look but said nothing more.

DaSilva sucked in air from the corner of her mouth. "Casualties?" she asked. Her lips formed a straight line as she waited for the answer.

"Nancy's team took heavy casualties. I don't have numbers. They pulled back to the chapel. Steve's guys took their place."

DaSilva's eyes momentarily squeezed closed, her eyebrows lowered, and her nose wrinkled before she regained composure. "Flanagan, I want you to cross the river with these folks and then evacuate any injured."

Flanagan's broad frame tensed. "I should be on the front line," he said, jabbing a finger in the direction of the heaviest fighting.

DaSilva shifted her weight and pulled her rifle tighter to her shoulder. "We're pulling everyone back toward you. You'll be the front line as everyone crosses."

Deep lines furrowed Sawden's brow. "We're abandoning the camp?"

"For today," DaSilva said. She rose slightly. Her expression softened. "Now let's move out and get these folks out of here."

The guards moved in a crouch down the row of vehicles and stopped, holding a fist in the air to halt Ayden and the others. They seemed professional—like they knew what they were doing, which was somewhat comforting. Maybe they had a tiny sliver of hope of making it out of this alive. But something didn't make sense. Ayden and his group were liabilities to these people, yet despite that, DaSilva and the guards were still putting their lives on the line for them.

"Why are you doing this?" Ayden couldn't help but ask.

"What?" DeSilva asked, peering over the top of the hood of a vintage truck.

"Saving us," Laney said. "You don't know us. You don't owe us anything."

Flanagan smiled. "Because."

Kim shot her a glare. "Because we've spent our whole careers and dedicated our lives to saving stupid people like you."

"Kim!" DaSilva snapped. "That's enough."

Flanagan rose an inch or two and pulled his rifle to his cheek. He scanned back and forth before declaring the space between the vehicles and the building safe.

"Thank you," Tina said softly.

"No need," Pasfield muttered.

When he reached the end of the row of trucks, Ayden was hesitant to step out into the open. Not knowing how many Chinese soldiers were out there or where they were located had every nerve in his body on edge.

Pasfield tapped Ayden on the shoulder. "You ready?"

Ayden nodded. It was a lie. He was far from ready. He'd never been so ill-prepared in his life. Right then, he vowed to himself that if he somehow made it out of this mess, he'd get prepared, somehow, someway. He'd get armed. This was America. There were millions of guns out there. He'd find a way to be ready when trouble found him again, and he knew it would.

EIGHT

Mueller

New Eden Compound
Somerset Township
Washington County, Pennsylvania
Day Six

On the morning of the sixth day following the EMP attack, the compound was buzzing with activity. Mueller was in the central meeting hall with Frank, going over the security reports, when Thomas Coupland, a longtime friend and one of New Eden's members who was late arriving, rushed through the door. His face was pale and drawn.

"Ty, I need your help," Thomas said, his chest heaving in and out. "My wife and kids are trapped in Pittsburgh. It's chaos there—riots, looting. I tried to get to them, but it's impossible on my own."

Mueller stood and put a hand on Thomas's shoulder. "Slow down, Tom. Where are they supposed to be?"

Frank handed Tom a bottle of water, and he began to explain as he drank. "They were at her sister's house, but they had to flee. She left a note saying they went to a business owned by her sister's friend. It's guarded by armed men, but I couldn't get through. I'm worried if I try again, they might get hurt or worse."

Mueller glanced back at Frank. It was all their nightmares to have their loved ones in this type of scenario. But a rescue mission was risky. Previously, before all this became their reality, they'd discussed the idea of such a plan. From the moment Laney announced that she was planning to hike the Appalachian Trail after graduation, he and his wife Monica had talked about how they might get her home. They'd spoken to friends from eastern Pennsylvania all the way to the head of the trail down Georgia, where she began her hike. They'd arranged for Laney to go to those designated people for help. Each of them had ham radios, and the plan was that once one of them radioed that Laney was with them, Mueller and Monica would strike out to bring her home. Mueller understood Tom's pain. At least his friend knew the location of his family.

"All right, we'll figure something out," Mueller said. "I need to talk to the security team. Why don't you go to the chow hall and grab something to eat? I'll send someone for you when we're ready to make a plan."

The relief on Tom's face was visible. "Thank you, Ty. I knew you wouldn't let me down."

As Tom headed off to the dining facility, Mueller convened an urgent meeting with his security team and advised them of the situation.

"Thomas needs our help. His family is trapped in Pittsburgh, and he can't get them out alone. I need volunteers for a rescue mission."

Nesbitt, Smith, Amos, and Giblin raised their hands immediately.

Mueller smiled. He knew he'd picked the right people. They were not only brave and capable but also loyal to their friends.

"Thank you. We'll need to plan this carefully. This isn't going to be easy."

"Never thought it would be. We talked about this possibility."

Mueller nodded. "Yes, we did, but I still wanted to give you all an opportunity to back out."

"No way," Amos said.

Smith and Giblin nodded.

"We trained for this. I'm not backing out," Giblin said.

"We can't stay here behind these walls forever. Eventually, we're going to encounter scenarios that require us to fight. Might as well be now." He smiled. "Besides, Tom's wife makes the best red beans and rice."

Everyone chuckled.

"Okay, folks. We have our team for this mission. That means that the rest of you will be pulling extra shifts until we return. Stay sharp. Make sure we don't have a repeat of the incident with Bierman, the sentry who fell asleep on duty."

"Oh, I don't think anyone will be falling asleep on duty again," Amos said.

Members of the security team had taken care of the issue before the council completed their vote. Kristopher Bierman was now in the infirmary recovering from the injuries inflicted by his fellow teammates.

"No! That will not be happening again," Nesbitt said.

"I still think we should have hung his ass!" Smith glared at Amos.

Nesbitt shook his head. "We're not murderers. A sentence like that needs to come from the council."

"If they decide to try him in a court-martial like Mueller said, he could still be sentenced to death for falling asleep on guard duty."

"Yeah, but do you really think the tribunal would do that?" Smith asked.

Nesbitt shrugged.

Mueller stood. "The team on the rescue mission, go gather your gear and meet me back here in twenty minutes. I'll inform Tom and grab my ruck and rifle, and we'll meet back here to go over the plan before heading out."

"You gonna tell Monica?" Amos asked.

"Of course." He told his wife everything. He'd explain the mission to her. She'd be upset. Not because she didn't think they should rescue Tom's family. She adored Mary and the kids. She'd be mad that they were risking their lives to get them but hadn't yet taken off to find Laney.

Mueller found Monica in their quarters, preparing supplies for the day's activities. She looked up as he entered, reading the tension on his face immediately.

"What's going on, Ty?"

Mueller sighed. "Thomas's family is trapped in Pittsburgh. He couldn't get to them, and he's asked for our help. I've put together a team, and we're going to get them out."

Monica's face tightened. Her left eyelid twitched as it did when she was mad at him.

"We should have discussed it before you agreed."

"I'm sorry."

"I get it. I really do. Tom and Mary are my friends, too, and you know I adore those kids, but we haven't even tried to find Laney. You said it's too risky. Suddenly, you're willing to head off to Pittsburgh, where we know violence fills the streets."

Mueller took her hand and looked her in the eyes. "You know I'd go after Laney in a heartbeat if we had any idea where she was. But Tom's family… we know where they are. They need our help now."

Monica looked away, her eyes glistening with unshed tears. She took a deep breath and nodded.

"I understand. I just… I'm scared, Ty. For you, for Laney, for all of us."

He pulled her to his chest. "I'm scared too. But we've got a plan. We've trained for this. And when we hear from Laney, we'll go get her, no matter what."

Monica squeezed him tightly. "Just promise me you'll be careful."

"Of course," Mueller said, kissing the top of her head. "I'll be back with Tom's family, and then we'll focus on getting Laney home the moment we hear from her." He bent and kissed her lips. "We'll get home. I promise."

Monica nodded, a smile playing on her lips. Mueller kissed her forehead and then turned to gather his gear.

As he walked away, he heard her whisper, "Stay safe, Ty."

He looked back, gave her a reassuring nod, and headed out to meet the team.

NINE

Ayden

Camp Evergreen
Knoxville, Maryland
Day Six

As they set out for the boats, fleeing the PLA soldiers, Ayden wrapped his arm around Clara's waist, supporting as much of her weight as possible. "Okay, try not to drag your foot," he said as he pushed away from the truck and followed Pasfield and the others.

Clara hopped on her good leg. "I'm trying. The damn thing just won't cooperate."

Ahead was a row of rustic-looking bungalows with small front porches. "It's not much farther," Ayden said.

Once they reached the first log shelter, the group stopped and stacked up behind DaSilva, who was pressed up against the side of the stone chimney. Flanagan and Sawden took off toward the next row of cabins, fifty feet from the first. Between them was a large firepit circled by stones and surrounded by Adirondack chairs. When the guards reached their destination, they surveyed the scene, looking for more gunmen before waving for Ayden and the others to follow. Laney went first, followed by Ayden and Clara. DaSilva and Kim covered the others until they were safely across.

Ayden's shoulder was screaming from carrying most of Clara's weight. He was beginning to feel the effects of exhaustion. A headache was forming behind his eyes, but he had to concentrate on making it safely to the next row of cottages. He just had to keep putting one foot in front of the other and tune out the pain.

Clara's face was flushed. He worried for her. She'd been shot days ago, and pushing too hard could be costly to her, but with Chinese soldiers waiting to mow them down, they couldn't afford to stop and take it slow.

When everyone had safely reached the second row of cabins, DaSilva's guards took off toward another grouping of shelters. A line of tall shrubs made it impossible to see what or who was on the other side.

Flanagan stopped, pressed his shoulder against the side of one of the cabins, and peered around it toward the tree line. A second later, he gestured for them to move again. As soon as he stepped from the cover of the log structure, a bullet cracked somewhere to their right, sending Flanagan diving back behind the corner of the building. More rounds peppered the shelters to their left. The PLA was everywhere!

Ayden and the others squatted, trying to keep out of the line of fire. Ayden draped himself overtop of his sister to shield her from the splitters raining down from the bullets hitting the logs.

"Keep your heads down!" Sawden shouted as he returned fire and then moved around the side of the building.

As Sawden disappeared, Ayden's heart flipped in his chest. A moment later, the gunfire concentrated on the back end of the cabin. It was terrifying being pinned down in this way with rounds striking nearby and not having a weapon with which to defend himself or his sister. He prayed nothing happened to Sawden, but he hated being so reliant on these people to make it to safety.

The shooting stopped, and Sawden reappeared. "Let's move!" he said as he took off for the next row of camp shelters.

DaSilva tapped Tina on the shoulder. "Follow him."

Tina pivoted to face DaSilva. Tears welled in her eyes and spilled down her cheeks. She looked like a deer caught in headlights.

"I got her." Sawden took hold of her by the shoulder. He stepped in front of Tina. "Stay on my left." The two sprinted off for the next row.

Pop! Pop! Pop!

A cacophony of gunfire erupted.

Sawden dropped to the ground in a heap, his head bouncing off the hard-packed earth. Tina froze, staring down at him. She looked in the direction of the gunfire and screamed.

Ayden ran over to her. "Get his arm," he said, grabbing hold of the guard's vest. Tina stared blankly at him for a second before sliding her arm under Sawden's armpit. As they struggled to pull the guard out of the line of fire, DaSilva and Pasfield ran past and dove beside a trash dumpster at the end of the next row.

"I'm hit, man. I'm hit," Sawden cried out.

"I got him," Flanagan yelled as he ran up.

He quickly grabbed hold, and they dragged Sawden to the cover of the steel trash dumpster. Flanagan immediately began ripping the man's vest off to find the wound.

Ayden glanced in that direction to see how bad the wound looked. Flanagan was applying pressure to his side near the armpit.

"Am I going to die, Flanagan? Oh, man, I'm going to die, ain't I?" Sawden said, lifting his head and staring at the wound.

"You're not going to die. I got you, bro," Flanagan said.

Ayden picked up Sawden's rifle and moved back toward the cottage to assist his sister.

DaSilva was still there, returning fire. "I'm out," she said, dropping back and reloading.

Ayden stepped around her, pulled the guard's rifle up, and

began firing to his left in the direction he thought the Chinese soldiers were firing from. Rounds bounced off the log structures. Ayden didn't believe any of them had found their target, but the enemy stopped shooting.

Ayden turned his attention to a fifty-foot-tall freestanding climbing wall about seventy-five feet from their position. He couldn't see anyone, but he was reasonably sure that was where the rounds had come from. A moment later, he spotted a shadowy figure move near the three-sided wooden structure. Ayden watched through his scope and waited for a head to appear. When it finally did, he squeezed the trigger. The enemy dropped, confirming he'd hit his target. An instant later, a volley of gunfire opened up on his position.

TEN

Ayden

Camp Evergreen
Knoxville, Maryland
Day Six

The gunfire came from the left this time. The Chinese combatants had either moved around the row of cabins to flank them, or these shots had come from somewhere else. An unknown number of hostiles were firing from the cover of vehicles in the parking lot of a building to the left of the climbing wall.

Ayden returned fire as he ran. Laney, assisting Clara, lagged behind him as they headed toward a larger log structure.

"Get them to the chapel," Flanagan shouted back, dropping down by the climbing wall. "I'll cover you."

"Let's move out," Pasfield said.

Laney pointed to Sawden. "What about him?"

Pasfield shouldered his rifle and rose to a crouch. "He's gone. We have to go."

As Flanagan checked the area for Chinese combatants, Ayden rushed to Sawden's side, removed the man's vest and tactical belt, and then grabbed the ammo from his pockets. It was like robbing from the dead, but he no longer needed them, and Ayden did. All that mattered was self-preservation at that point. Ayden was keenly aware of how much they'd abandoned civilized behavior already.

"How much ammo did he have left?" Pasfield asked as he leaned against the dumpster.

Ayden pulled four empty thirty-round magazines from a pouch from the belt and then counted the full mags remaining in the tactical vest. "Four magazines."

"Grab his knife," Pasfield said, pointing to a thigh holster.

Ayden removed it and handed it to Dominic. It wasn't much, but it was better than having no weapon at all. Then he scanned the distance between the dumpster and the northeast corner of the chapel as he assisted Clara in putting on the vest and adjusting it to fit her more petite frame.

"It's clear," Pasfield said, taking off toward the timber-framed chapel building.

Clara stood with her arms across her chest, gripping the top of the vest. He wished he had a weapon to give her. She'd shown so much more confidence when they'd battled the gangs in Harlem, but he understood the vulnerable feeling of being in this situation without a means of defending oneself.

Laney tapped Clara on the shoulder. "Lean on me. We'll follow behind Ayden."

Ayden shouldered the rifle, and together they set off after Pasfield.

As they approached the building, Kim raced ahead. DaSilva and Pasfield appeared in Ayden's peripheral vision. The three of them reached the corner of the chapel simultaneously and dropped down behind the four-foot-high wall of sandbags for cover. Pasfield returned fire, emptying a magazine before stopping.

While he reloaded, Ayden poked his head up and fired until he was out of rounds. It slowed the enemy's return fire, but only temporarily. When a bullet hit the sandbag in front of his face and kicked debris into his eyes, Ayden was forced to stop firing and drop back down.

"We can't stay here. There are too many of them. We have to get inside and make it around to the west side of the building," DaSilva said. Around her neck, DaSilva's rifle dangled on its sling. She holstered her empty pistol.

Pasfield sprinted to the door and yanked on the handle. It didn't open. He fired, and the glass shattered. "Hurry!" he yelled.

Rounds slammed into the log, siding to his left as he flung open the door.

Ayden fired on full automatic as DaSilva and Laney helped Clara reach the doorway. Someone tapped on Ayden's shoulder, and then Flanagan dropped down beside him. "Go with them. I'll hold them back."

"No! Not by yourself!" Ayden said as he reloaded his rifle. "We need you to get us to the boat."

The soldier glanced back toward the chapel's door. "Okay. I'll cover you while you get inside. You cover me when you get there."

"Understood," Ayden said.

Ayden and the others followed Kim up the steps.

Once they'd made it inside the building, Pasfield spoke into a radio attached to his vest.

"Bravo one-niner. This is Bravo two-three."

A concerned expression crossed his face.

"Bravo one-niner. This is Bravo two-three," he repeated.

A knot formed in the pit of Ayden's stomach. What did it mean that there was no answer? Was the camp totally overrun? Were they doomed? His pulse pounded in his ears as he ran. It was like he was going in slow motion. Was this really happening?

While DaSilva helped Clara onto the floor just outside a bathroom, Laney paced back and forth in front of the elevator, chewing on her thumbnail. She was breathing hard, which Ayden suspected was more out of anxiousness than from running.

"Bravo two-three. This is Bravo one-niner." The following

words were drowned out by heavy gunfire, and then "SITREP!" crackled through Pasfield's radio.

"Bravo one-niner. This is Bravo two-three. We're in the northeast corner of the chapel. We're taking heavy fire from two teams of six to ten hostiles. Requesting additional support. Over."

"Bravo two-three. Hold your current position. Sending Alpha two-six to your location. Over."

"Roger that. Holding current position. Bravo two-three out."

Ayden felt a rush of relief at hearing that help was on the way. He hoped they'd be able to hold out until they arrived. DaSilva didn't look all that relieved, though.

"How long, Pasfield?" DaSilva asked.

"They were at the checkpoint on the freeway. Ten. Fifteen minutes."

"Ten or fifteen minutes?" Laney asked, her voice pitching high.

"They're on foot and have to fight hostiles to get here."

Laney's face contorted. She opened her mouth to say more but didn't, then she pivoted and hurried down the hall.

Ayden understood her concern. They were trapped like cornered animals. But all he could think about was Clara and what would become of her if he didn't make it.

"How much ammo do you have left?" Pasfield asked as he ejected a magazine from his rifle and replaced it with a fresh one.

Ayden counted the magazines in the pouch on his vest. "Three."

"Give me two of them. We'll have to make each shot count and conserve ammo. Don't shoot unless you see the enemy, okay?"

"Got it," Ayden said, handing him the mags. He hoped it wouldn't come to that. He prayed the hostiles wouldn't try to get inside. The minutes crawled by as they waited for help to arrive.

"You watch that door there." Pasfield pointed to one they'd just come through. "I'm going to check the doors on the other side of the building."

"What? No. What if they break in?" Laney asked, stepping in front of him.

"I won't go far. I'll be right back."

Laney slid down the wall and sat on the floor beside Clara.

"Maybe in the meantime, we should find something to barricade the door," Ayden said.

"Russell and his team will be here shortly," DaSilva said.

Ayden heard her confident words, but her face said something else entirely. He could see the tension in the rigid lines of her body. He found it hard to resist stealing quick glances over at Clara. She looked pale and sweaty. This was too much for his sister in her weakened condition.

"I need to use the restroom, Ayden," she said. "I think I'm going to be sick."

Ayden moved to her side and pulled Clara to her feet.

"Make it quick," DaSilva said. "We have to be ready to move when Russel gets here."

Clara acknowledged DaSilva's statement with a thumbs-up as Ayden slid his arm around her, and they slipped inside the restroom. Ayden led Clara over to one of the stalls.

"I can do the rest myself," she said, reaching down to unbutton her pants.

"I'll be just outside." Ayden backed out and returned to the hallway.

"What happens when we reach the boat ramp, DaSilva?" Kim asked. "Do you expect to hop on a boat and float away?"

DaSilva pivoted slightly as if about to say something and then shifted her weight to the opposite foot. Her focus returned to the door. After a long silence, she said, "I think we're going to have to abandon the camp."

"And the people?" Kim asked.

"You heard them. They're gone. Russel's team is all that's left. We can't retake the camp with only eight people. If we don't act quickly, we could all be trapped behind enemy lines."

"Wait. You think the PLA has taken that much territory?" Ayden asked. "What about our troops—the ones up at Sharpsburg?"

"Until we receive word otherwise, we have to assume they've pulled back as well."

"We don't know that," Kim said.

"Why would the PLA send soldiers after us if they were fighting the National Guard in Sharpsburg?" DaSilva asked.

"Why would they send them after your camp in the first place?" Laney asked.

"We kind of stirred up the hornet's nest," Kim said, smirking.

"We've been sabotaging their special forces teams as they scout the bridges and the boat ramps," DaSilva said.

"We put the target on our backs. The last mission led them right back to us. I knew we shouldn't have put Maxine in charge," Kim said.

"She has—had the most experience. They took the appropriate countermeasures. The enemy had the advantage of eyes in the sky."

"Yeah, and we're lucky they didn't just drop a bomb on us from one of those drones," Kim said.

"So what now?" Laney asked. "We just tuck tail and run and hope they don't decide to cross the Potomac after us?"

"Once we're out of the area they're operating in, they won't pursue us. We're no longer a threat to them at that point."

"What about our military?" Laney asked. "Is there nothing they can do to stop them?"

DaSilva's face flushed. She glanced away.

"What aren't you telling us, DaSilva?" Ayden asked.

DaSilva said nothing.

"DaSilva?" Ayden repeated.

"It's chaos. Without reliable comms with the Pentagon, each battalion is operating blind."

"Who's in charge then?" Ayden asked.

Slowly, she turned to face them. Her back straightened, and her shoulders stiffened. "The Pentagon's gone," she said matter-of-factly.

"Gone? Nuked gone?" Dominic asked.

She nodded.

"Who's going to lead this war then?" Ayden asked.

DaSilva's gaze fell to the floor. "After they launched the nukes into the atmosphere, causing the EMP, they launched nuclear strikes on Washington and various other places."

It was too horrible to contemplate. The idea that their entire government could be wiped out in an instant was unfathomable. What would that mean for the country and its ability to recover? Was it even possible?

"What about radiation and fallout? Are we all going to die?" Tina was nearing hysteria.

Ayden's mind went blank. His worst fears had been confirmed. The president had been in that motorcade and had been hit by the drone strike. He'd fled DC—maybe before it was nuked but had obviously been tracked by the PLA. It didn't feel real. None of it felt real. This couldn't be happening. America could not have been brought to her knees like this. Not like this. Not this easily.

"From what we've learned, the military's responses are being commanded from the president's doomsday plane," DaSilva said.

"By whom?" Clara asked. "We witnessed the presidential motorcade get blown up in Federick yesterday."

Tina's mouth dropped open. "The president is dead?"

"Whoever was in the president's car is," Ayden said.

"I can't say who is commanding the military from the doomsday plane. That wasn't told to us," DaSilva said. "It's just comforting to know that someone is in control and doing something."

"How do you know?" Tina asked. "How can you be sure?"

"One of our Coast Guard cutters received word. We relayed the information to another party," DaSilva said.

"What about our allies? What about Canada and Mexico? Were they affected by the EMP? Were we the only ones?" Laney asked.

"As far as I know, Canada and Mexico weren't hit," DaSilva said.

"Well, that means they'll come to our aid soon, right?" Ayden asked.

"If they can. They may wait until our naval forces arrive back home. They're on their way now, but they will be concentrating most of their attention on the West Coast, I'm told."

"Why? Don't they know about the PLA soldiers here?" Laney asked.

"I'm not sure. The concern at the time was with the Russian forces on the West Coast," DaSilva said.

"This is unreal," Ayden said.

"DaSilva, back to my original question, what do we do when we reach the boat ramp?" Kim asked.

"We'll cross over into West Virginia and make our way to our rally point."

"How are we supposed to get there without vehicles?" Kim asked.

"We have a vehicle," DaSilva said. "We prepositioned one two days ago when we first learned that PLA troops were coming this way."

"My motorhome is back at your meeting hall," Joyce said. "How are we supposed to escape the area?"

"You said you were on your way to Pennsylvania—Washington County, I believe."

"Yes," Laney said. "In western Pennsylvania."

DaSilva glanced at Kim and nodded. "We'll help you get to Kearneysville, West Virginia, and then you'll be on your own." She and Kim exchanged another glance. "We have to join the soldiers and hold back the PLA."

Kim smiled and then let it fall.

"Bravo two-three. This is Alpha two-six. How copy? Over," crackled over Pasfield's radio.

"Alpha two-six. I read you, Lima Charlie. Over."

"We're moving around to the southwest side of the chapel. Can you make it to that exit? Over."

"Alpha two-six, affirmative. We'll meet you at the southwest exit. Bravo two-three out."

Wondering what was taking his sister so long, Ayden ran into the restroom to check on her. Clara was leaning over the sink. An instant later, an explosion rocked the building. He grabbed Clara's arm and wrapped it around his neck. "We have to go!" he yelled as dust and smoke filled the restroom.

ELEVEN

Ayden

Camp Evergreen
Knoxville, Maryland
Day Six

Outside the chapel's bathroom, Ayden had to carry his sister over debris to reach the exit. Tina clung to Laney while Dominic helped his grandmother navigate around parts of the outer wall that had come down in the explosion. As they all made their way down the corridor toward the exit, they passed the arrival hall. Ayden got a view of the interior damage to the front of the building.

"They're using RPGs and mortar fire. We need to double-time it before they bring the whole building down on top of us," Kim said, moving past them.

The multistory chapel's windows were gone, replaced by a pile of twisted metal and shattered glass.

"This way! Keep coming," Pasfield called to them.

"Hurry!" Kim shouted.

"Let's go! Let's go, people," a gruff voice shouted from the doorway.

The reports of automatic gunfire echoed nearby.

When Ayden and Clara reached the end of the long hall, a man in military combat fatigues awaited them.

"Go! Go! Go!" he yelled, gesturing wildly with his hand.

"Where's Russel?" DaSilva asked, stepping past him.

The soldier turned and shouldered his rifle. "He's assisting Fox Team. He'll join you at the boat ramp."

At the doorway, Pasfield took Clara from Ayden's arms and handed her off to one of the soldiers. Satisfied his sister was in safe hands, Ayden assisted Joyce and the others to exit the building.

The gunfire sounded even closer now. Ayden hoped the team that had been sent to collect them had enough ammo to resupply him. He didn't like the prospect of crossing the open ground to the boat ramp without being able to defend himself and the others.

As they hurried past a cluster of primitive shelters and headed toward the river, the sound of the gunfire faded. Ayden spotted soldiers standing at the river's edge—only four. He didn't think that would be nearly enough to take on the group of PLA soldiers. Ayden's stomach tightened. He just wanted all this to be over. He'd had enough of fighting and death. He tried not to think about what they would face after leaving Maryland. He could only hope things weren't as bad in West Virginia.

Ayden thought of Mia and the boys—and the Russians. Not knowing what was going on with them out in Wyoming was torture. He glanced over at Laney. He prayed her father had heard something about that area of the country. He'd like to know if they were running from one war zone into another. He felt a sudden pang of guilt for even thinking of dragging his sister across the country. If he was really thinking of her safety, they'd head in the opposite direction—either north into Canada or south into Mexico.

Ayden followed Pasfield and the others down a dark, tree-lined gravel path. When it opened, he could see moonlight shimmering on the surface of the Potomac River. Four sixteen-foot flat-bottomed aluminum fishing boats were half in the water on the boat ramp.

"How's it going out there, Garcia?" Pasfield asked as he lined up behind the soldiers.

"Better than here, but not by much. You're lucky Sarge ordered us to come save your ass," the stockier of the two soldiers said.

Ayden noticed he wore a different uniform than the US soldier who'd stopped them on the way north. This man's blue uniform with USCG written across his vest told Ayden he was with the United States Coast Guard. Even though they were in different branches, their familiarity with one another made it obvious they'd met and worked together before all this.

"What about the bridge?" Pasfield asked.

"Charges have all been placed. I just hope we don't have to blow it. We could use you to hold our position."

Pasfield nodded. "I've got obligations here, but once I see these folks to safety, I'll head that way."

"Let's go, puddle pirate," the second soldier said, chopping the air in the direction of the path.

Garcia flipped him the bird and pivoted to face Pasfield. "Eat shit, Santos."

"What are the conditions in Pennsylvania?" DaSilva asked as she approached.

"They seem to be concentrating their efforts on Harrisburg at the moment. Dog Company took out one of their special forces companies near Gettysburg," Garcia said over his shoulder.

"We need to move," Santos barked.

"We need more ammo," Pasfield said.

"Santos, you got any extra 5.56?" Garcia called out.

Santos walked over. "I've got two mags." He held out the ammunition to Pasfield.

"Can I get one of those?" Ayden asked.

"No!" Kim snatched one from Garcia's hand.

"Kim, you go first, and then DaSilva, and… I forgot your name?" Pasfield said, gesturing at Ayden.

"Ayden."

"DaSilva, you got the girls? I need Ayden's help watching our six."

"Of course."

Ayden moved to Pasfield's side as DaSilva and Kim followed Garcia and Santos to the boats. A refreshing breeze hit Ayden in the face as he turned toward the river. The sun was coming up as the others each climbed into one of the four boats. Pasfield and Ayden remained on the ramp. Pasfield watched for hostiles to their left and Ayden scanned to their right as Flanagan and the soldiers pushed them deeper into the water. When the trolling motors hummed to life, Pasfield tapped Ayden on the shoulder, and the two climbed aboard the nearest boat.

They were within ten feet of the shore when the shots rang out. Pasfield shoved Tina to the bottom of the boat seconds before several rounds hit the boat to Ayden's right. The pinging noise it made caused Ayden's butt to pucker. Ayden craned to see if his sister was shot as the driver of his boat began swerving in a zigzag pattern to avoid incoming rounds.

He and Pasfield opened up on the four PLA soldiers on the boat ramp while DaSilva and the others fired upon those lining the shore, causing them all to dive for cover.

"Go!" Pasfield shouted to Flanagan, who was steering the boat.

"Open her up and get us the hell out of here, Flanagan," Pasfield shouted.

"It's open. This is as fast as it goes."

As they reached the middle of the river, the PLA soldiers began returning fire. An instant later, an explosion lit up the sky behind them, and then another landed on top of the Chinese fighters.

Moments later, the first boat reached the shoreline on the opposite side. Santos and DaSilva were the first ones on shore. They greeted the next boat and quickly assisted the passengers onto dry ground.

"Run!" Santos said. "Get to the inn!" He chopped the air in the direction of a two-story hotel with its back door standing open.

When Ayden's boat hit the shore, Pasfield leaped from the vessel and spun to face the opposite shore. Ayden jumped onto the boat ramp and moved to his side.

"Keep moving. That way," Pasfield said.

Ayden ran in that direction but kept peering back, looking to see if the soldiers were following. He didn't want to get separated from them. "Where are the soldiers?" he asked as he ran alongside Pasfield.

"They're going back to join their units."

"Are we safe on this side of the river?"

"For now," Pasfield said as they joined with the others. He nodded toward Flanagan."Flanagan, you know where to take them."

"You're not coming?" Kim asked.

"No! I need to help them hold the bridge."

Pasfield turned back before reaching the hotel. "I'll meet up with you all at the rally point if I can, but don't wait for me."

"Where's the rally point?" Laney asked.

"Crap!" Pasfield cursed. He pressed the button of the radio attached to his vest as he turned back toward the boat ramp. Before he could speak, a barrage of gunfire erupted.

Ayden dropped to the ground behind a row of low shrubs.

"Alpha two-six. What is your position?" Pasfield yelled into his mic as he turned back toward the house. "Ayden! Go, dude! Get to the house!"

Ayden popped back up about the time Pasfield reached him. They were running away from the gunfire, but it was hard for Ayden to pinpoint where it all was coming from.

"Alpha two-six! How copy?"

No response came.

TWELVE

Mia

Christiansen Ranch
Farson, Wyoming
Day Six

Morning brought a flurry of activity to the Christiansen ranch. Mia stood on the front porch, watching her father, Neil, and the wranglers as they set about fortifying the cabin. The sense of urgency was palpable, each man moving with purpose as they prepared for the potential threat looming over their home.

Neil, his weathered face set in determined lines, directed the wranglers with calm authority. "All right, let's get those plywood boards up on the windows first," he called out, pointing to the large sheets of wood stacked against the cabin wall. "Make sure you leave small gaps for observation."

Dirk, the ranch manager, nodded and began organizing the wranglers. He handed out hammers and nails, and the rhythmic sound of hammering soon filled the air. The cabin's windows, once open to the elements and offering picturesque views of the surrounding landscape, were quickly transformed into fortified barriers. The plywood was cut to fit perfectly, leaving narrow slits that would allow them to see out while remaining protected.

Mia's gaze shifted to the doors, where her father and another wrangler were installing heavy metal bars and additional locks. Each clang of metal against wood reverberated through the cabin. Neil's hands were steady as he worked, his focus intense. He exchanged a few words with the wrangler, who nodded and set off around the cabin to secure the back door with similar reinforcements.

The front porch, where Mia stood, was soon buzzing with activity. Sandbags were being carried and stacked around the perimeter to create makeshift defensive positions. The wranglers were quieter than Mia had ever heard them, their faces filled with tension. Even still, in the midst of this daunting task, there was a sense of camaraderie among them.

Mia watched as Dirk and one of the younger wranglers began digging trenches around the cabin. The earth yielded to their shovels as they carved out protective barriers. The trenches would serve as additional defense, giving them cover if they needed to repel an attack. The sight of the raw earth being turned up was both reassuring and unsettling, a tangible sign of how crazy their world had become.

Melody, Mia's mother, joined her on the porch, her eyes scanning the activity with a mixture of pride and worry. "They're doing a good job," Melody said softly, her voice barely audible over the noise of construction.

Mia nodded, her throat tight with emotion. "Yes, they are. Dad seems so calm."

"He always does in times like this," Melody replied, placing a comforting hand on Mia's shoulder. "But we all need that right now."

As they watched, one of the wranglers approached with a large bundle of barbed wire. Dirk directed him to start stringing it in rows across the field between the house and the road to create a first line of defense that would slow down any unwanted visitors. The wrangler worked quickly, unspooling the wire and securing it to the ground with short posts, each strand a barrier of sharp metal meant to protect.

"I've heard the wire might even slow down tracked military vehicles," Dirk said.

Melody pressed her hand to her cheek. "Let's hope so."

Mia's eyes were drawn to the barn, where a group of wranglers was busy securing the livestock. Sensing the unusual activity, the animals were restless, their lowing adding to the noisy scene. The wranglers worked to reinforce the stalls and ensure the horses would be safe and contained. They would need them if they had to bug out into the mountains.

With every passing minute, the cabin and its surroundings were transformed from a peaceful homestead into a veritable fortress. The sense of security was tempered by the realization of why these measures were necessary. The threat of the Russian military, still abstract but terrifying, loomed over them like a dark cloud.

Mia took a deep breath, the cool air filling her lungs as she tried to steady her nerves. The sight of her father and the wranglers working so tirelessly, doing everything they could to protect their home, filled her with a mixture of hope and dread at the uncertainty of what lay ahead. As the last of the fortifications were put in place, Neil called for a brief pause. The wranglers gathered around him, their faces lined with exhaustion and determination. "Good work, everyone," Neil said. The corners of his eyes crinkled. "We've done what we can for now. Let's take a moment to rest, and then we'll continue preparing."

The wranglers nodded, some dropping to the ground to rest their weary bodies, others heading to the bunkhouse to grab a quick bite to eat.

Mia stepped down from the porch and limped over to her father, who was inspecting the fortification at the front of the cabin. "Dad," she said softly, drawing his attention. "Did Dirk happen to say anything about what might be happening in the East?"

Neil looked at her, his stern expression softening. "No, sweetheart." He took her hand. "I know you're worried about Ayden. I was going to have Dirk ride over and see if Simmons had heard anything new today. I'll have him ask about New York."

"Thanks, Daddy." She stared off toward the road. "I know the odds of him making it back to me and the boys are slim, but not knowing…"

Neil wrapped his arms around her and pulled her close. "I know, sweetie. That's how I felt when I couldn't find you."

"But you did. I'm home, safe."

"And we'll have to believe that somehow, Ayden is as well, and he'll find his way here." He looked her in the eyes. "I know this: That boy loves you and those kids, and I'd bet anything he's doing everything within his power to get back to you."

"I hope so," Mia said.

THIRTEEN

Mueller

New Eden Compound
Somerset Township
Washington County, Pennsylvania
Day Six

Mueller and his team gathered around a large map of Pittsburgh laid out on the table. Mueller began to outline the plan to rescue Tom's family. "All right, listen up. Here's the plan: we'll take the Suburban and use back roads to avoid main highways. Once we get close to the city, we'll go on foot. Nesbitt, you'll be our scout. Amos, you're our point man. Smith, you'll handle communications and provide cover. Giblin, you're on lookout and rear guard. Thomas, you'll stick with me."

Nesbitt jabbed a finger at the map. "What's the best route in?"

Mueller moved around the table. "We'll approach from the west, through the industrial area. It's less populated and offers better cover. We'll have to navigate through gang territories, so stay alert. Our goal is to get in, locate the family, and get out quickly. Minimize contact and avoid confrontation if possible."

"What if we do run into trouble?" Smith asked.

Mueller glanced up from the map. "We engage only if necessary. We're not looking for a fight. The priority is to get Thomas's family out safely. Use smoke grenades for cover if needed. Remember, stealth and speed are our allies here."

"Understood," Amos said. "What about the exfil?"

"Once we have the family, we'll regroup at the rendezvous point here." Mueller pointed to a spot on the map indicating a dry cleaner, which Tom had said hadn't yet gone up in flames. "From there, we'll head back the same way we came. Everyone clear on their roles?"

The team nodded, the gravity of the mission evident on their faces. Mueller felt a mix of anxiety and excitement. They'd trained for years for missions like this, and he had to admit to a certain level of excitement about finally utilizing those skills.

The team loaded up into the 1970 Chevrolet Suburban, the vehicle stuffed with their backpacks full of supplies and weapons. The drive was tense but uneventful as they took the back roads to avoid potential threats and the mass of refugees filling the main roads. As they neared Pittsburgh, the signs of chaos became evident—smoke rose in the distance, and the sound of sporadic gunfire seemed to rise with it.

Smith pulled the SUV into the construction company's parking lot and parked it among the many work trucks near the back, which abutted a green belt. The team hiked through the dense tree cover, crossed the railroad tracks, and then exited, intending to take Woodruff Street north to West Carson Street. Instead, they encountered a large group traveling south toward them.

"Turn right," Mueller said, chopping the air with his hand in that direction. "We'll take Sawmill Run Boulevard to Boggs Avenue."

As they made their way toward the industrial area, the residential streets were eerily quiet, with abandoned cars and debris littering the roads. Less than a mile later, the homes gave way to commercial buildings. Mueller and his team rounded a corner just as a group of looters ran toward them. Mueller held a fist into the air. “Hold your position. Let them pass.”

The team dropped behind an abandoned SUV. They watched as the looters ransacked the stores, oblivious to their presence. The street was lined with tall, decaying brick buildings, their windows shattered, and graffiti-covered walls that indicated the area had been economically depressed for years prior to the event. Smoke from distant fires hung in the air, casting an eerie haze over the scene and affecting Mueller’s sinuses. He suppressed a sneeze, wishing he’d thought to bring his allergy spray.

One of the looters, a tall and muscular man, carried out a stack of boxes. Behind him, a woman and a young girl held shopping bags overflowing with looted goods. The couple and the child ran across the street and slipped down a side alley.

“Tom, you and Smith check that alley. Make sure they’re gone,” Mueller said.

“Amos, Nesbitt, you’re on me. We’re moving to that delivery van on the corner.” Mueller stepped out from behind the vehicle, his focus on the store the couple had just emerged from. “Stay sharp,” Mueller said. “Threats could come from anywhere.”

Suddenly, a voice echoed from the alleyway. “What are you doing in our territory?”

Mueller dropped back, seeking cover as Tom responded to the man.

“We don’t want any trouble. We’re just passing through.”

A second man, tall and broad-shouldered, with long, stringy hair, stepped from the mouth of the alley, pistol aimed at Tom. “That’s gonna cost you.”

An instant later, three more people emerged behind the man. Each held a pistol. Mueller aimed the crosshairs of his rifle scope on the teen to the right of the broad-shouldered man. The kid looked terrified. His pistol shook in his trembling hands. Mueller needed to defuse the situation before someone got killed.

Smith, standing just to Tom's side, laughed. "Pay? You must be kidding. Look at you, standing there holding that pea shooter like some gangster wannabe thug. You know you can't hit anything with it pointed sideways like that, right?"

Mueller sprinted toward them, followed by Nesbitt and Amos. This was escalating quickly and getting out of control.

"Oh yeah? You wanna screw around and find out?" the looter spat.

Smith scoffed. "Please! I will drop you before you can squeeze that trigger."

The man threw his chin in the air and jabbed the pistol in Smith's direction. "This block is ours. I own you now."

Tom raised his hand. "Please, let's just—"

The nervous teen reacted, flinching. An instant later—

Boom!

The kid's pistol went off.

"Move! Move! Move!" Mueller shouted as Smith tossed the grenade.

FOURTEEN

Ayden

River's Edge Inn
Bakerton, West Virginia
Day Six

Clara leaned against the doorjamb of the inn, waiting for him as Ayden raced up the driveway toward her. Near the rear deck of the inn, DaSilva, Kim, and Flanagan were scanning the river's edge through their rifle scopes for threats.

"Alpha two-seven!" Pasfield radioed. "Santos!"

"Bravo two-three. Bravo two-three," finally crackled through the radio. "We're on the southwest corner of the chapel parking lot, taking heavy fire. We've got at least a dozen advancing from the east side of the camp. There are more making their way across from the front. Two-six is down surgical."

"Crap! Crap! Crap!" Pasfield said, pacing back and forth.

"Alpha two-four. This is Bravo two-three. How copy? Over."

Ayden didn't hear a reply from Alpha two-four.

"DaSilva. Flanagan. We're going to head to the street. I'm going to take the rear and cover your six. You stay close to the building by the shrubbery. When you reach the street, move from vehicle to vehicle. Call out if you see anything. We have to get to our bug-out vehicle before the PLA crosses the river."

Ayden's mind imagined the worst, conjuring images from all the war movies he'd ever watched. Those films had made the battlefield look like hell on earth, and they'd had the ability to call in air support. What hope did he and this group have?

Flanagan led the way, followed by Dominic, Lunch Box, and Joyce. Laney and Tina each grabbed one of Clara's arms, and together, they half-carried her out of the inn behind Joyce. DaSilva and Kim fell in behind them, rifles shouldered and scanning for threats.

"Go, Ayden! We have to get to the box truck parked at the fire station," Pasfield said, running alongside him.

At the end of the street leading into the small riverfront subdivision, instead of turning right or left on the main road, Flanagan crossed over and continued west. The route dead-ended at a cul-de-sac.

Laney, Clara, and Tina stopped as Flanagan continued across a lawn and down the side of one of the homes. As Ayden and Pasfield caught up to them, Clara's chest was heaving in and out as she struggled to catch her breath.

"Let's go," Kim shouted back at them.

"I can't," Clara cried. "I can't keep going. My hip is killing me from hopping on one leg."

Ayden ran over, shoved his rifle at Laney, and scooped his sister into his arms. As he set off across the cul-de-sac, Laney flung the rifle strap over her head and shouldered the weapon.

"Try not to shoot any friendlies," Pasfield said, gesturing for her to follow Ayden.

"Zip up your fly, bozo. Your brain's hanging out," Laney responded back.

Ayden didn't hear anything back from Pasfield, but Laney was smiling when she reached the side of the inn where everyone had stopped, waiting for Flanagan to scout ahead to make sure the way was clear.

As Laney approached, Tina held out her hand, and the two fist-bumped. "Good comeback!" Tina said.

"Pay attention, ladies," DaSilva said. "Voices low. The PLA could be anywhere."

"Sorry!" Laney whispered. She moved past Tina and Joyce and stopped beside Kim. "So we're heading out to your van, but then what? Where after that?"

"South!" Kim said.

"No!" Laney said, a little too loud.

That earned her a scowl from DaSilva. The older woman placed her finger to her lips.

"I need to go north to Pennsylvania," Laney said, more quietly.

"I understand," DaSilva said. "We can get you as far as Kearneysville, West Virginia. From there, we go south, and you'll head north."

"How far away is Kearneysville?"

"Ten miles west of here," Kim said.

Flanagan returned, waving them onward. Twenty minutes later, they crossed a farmer's field and exited across from a fire station. Parked in the gravel lot adjacent to the building was an older model, yellow box van. Flanagan rushed across the street, dropped to the ground, and retrieved a set of keys from the driver's side wheel well. By the time Ayden and Clara reached the truck, he had the door rolled up and was assisting Joyce inside.

Minutes later, Ayden and his group were sitting in the back of the box van in the dark, listening to their own heavy breathing.

DaSilva, seated next to Joyce, flicked on a flashlight and pointed its beam at the floor, illuminating Pasfield's feet.

Pasfield sat near the door with his back against the side. He retrieved a flashlight from his belt, turned it on, and sat it on the floor beside him. He busied himself by consolidating his remaining ammo from two partially full magazines into one. "We're going to need to hit one of our caches before we reach Kearneysville," he said.

DaSilva rose and banged on the wall between them and the cab of the van. A second later, the van stopped, the door rolled up, and Kim's face appeared in the opening. "Time to hit the cache at the church. We're all out of ammo."

"Yes, ma'am," Kim said, closing the door.

The van took off again and stopped a few minutes later outside a church. "Everyone, just wait here. This won't take long." Pasfield jumped down from the van.

Ayden used the time to examine Clara. He placed his hand on her forehead. "How's your pain?"

"I'll survive."

"Do you need pain meds?" DaSilva said. "I've got Percocet and ibuprofen."

"How about just an ibuprofen?"

DaSilva retrieved the pill bottle from one of the side pockets of her pants. "We'll have water in just a minute. I'll take a look at her bandage when we get to Kearneysville. I can give you some fresh gauze to take with you."

"Where are you heading?" Tina asked.

"South," was all DaSilva would say.

"Is it safer in that direction?"

"For now."

The crew was quiet, and a short time later, Pasfield and Kim returned carrying duffle bags and backpacks. Kim tossed hers into the back of the van and returned to the driver's seat as DaSilva rummaged through the bags and retrieved a bottle of water. She handed it to Clara and then passed out more to the van's other occupants. Ayden opened the bottle for Clara and then drank his own, taking large gulps. He couldn't recall ever being so thirsty.

They rode in silence the rest of the way to Kearneysville. As they did, the effects of the adrenaline began to wear off, and Ayden found himself with the shakes despite the overly warm temperatures inside the box van. Exhaustion seeped into every muscle in his body, and all he wanted was to lie down on the floor of the truck and sleep. He rested his head against the side wall and closed his eyes, but the scene from the battle began to replay in a loop. Sighing in frustration, he forced away the images by concentrating on how they were going to make it all the way to Washington County, Pennsylvania, on foot. They had no food or water and no way to defend themselves. His stomach then growled loudly, and Tina snickered.

"Someone's hungry," she said.

DaSilva tossed Ayden a protein bar. "We have supplies stashed in Kearneysville. We can't spare much, but at least you'll eat today."

He split it in half and gave the rest to his sister. As they ate, Pasfield tossed more snack bars to the others.

"You'll want to scavenge the area in Kearneysville before heading north. There's an orchard that had fruit when we scouted it two days ago."

"Martinsburg is going to be the best place to find food and shelter items. Look for tarps, ropes, or something to carry water. A pot for boiling it. Don't—whatever you do—do not drink water you haven't boiled. You will regret it. It could kill you."

"My dad said dehydration is your biggest enemy on the road," Laney said. "You get the poops from bad water, and you'll get dehydrated quickly."

Pasfield nodded. "Most places are going to have been looted out by now. Think out of the box—places like offices, churches, daycares, and fitness centers for food and bottled water and juices. You might find tents and camping gear inside storage units. You'll need a good set of bolt cutters to break the locks, though."

"What about weapons?" Laney asked. "My dad suggested hitting a home goods store or garden center and looking for sharp tools."

"That would be great if they haven't been looted already. There are a number of things you can use to make an effective close-combat weapon. You just need to be innovative."

The truck stopped, and Pasfield rolled up the door. Ayden shielded his eyes from the bright sunlight as DaSilva brushed past him. They were parked in the lot of a mini-storage facility. Lining the fence was a row of boats and motorhomes.

Dominic and Joyce set out for them. "Maybe we can get one of them started," Dominic said.

"You could try," DaSilva said. "I wouldn't waste my time, though. They've likely been sitting a long time, and the batteries are probably dead."

"Worth trying," Joyce said, disappearing between a pontoon boat and an older-looking RV.

FIFTEEN

Ayden

Kearneysville Mini-Storage
Kearneysville, West Virginia
Day Six

While Dominic and Joyce checked out an older model motorhome to see if they could start it, Pasfield pulled a pair of bolt cutters from his duffle bag and headed toward a storage unit in the middle of the first row a short distance away.

"What's Pasfield doing? Don't we have the keys?" Kim asked, pointing to the backpacks.

"To our units, but when we were here stowing our cache, we saw a guy unloading a truck at that locker." DaSilva reached into one of the bags, retrieved a large set of keys, and handed them to Flanagan. "The unit numbers are on the keys."

"What's in the unit Pasfield is breaking into?" Laney asked.

DaSilva smiled. "Let's go see."

Ayden reached for Clara.

"Go ahead. I'll wait here in the van," she said.

Ayden handed her the rest of his water and followed DaSilva

and the others to the unit Pasfield had just opened. A smile formed on Ayden's lips as Pasfield rolled up the door to reveal a locker full of sports equipment, including bats, fishing rods, tackle boxes, shoes, backpacks, sports bottles, and a duffle bag to carry it all in.

"Nice," Laney said, grabbing one of the metal bats and slapping the palm of her left hand with it.

Tina stepped inside and began shoving the sports water bottles into the duffle while Ayden inspected the fishing rods.

"Just up the road a little way is a nature park," DaSilva said. "I'm told it has a spring-fed lake stocked full of fish. It would make a nice spot to stop for the night and rest, catch some fish, and fill up your water bottles for the road."

"And bathe," Joyce said.

"I'd love to wash my hair." Tina held up a clear pouch filled with hygiene products.

Ayden ran his tongue across his teeth. He'd never gone so long without brushing. He glanced back at Clara. They could use an evening to rest. He wasn't sure how far she would be able to walk before the pain became too severe, and he was so exhausted he wasn't sure he could assist her more than a mile or so. The thought of filling his stomach with rich aquatic protein was very appealing.

"I vote we find this nature preserve and rest and recalibrate for the night," Ayden said.

"I'd really like to get a lot farther from those PLA troops before we stop," Laney said.

Ayden nodded. "I know. Me too, but on foot…" He nodded toward Joyce, who had just exited the back of one of the motorhomes wearing a disappointed look.

"Finding transportation should be our top priority then," Laney said.

She fixed her gaze on the older woman. Ayden could see the concern on her face. She'd counted on Joyce's motorhome to get her to her parents' compound. Now all she had was the liability of a group of people who would only slow her down.

"You know, Laney…" Ayden handed her the backpack he held in his hands. "You owe us nothing. We'll only slow you down. You're free to make your way home without us."

Tina spun around and grabbed Laney's arm. "You won't leave me, right?"

Laney shook her head. "Of course not." She reached out and plucked a strand of Tina's hair and tucked it behind the young woman's ear. "We're going to find a new ride."

Tina pivoted and scanned the line of RVs and boats lining the chain-linked fence. "I wish the river were safe. I bet we could get one of those boats to start."

DaSilva shook her head. "The river is definitely not safe."

"We're loaded up," Kim called from the van.

DaSilva extended a hand to Ayden. "Good luck."

"Thank you for everything," Ayden said as they shook.

"Yes," Joyce said, walking up. "You've restored my faith in humanity. You didn't know us from Adam, yet you put your life in danger to get us here safely."

"We're all Americans, and pulling together during trying times is what we do," DaSilva said.

Laney reached her hand out to the older woman. "Can I ask, were you in the military?"

DaSilva smiled. "CIA."

"You were a spook?" Tina asked, wide-eyed.

DaSilva chuckled. "We were."

"Kim too?" Laney asked, shifting her gaze to the van.

"No, she's Homeland Security."

Laney smirked. "That figures. They did a piss-poor job securing the homeland."

"Not much you can do when your hands are tied at every turn," Pasfield said, handing Ayden the pair of bolt cutters he'd used to break the lock on the unit.

"We did our parts. Washington was warned."

"Is that why you have stashes like this?" Laney asked,

gesturing to the van.

"And a camp like across the river," Ayden said. He furrowed his brow, recalling what Clara's neighbor had told them about his uncle being forewarned about the attack. "You knew in advance and set yourself up to survive?"

DaSilva glanced away. "Washington didn't believe this kind of attack was possible. They downplayed every piece of intelligence we sent them concerning the joint operations between Russia, China, and Iran. DC pursued diplomatic channels and threats of sanctions, taking a mutually assured destruction defense strategy, believing that our second-strike capabilities countered our adversary's first-strike threat. All the while, our enemies were planning this devastating attack against our infrastructure undeterred."

"You failed to answer the question," Joyce said. "You prepositioned supplies knowing this was going to happen." She glared at DaSilva. "And didn't tell the American public so we could prepare too?"

DaSilva was silent.

"It would have caused a mass panic," Pasfield said. "That was the consensus. People might have fled their homes, which would have killed even more people. Despite the conditions, remaining in their homes was the safer strategy."

"How so?" Ayden asked. "Manhattan was ripped apart by violence. Buildings were falling down around us. The gangs totally took over the streets almost immediately. Staying in our apartment wasn't an option."

"For most people, it is the best option under the circumstances." Pasfield gestured to a group of single-family homes nearby and then turned toward an apartment complex across the highway. "For them, bugging in is the safest strategy. They may have to scavenge for food and occasionally leave to find water, but they have roofs over their heads and some measure of safety within the familiar walls of their residences." He waved his hand in the air. "Out here, with no place to go, they're at the mercy of the elements, people who mean them harm, and the PLA. Besides, do you think they could just walk off into the woods and survive off the land? Most Americans have no idea what it takes to feed themselves without a grocery store." He tilted his head to the side and raised an eyebrow. "You ever eat bugs for a week?"

"Bugs? Yuck!" Tina contorted her face.

"You're going to have to be willing to eat whatever you can find to live now, including bugs," DaSilva said. She turned toward the box van. "Survival is a head game. You need to make up your mind if you really want to live and decide whether you are willing to do whatever it takes to do so."

Ayden considered DaSilva's and Pasfield's words as the two walked toward their van. He made up his mind as he followed them back to his sister. He would do everything within his power to ensure that Clara and their traveling companions would make it. The best way he knew to achieve that goal was somehow to get them all to Laney's father's compound.

Kim walked up to Laney and unholstered her pistol.

Laney took a step back, eyeing her warily.

Kim held the firearm out to Laney. "You said you were familiar with firearms."

Laney's hands remained at her sides. "My father taught me from a young age."

"Here," Kim said. "Take it."

Laney glanced back at Ayden with a questioning look.

Kim's abrupt turnaround confused him as well.

After taking the pistol from Kim, Laney dropped the magazine and racked the slide, examining the weapon before reinserting the ammunition. "Nice Glock 19, but it needs to be cleaned," she said.

Pasfield tossed her a small gun cleaning kit while Kim removed two extra magazines from one of the pouches on her belt.

"How many rounds are left in that rifle?" Flanagan asked, gesturing to the firearm dangling across Ayden's chest.

He checked the weapon. "Five."

Flanagan reached into his back pocket and then held out an extra mag. “It’s chambered in 5.56. You can safely shoot .223 ammo in a rifle chambered for 5.56, but never shoot 5.56 ammunition in a rifle chambered for .223.”

Ayden stared back at him, unblinking. “Okay!” Ayden wasn’t a gun guy and had no idea what he was talking about.

“I usually shot 6.5 Grendel or 300 Blackouts,” Laney said, stuffing her new pistol into her waistband.

“Here,” Pasfield said, handing her a waistband pistol holster. “So you don’t shoot your pee-pee off.”

Laney rolled her eyes, then smiled as she took the holster from him. “Funny, bro, but if I wanted to hear from an asshole, I’d fart.”

Pasfield laughed. “Admit it, you’re gonna miss me.”

“Yeah, just like period cramps,” Laney said sarcastically.

Pasfield wrinkled his nose and reached out his hand. He chuckled as Laney fist-bumped him.

As he began to walk off, Laney called out to him. “Pasfield, try not to shoot yourself in the foot.”

Pasfield guffawed and shot her the bird. “Do me a favor, Laney. Have your dad send out a message on the radio when you reach home so I know where to send my sympathy card.”

“Ha! Ha! That’s funny, Past Your Prime,” she said, making a play on his last name.

He faked a laugh. “Past your prime!” He jabbed a finger in the air. “Sorry, I can’t hear you over the sound of how awesome I am.”

Laney waved with her middle finger as Pasfield and DaSilva climbed into the back of the box van.

“Keep your heads on a swivel out there,” Flanagan said, climbing into the passenger seat.

As Kim got behind the wheel, Ayden slung his backpack over his shoulder and took Clara’s arm.

“Are we ready?” he asked.

“Not really, but let’s do it anyway,” Joyce said.

“How far is this nature preserve?” Clara asked, hopping on one foot as they headed for the highway.

Ayden shifted the rifle to his opposite shoulder. “Not far, I hope.”

Dominic grabbed the fishing poles and tackle box and headed out ahead of them. Joyce and Tina each picked up backpacks from the ground while Lunch Box carried the duffle bag filled with empty water bottles.

“Keep your heads on a swivel,” Ayden said, repeating Flanagan’s advice.

Laney passed them. “Roger that!”

SIXTEEN

Mueller

Boggs Avenue
Pittsburgh, Pennsylvania
Day Six

Gunfire rang out along Boggs Avenue.

Tom fell, clutching his chest, blood spilling through his fingers.

"Tom!" Mueller shouted, running toward him.

The teen stood there, eyes wide, staring down at him as chaos erupted around him.

Smith reacted quickly, raised his rifle, and fired back, hitting the broad-shouldered man in the chest, but the return gunfire was brutal. The team responded swiftly, engaging the gang members in a brief but intense firefight.

Mueller's vision tunneled as he focused on returning fire, every shot aimed with precision. The looters, caught off guard by the team's skill and coordination, quickly retreated back down the alley.

He rushed to Tom's side, but it was too late. His friend's breaths came in ragged gasps. Mueller choked back grief, his throat tightening and eyes stinging with unshed tears. His hands trembled as he pressed them against Tom's wound in a futile attempt to stop the bleeding. The reality of the situation crashed over him like a wave, almost knocking the breath out of his lungs.

"Ty… take care of them," Tom whispered before his body went limp.

"I will, Tom. I promise," he murmured, his voice breaking.

Mueller's mind was a storm of emotions. Every heartbeat seemed to echo the guilt that gnawed at him—his plan had gone horribly wrong, and it had cost his friend's life. He hung his head, his shoulders slumping under the crushing burden of his failure. How could he have let this happen? He had promised to keep them all safe, and now Tom was gone. How would he tell his wife? How would he look Tom's children in the eye?

"We need to move," Amos said, grabbing Tom's right arm and throwing it around his neck. Smith grabbed the other side. "We can't stand out here in the open."

Now on autopilot, Mueller snapped back to the task at hand, his training kicking in. "There!" He pointed to a detached garage behind one of the buildings. The team moved swiftly and silently back to their safe position.

Giblin kicked open the man-sized door and rushed inside. He reemerged seconds later.

"Clear!" he said, and Amos and Smith carried Tom's body inside.

Mueller's heart was heavy as they laid Tom's body gently on the ground, covering him with a blanket they found in the back seat of the car inside the garage. The team stood in somber silence.

Amos moved to the window that overlooked another alleyway. "We can't see much from here."

"We'll wait them out," Mueller said. "Give it a few minutes, and then we'll scout the next few blocks." Mueller paced in front of the roll-up doors for a moment before taking a seat on the floor, the cold concrete offering a brief respite from the heat.

Smith, his face pale with anger and fear, broke the silence. “Tom’s dead, Ty. What’s the point of continuing this mission? We’re risking our lives—for what?”

Mueller’s hands balled into fists, nostrils flaring. He couldn’t believe Smith would suggest abandoning Tom’s family. “We gave our word, Smith. A man’s word is worth everything. Without it, he’s nothing. Tom’s wife and children are as much a part of this group as you or me. They deserve to be rescued as much as my daughter or yours.”

Amos, his face set in a fierce look, stepped forward. “Mueller’s right. We owe it to Tom and his family. We can’t abandon them now!” Amos’s hands were trembling with barely contained rage.

Nesbitt, usually calm and collected, looked at Smith in disgust. “How can you even think about leaving them? We trained for this, Smith. We knew the risks. Are you really going to wuss out now?”

Smith stiffened, working his jaw. “I don’t want to see anyone else die.”

“None of us do,” Mueller said, his voice firm but edged with contempt. “But we can’t let fear dictate our actions. We honor Tom by finishing what we started. If we don’t stand by our principles now, we never will.”

Mueller rubbed the back of his neck. How could Smith be so willing to abandon their mission? Had he misjudged Smith’s character all this time? Could he ever trust him again? Doubt gnawed at him, but he pushed it aside. They were there now. He’d just have to keep a close eye on the man.

Smith finally nodded, his posture softening. “I’m sorry. You’re right. We can’t abandon his family.”

With the team reluctantly back on the same page, Mueller moved toward the door, eased it open, and listened. Hearing only silence, he emerged from the garage.

“What about Tom?” Amos asked, standing beside his body.

“We leave him here for now. We’ll retrieve him on the way back if we can,” Mueller said.

SEVENTEEN

Ayden

Kearneysville Mini-Storage
Kearneysville, West Virginia
Day Six

After watching DaSilva and her group depart the mini-storage facility, Ayden and his companions trudged down the highway to Martinsburg. The sun blazed unforgivingly, intensifying their desperation. Clara's steps were heavy, her breathing labored, and sweat streamed down her face. Joyce's pace was slowing, and her age showed more with every mile.

Ayden scanned the horizon, his mind working furiously. "We need something on wheels—anything that can carry a load," he muttered to Dominic, who nodded in agreement.

A few miles up the road, Ayden spotted a yellow and red frozen food delivery truck. "The sight of that makes my mouth water."

"Oh, man!" Dominic said. "Have you ever tried their fire-braised pork or the penne with prosciutto?"

"I've never heard of the company," Clara said.

Joyce wiped her forehead with the back of her hand. "They

sold out to some Korean company and changed the name. I heard the food wasn't as good now."

"Should we check it out?" Clara asked.

Ayden shook his head. "After six days, all the food will have thawed. It won't be edible."

Laney stopped walking and turned around. "We should at least take a look," she said, spinning toward the food truck. "We have to explore every possible source of food and supplies." Laney handed Tina her bat, unholstered her pistol, and ventured off toward the frozen food delivery vehicle.

"I would love one of their ice cream sandwiches." Tina shouldered the bat as they headed that way. "You think their cookie and brownie dough would still be okay to eat?"

Ayden deferred to Joyce.

She raised an eyebrow. "Maybe. Most things you can tell by the appearance or smell if they've gone bad."

"I wouldn't risk it," Ayden said. "Food poisoning could be deadly out here."

"If it's still cold, it might be all right," Lunch Box said.

"Only if it's still below forty degrees inside there," Ayden said as he and Clara followed after the others.

"You think that's possible after six days?" Tina asked as they neared the food truck.

Ayden leaned Clara against the side of a sedan and then removed the bolt cutters from his pack. "We're about to find out."

He snapped the locks and swung open the door. The interior was cool to the touch but not cold and definitely not still frozen. He pulled out one of the white bins, probing the bags inside. He frowned. "It doesn't feel like forty degrees in there."

Tina nudged him aside, yanking open a bag. She sniffed it and immediately recoiled. "Nope! That's gone bad."

Despite their hope, a thorough check of the other compartments confirmed their fears: all the food was spoiled. Reluctantly, they left the food delivery truck with its doors gaping open. None of them were hungry enough to risk food poisoning.

Soon, the group approached an ambulance service building. Two of the bay doors were up. It had likely already been looted of anything helpful, but as Laney had said, they needed to exploit every opportunity to find supplies.

"Should we check it out?" Tina asked. "Maybe they have medical supplies inside."

"I don't think I have the energy to veer that far off the highway," Clara said.

"How about Ayden and I go," Dominic said. He walked ahead to a nearby pickup truck and lowered the tailgate. "You guys can have a seat here while Ayden and I check it out. We'll make it quick. Laney can stand guard over you with her pistol."

Clara nodded, and Ayden helped her settle onto the tailgate before he and Dominic approached the ambulance service building. Although the bay doors stood open, the facility's garage looked untouched, which seemed odd. Inside the building, they found a treasure trove of potentially useful items. Shelves lined with medical supplies were a welcome sight: bandages, antiseptics, an assortment of splints, but no painkillers or antibiotics. They did find a bottle of ibuprofen in a desk drawer, along with a package of peanut butter crackers and a bag of chocolate candies.

Venturing farther, they checked the ambulances parked outside. In the back of one, they discovered enough supplies to fully stock a first-aid kit and a hydraulic lift stretcher, which would be invaluable for transporting Clara.

Dominic exited the building, pushing an office chair loaded down with their finds. "It's not a wheelchair, but I think I can push my grandma in it."

"I think it will work. We won't be doing anything off-road with them, but the ladies will be more comfortable, and we'll be able to move faster," Ayden said.

Loaded with as much as they could carry, they hurried back to the highway, hopeful that these supplies could ease their journey and perhaps save a life.

Clara greeted them with a weak smile at the sight of the gurney. "What's that for?"

"You. Now you can elevate your leg and ride in style."

"It doesn't look like it will be any easier on you since you'll have to push it."

"We'll travel faster, so that will help." Ayden pushed the gurney near the tailgate. "Hop on and let's try it out."

"What's the chair for?" Tina asked, gesturing to Dominic.

"For Gran!" he said. "Your chariot, my lady!"

Joyce gave him a sideways glance. "In that? Where will I put my feet?"

"On the wheelbase. Just try it. I promise I won't go too fast."

Joyce took a seat, placing her feet near the front wheels.

Dominic laughed as he spun her in a circle. "Remember when I used to play in your office chair while you cooked dinner?"

"I recall you asking a thousand questions. I've never known such a curious kid."

"Grandpa used to limit me to five questions before dinner," Dominic said.

Joyce's eyes filled with tears.

Dominic bent and wiped them away with his finger. "I'm sorry, Gran. I didn't mean to…"

"It's okay. It's good to remember him." Joyce gazed up at her grandson. "He was such a good man. He should never be forgotten."

Dominic smiled, his eyes glistening. "And he never will be forgotten as long as I live."

Ayden used his foot to pump the gurney up to a comfortable height for him to push and then stuffed Clara's backpack and his duffle bag into the space beneath it.

"Ready?" he asked.

"Let's roll," Clara said.

Joyce and Dominic continued to reminisce about her husband, Stanley, as Ayden wheeled Clara between the pickup and a sedan. The group proceeded north, making their way along the left-hand lane, occasionally weaving between abandoned vehicles.

The next stop was an abandoned office building. Ayden assisted Clara from the walkway to a set of double glass doors. Dominic pulled on the handle. It was unlocked.

Inside, behind the first door on the right, colorful mats and small chairs were scattered about—the remnants of a childcare center. Ayden's eyes widened as he spotted several large water bottles in a storage closet, along with a stack of juice boxes. "These will keep us hydrated until we find somewhere to fill our sports bottles," he said, loading his arms with them.

Tina opened one of the cabinet doors. "Ah, too bad! I was hoping for those little fish-shaped crackers." She turned to Laney. "Remember those from daycare when we were little?"

"Yes, but I never went to daycare."

Tina narrowed her gaze. "Never?"

Laney shook her head. "Nope. My parents worked opposite shifts so I'd never have to be raised by strangers."

"That wasn't an option for my mom. I didn't have a dad," Tina said.

"I remember daycare. My mom was a teacher at my childcare center," Dominic said. His expression changed suddenly. He glanced over at Joyce.

She wore a pained look. She took a deep breath and forced a smile. "And she loved that job."

"Where is she now?" Tina asked.

Dominic and Joyce just stared at one another.

"I'm sorry," Tina said. "Was that too personal? I tend to do that. I just don't think before I speak sometimes." She placed her hand on Dominic's shoulder. "Please forgive me."

"No! It's okay," Joyce said. "My daughter passed away when

Dominic was six. Cancer. Pancreatic. It was sudden." Joyce wiped a tear from her cheek.

Dominic placed his hand on her shoulder. No one spoke for a moment.

"We need to keep moving, everyone," Laney said. "Martinsburg isn't far. We can look for more supplies there."

"Maybe we'll find a solution for boiling and carrying water along the way," Clara said.

"We could use a large pot, maybe find one in a restaurant or a school cafeteria," Tina suggested as Dominic wheeled Joyce toward the door.

Back on the road, the conversation turned to families and childhood memories.

Lunch Box nudged Laney as they walked. "So your parents were always around, huh? That must have been interesting, especially with them being so… cautious?"

Laney chuckled, the tension easing from her shoulders. "Yeah, 'cautious' is one way to put it. My folks have always been full-on doomsday preppers. Always preparing for the worst. Our basement was like a miniature warehouse, stocked with enough supplies to last years."

"Really?" Tina's pitched. "What kind of stuff did they store?"

"Oh, you name it—canned foods, dried goods, medical supplies, water filters, and tons of survival manuals. Every weekend was a new drill: bugging out, evading capture, you name it."

Tina laughed, shaking her head. "Sounds like you were trained for this kind of situation way before it was necessary."

Laney nodded, her expression a mix of pride and wistfulness. "I guess they had a point. Look at where we are now. I used to think they were crazy, but all those skills have definitely come in handy."

Clara, who had been listening, joined in. "Did you ever feel like it was too much? I mean, growing up with that kind of intensity?"

"Sometimes," Laney admitted. "I didn't have many friends over. You can imagine a sleepover with emergency drills at midnight doesn't really go over well with other kids. But it made me who I am. Prepared, cautious, and maybe a little tough to get close to."

Joyce smiled at Laney. "It's that preparedness that's keeping us a step ahead now. You're a valuable member of this group, Laney."

"Thanks, Joyce. That means a lot."

As they continued their journey toward Martinsburg, the conversation turned to lighter memories of childhood. Each shared stories that fostered a sense of closeness and helped fortify their resolve to help each other survive and thrive in a world that had thrown them unimaginable challenges.

After listening to Laney's and Dominic's stories, Tina shared her own upbringing. "I was raised in a small apartment by my mom, just the two of us. She worked a lot, so I spent a good deal of time on my own or with friends. We didn't have much, but she made it feel like enough," she said with a mix of fondness and melancholy.

Curious about Ayden and Clara's background, she turned to them. "Laney mentioned you guys grew up in Manhattan and spent summers in Europe. That must have been something."

Ayden nodded, and Clara picked up the thread. "Yeah. But it sounds more glamorous than it was. Our parents ran a finance business off Wall Street, so they were always busy. Most summers, they sent us to Europe with our nanny. We got to see a lot of places —Paris, Rome, Barcelona—but it was usually just us kids and the nanny. We didn't spend much time with our parents."

Tina's eyes widened slightly. "That's kind of sad, missing out on time with your family, even in all those beautiful places."

Clara smiled softly. "It was. But those trips gave us a view of the world not many get to see. We'd explore museums and historical sites and just soak in the culture. It shaped a lot of who we are."

Tina seemed thoughtful, then said, "It sounds amazing to have seen those places, but I guess I can't imagine being away from my mom that much."

Clara nodded. "One day, when things settle down, you'll see them too, Tina. The world's beauty isn't going anywhere. Places like the Louvre and Notre Dame have stood the test of time, and they'll be there waiting."

"Clara's right," Joyce said. "Just like after World War II. My parents lived through tough times—the Depression and then the war. But they always said how everything looked so bleak, yet recovery came. Europe and Japan rebuilt from the ashes, more vibrant than before." Squaring her shoulders, she looked around at the group. "We'll get through this and rebuild too. And, Tina, you'll have your chance to travel, to take in all those wonderful places, and maybe show them to someone special one day."

EIGHTEEN

Ayden

New Leaf Garden Center
Kearneysville, West Virginia
Day Six

An hour later, Dominic caught sight of a run-down nursery and garden center just off the highway. The place was overgrown with weeds, but it was a hopeful mess. "Let's check it out," he said, gesturing toward the dilapidated structure.

"What would we hope to find in a place like that?"

Dominic smiled. "I worked at a nursery one summer. You'd be surprised what you might find."

"Could you elaborate before I walk all the way over there?" Tina asked with one hand on her hip.

"Waterproof plastic sheeting, for one."

Tina smiled. "For making a shelter?"

"Exactly!" Dominic nodded. "There could be twine. We would need to braid several strands together to make suitable cordage to support the weight of the plastic."

"It's worth exploring," Ayden said.

Dominic pushed Joyce in the chair down the off-ramp while Ayden followed him and the others, rolling Clara on her gurney. They stopped in the parking lot outside the plant shop's door.

Ayden reached out to help his sister get down from the stretcher. As he did, Clara groaned.

"Just leave me here. My hip can't take more hopping on one foot."

"I'll stay here with Clara and Joyce," Laney said, with her pistol at her side.

Ayden gave them a thumbs-up gesture. "Okay. We'll poke around a bit and then get back on the road."

Inside, amidst the chaos of upturned soil and broken pots, they did indeed find a spool of twine, along with a roll of black plastic sheeting stuffed under a long, wooden table. "It's thick," Ayden said. "It looks like enough to make each of us a shelter covering."

Tina pointed toward a collapsed shed in the back. "There might be something useful in there."

Dominic, Ayden, and Lunch Box went to investigate. Inside, Ayden found a small propane torch and held it up. "Yes!"

"Now that's a fire starter," Dominic said. "So the basic needs for survival are food, water, and shelter. We have enough plastic for a temporary shelter. Check! Hopefully, we can catch dinner with the fishing rod and tackle, so there's the potential for food. Check! We have the means to make a fire, cook it, and boil water if we have wood. We still need a pot or something to boil it in and a water source."

Ayden scanned the side of the building, noting several planting pots of various sizes stacked near the door. "You know anything about terracotta pots?"

Dominic shrugged. "No, why?"

"We might be able to boil water in them."

Tina stepped around the corner of the building. "Laney," she called out to catch her attention. "Are terracotta pots safe to boil water in?"

"Only if they're not glazed. Glazed could contain lead," Laney yelled back.

Ayden walked over, picked one up, and rotated it in his hands. "How would you know if it's glazed?"

"The glazed ones will be shiny without the porous look of clay," Tina said. "Those look unglazed to me."

"Sweet!" Lunch Box said, stuffing a six-inch clay pot under his arm.

Dominic picked up a larger one. "This one would be nice, but what could we use to plug the hole in the bottom?"

Tina offered a blank stare. She lifted one shoulder. "Wax, maybe?"

Lunch Box chuckled. "That would be fine if you don't want to use it for boiling."

Tina's mouth formed an O.

"Wax melts," Ayden said.

Tina glanced around, turning in a circle. She gestured to a foam block.

"Nope. Flammable." Lunch Box walked over and picked up a pot without a drainage hole. "This one should hold water."

Ayden walked over to inspect the pot as well. "We could make a teepee tripod with branches if we had wire or chain. Otherwise, we'll have to find rocks to sit it on in the fire."

Dominic set off, searching through the tall grass and weeds that lined the building. "I saw some wire here somewhere. It got caught on my shoe." A moment later, he bent down and retrieved a three-foot-long piece of thin wire. "Bingo!"

"Looks like we're set. All we need now is food and a body of water," Tina said.

"Yep!" Dominic smiled back at her. "Things are looking up."

Ayden wouldn't have gone that far. Things were anything but bright, but at least it hadn't taken them long to find supplies that would help them survive. Without them, they likely wouldn't last long out there on foot, two hundred miles from their destination in

Washington County, Pennsylvania. He pushed aside thoughts of making it to Wyoming—at least for the moment. It was too stressful with the odds so stacked against them. Before they lost the motorhome, he'd at least had some rational basis to believe he stood a chance. Now, it would take a miracle, and amidst their current circumstances, he wasn't holding out hope he'd receive one.

He glanced up at the sky. They still had at least six hours of daylight before they'd need to find a camping spot for the night. Ayden estimated they'd likely make it maybe eight or ten miles before then—depending on how many stops like this they made. He stepped over a pile of opened bags of potting soil and turned back toward the front of the building where they'd left Laney, Clara, and Joyce. As he rounded the corner of the building, Clara screamed Ayden's name.

Then a noise caught his attention.

The sound of the racking of a shotgun turned his blood to ice as his brain registered the source.

He stepped out into the parking lot, and immediately, his gaze landed upon his sister, still seated on the gurney. Joyce stood at her side. Their hands were in the air. At the foot of the gurney was a badly disfigured young woman carrying a baby on her back.

His gaze dropped to the shotgun in her hands.

She spun toward him. "Drop the rifle!" she yelled. "I said to drop the rifle," the young woman repeated.

Ayden studied her face. What he found there was fear. He hoped he could talk their way out of the situation before anyone got hurt. Her face and hands had been badly burned. The hair on one side of her head looked as if it had melted to her head. She'd been in some sort of accident.

The AR-15 dangled on its sling across Ayden's chest. He scanned the parking lot, searching for Laney, but there was no sign of her.

The young child on the woman's back began to cry, but she ignored him.

"Drop the rifle, or I'll blast a hole in you the size of a grapefruit."

"We're just looking for things to help us survive. We're sorry. We'll go now," Clara said, holding her hands out in front of her.

"You need medical assistance," Ayden said. "We have supplies. We can help you."

The woman bristled.

"We have gauze to bandage your wounds. We don't have anything stronger than ibuprofen for painkillers, but you are welcome to them."

The woman's gaze bored into Ayden. "I want your rifle and ammo."

"I can't do that. I have a responsibility to protect my group."

The woman nodded toward her shotgun. "You're doing a great job so far. Now do as I said and drop the rifle!"

Laney appeared in Ayden's peripheral vision. Her pistol was raised and aimed at the woman's back. "Not gonna happen!"

As Ayden shouldered his rifle, all he could think was *Please, Laney, don't shoot that baby.*

The young mother spun around, backing away. She twitched the barrel of the shotgun from Ayden to Laney and then back to him. "I'll shoot! I swear I will!" she shouted, still backing away.

The child continued to wail.

"Laney!" Ayden tried to get her attention. There was still time to defuse the situation.

"Listen, dear," Joyce said, moving toward the young mother. "We aren't a threat to you. Just put the gun down. You don't want to hurt anyone."

"Stay back," the woman shouted.

"Is the child hurt?" Joyce asked, her voice soft and full of compassion.

"No!" The woman's tone was defensive.

"Sweetheart." Joyce held her right hand out to her. "I know you're scared." Joyce glanced back at Clara and the others. "We all are. We're just trying to survive like you. We're not here to hurt anyone."

The young mother's posture softened slightly.

"Is the baby hungry?"

Ayden thought Joyce's strategy was smart. She was getting the woman to focus on the needs of her crying child.

"We don't have baby formula, but we have juice." Joyce pointed to the supplies packed beneath Clara's gurney.

The woman clutched the shotgun tightly, her eyes darting between Joyce and the gurney.

"Why should I believe you?"

"Because we want nothing from you but to go away safely," Clara said.

Tina kneeled next to the stretcher.

"Stop!" the young mother shouted.

"I just want to show you the juice boxes. We found them at a daycare. Unfortunately, they didn't have any of those little yellow fish."

"Gold," the woman said.

"Gold?" Tina looked perplexed. "We don't have any gold."

"The crackers—they're called Goldfish."

"Yes! I loved those things as a kid," Tina said, reaching for the duffle bag. She dropped it to the pavement and started to unzip it.

"No! Stop! You could have a gun in there."

"Like this one," Laney said, twitching the barrel of her pistol.

"No one wants to hurt you. It's the opposite, in fact," Joyce said. "We'd like to help you if you'll let us."

"People don't help strangers," she said, her gaze flicking to Clara.

"We're all pretty much strangers to one another, really." Clara gestured to Joyce. "We met on the road." She smiled. "My brother..." Clara nodded in Ayden's direction. "We broke into her motorhome after we were stranded following a carjacking in New Jersey."

The young mother shifted her gaze to Joyce. Dominic stepped up and took his grandmother's hand. "My grandpa gave his life to help them."

The young mother's expression softened as Joyce nodded.

"We were on our way to find my grandson here. He was on the Appalachian Trail with Tina and Laney and Christopher." Joyce nodded toward Lunch Box and then glanced back at Clara and then at Ayden. "They helped me reach him after my Stanley was murdered."

"So, you see, helping strangers and receiving help is how we've all survived this so far," Clara said.

"Please let us help your baby. I swear, it's just juice," Tina said. "I can set it here on the ground, and you can retrieve it after we leave."

The young mother pursed her lips, moving from foot to foot. Eventually, she nodded, and then a stream of tears flowed down her cheeks. "Can I have one for my other son too?"

Tina offered her a compassionate smile. "Of course!" She reached into the duffle and pulled out a six-pack of juice boxes. "Is it just the three of you?"

The mother nodded and then tilted her head to wipe her cheek on her shoulder. She stared at the gurney. "My son…" She cleared her throat. "My son. He's eleven. He hurt his leg, helping me escape the fire. He can't walk, and I can't carry both of my boys."

Clara slid off the stretcher. "Here," she said, pushing it toward the woman. "Take this. I can walk."

Clara hopped on one leg as she steered it toward her.

The mother lowered the shotgun. "What happened to your leg?"

"I was shot by some gangbangers in Harlem."

"Harlem? That's pretty far away."

"We've been on the road since this happened," Ayden said, rushing to his sister's side and taking her arm.

"Don't you have family that can help you?" Clara asked.

"I have a sister north of Martinsburg about fifteen miles from here, but Josiah can't walk even a block."

Ayden's voice was calm and steady. "We can help you get to your family. You don't have to do this alone," he said gently.

The woman hesitated, her gaze softening as she glanced at the wailing child on her back. The fear in her eyes spoke volumes about her ordeal. Ayden took a slow, non-threatening step forward. "We have medical supplies," he reiterated. "And we're heading in the direction of Martinsburg. If that's where your family is, we can take you there."

Laney slowly lowered her weapon and backed away, giving Ayden the space to negotiate.

Joyce moved up next to the gurney. "We're not here to harm you. We've seen enough of that for a lifetime. Let us help you and your children."

The woman's grip on the shotgun loosened slightly, and she finally lowered it, the fight seeming to drain from her posture. "I… I need to get to Martinsburg. My sister… she's waiting for me there," she stammered, the admission seeming to unburden her.

"We'll help get you there," Ayden said in a reassuring tone.

The group quickly discussed their new plan.

"There's room enough for both Clara and the boy on the stretcher," Laney said.

"True," Clara said. He can sit in my lap, or I can lie on my side and—"

"Why don't we do that and keep an eye out for another ambulance in the next town," Laney said, searching each face for agreement.

Everyone smiled and nodded.

"What's the baby's name?" Tina asked, handing his mother a juice box.

"Tobias," she said. "I'm Elsa. We're from Hillsboro, Virginia. We started out with my boyfriend a few days ago. We were with this group—his neighbors. Things got ugly after they robbed a drug dealer. His people did this to me." She choked up. "They locked me in a shed and set it on fire. My boyfriend and the kids escaped. He stashed the kids in a nearby house and came back for me. They killed him. My son followed my boyfriend there without him knowing. Josiah was able to break down the door with an axe to get me out, but he tripped on some garden tool, and it lodged in his leg."

"That sounds terrifying," Tina said.

Elsa nodded. "It was horrific. I pulled it out and managed to stop the bleeding, but I think my boy's leg is infected now."

"Sounds like you and your children have been through hell," Laney said. "That sucks. I'm so sorry."

"How about you take us to your son? We'll look at his wound, see if there is anything we can do to help, and then head out to find your sister's house," Ayden said.

NINETEEN

Mueller

Pittsburgh Self Storage
Pittsburgh, Pennsylvania
Day Six

The team paused on McKean Street, an area that used to bustle with activity but now lay in a ghostly silence. Tall brick buildings flanked the narrow street, their windows dark and lifeless. A sign for "Pittsburgh Self Storage" hung on one of the walls. Graffiti marred the walls, and weeds pushed through the cracks in the concrete.

Above them, a sky bridge connected two buildings, casting a long shadow over the street below. The air was thick with the smell of smoke lingering from the chaos farther into the city. The only sounds were their own footsteps and the distant echoes of unrest.

Mueller signaled for the team to take cover behind the large concrete block wall lining the street. They crouched low and scanned the area for any sign of movement.

"This is the spot," Mueller said in a hushed tone. "We'll surveil the situation from here before moving into the neighborhood where Tom's family is supposed to be. Nesbitt, you know what to do."

Nesbitt moved ahead cautiously, using the abandoned cars to his advantage, while the rest of the team remained hidden, weapons at the ready.

A few moments later, Nesbitt returned. "Looks clear for now, but we need to move quickly. There are signs of recent activity—smoldering trash and debris."

Mueller and his team huddled behind the concrete blocks on McKean Street, going over the plan one last time. The goal was to extract Thomas's family from Costantini's Restaurant and Bar on Carson Street without attracting the attention of the gangs controlling the area.

"All right," Mueller said in a hushed tone. "Listen up. Here's the plan: Nesbitt, you and Smith move ahead to scout the vicinity of the restaurant. Look for any gang activity or obstacles we might face. If we do encounter gang members, Smith will create a diversion using smoke grenades and sound distractions. We need to pull them away from the restaurant. Once the area is clear, Amos and I will approach the food establishment. Giblin, you'll cover our rear. I'll go inside to get Tom's family. Amos, you keep watch outside and be ready to assist if needed. We'll use the same route to get back, recover Tom, and again take the back roads. We need to move fast and stay low."

The team nodded, understanding their roles. Mueller glanced at Smith. "You all in, here, Smith?"

"All in! Let's do this," Smith said.

"Stay focused, everyone," Mueller added. "We're bringing them home."

As Nesbitt and Smith slipped away, the rest of the team waited, checking their rifles and doing one last check to make sure none of their gear rattled or made noise that might give them away.

A few moments later, Nesbitt and Smith returned.

"I spotted two gang members patrolling the street," Nesbitt

said, "but they're not paying much attention. We can use the alleyways to avoid them."

Nesbitt and Smith led the way down a side alley. Soon, they neared the restaurant, and Nesbitt and Smith struck out again to scout the immediate vicinity. After they returned, Mueller clenched his jaw as Nesbitt reported gang activity near the business.

"You know what to do, Smith," Mueller said.

Smith reached into his backpack and grabbed a couple of smoke grenades and flash-bangs, then placed them in pouches attached to his tactical vest and belt.

Mueller nodded, signaling him to move into position. Smith tossed a flash-bang grenade into a nearby alley, setting off a loud sound and drawing the attention of the gang members. They moved toward the noise, giving the team an opening.

This time, Mueller and Amos led the way, sticking close to the buildings and using every available cover. Giblin followed a short distance behind to cover their retreat.

The area was eerily quiet; the only sounds were the distant echoes of unrest.

As they approached, they saw the building where Tom's family was seeking shelter. It was fortified with makeshift barricades and armed guards patrolling the perimeter. Mueller signaled for the team to spread out and take positions. He and Amos stepped forward, hands raised to show they meant no harm.

"We're here for Thomas Coupland's family. They were supposed to be here," Mueller said, his voice steady.

One of the guards, a burly man with a wary expression, confronted them. "Who are you?"

"I'm Tyson Mueller. We just need to get the Coupland family, and we'll be on our way."

"Go see if Mary knows this guy," the burly guard said.

One of the guards slipped inside the building. A moment later, he returned, leaned in, and whispered something to the burly man.

After a tense moment, the guard nodded and signaled for the

others to stand down. They were led inside, where they found Thomas's wife and children huddled together, weary-looking but unharmed. The reunion was emotional and bittersweet.

"We need to go now," Mueller urged softly. "Stay close and stay quiet."

"Where's Tom?" Mary asked.

Mueller's gut clenched. He couldn't tell her there. What would he do if she fell apart? No. He needed her to be able to hold it together for him to get her and the children to safety.

"Tom's guarding our retreat with Giblin."

"Oh, Giblin. I like him. He has kind eyes," Mary said.

She held out her hand, and Mueller assisted her to her feet. Mary took her son's hand, and Mueller scooped her daughter into his arms.

"Thank you, everyone—for taking us in," Mary called over her shoulder as they moved through the door.

With the family in tow, the team began their exfil, retracing their steps through the industrial area. Every sound seemed even more threatening now that Mueller was responsible for the lives of Tom's wife, Mary, and her children.

They were navigating a narrow alleyway, hemmed in by tall, decaying brick buildings. The alley was strewn with debris and broken glass, potholes full of nasty water, fast-food waste, soiled diapers, flattened cardboard boxes, and piles of wood—all the remnants of a world that had descended into chaos. As they approached the end of the passageway, the faint murmur of voices reached Mueller's ears. He raised his hand, signaling the group to halt. He handed Tom's little girl to Mary and then peered around the corner. The sight of gang members loitering nearby made him recoil.

Tom's daughter began to cry, catching their attention.

"Back! Back!" Mueller barked, spinning toward the opposite end of the alley to retreat. But more men blocked their escape.

The gang leader rushed toward them and stood at the entrance with his arms across his chest. He was short and overweight, his arms covered in tattoos that snaked up to his neck and disappeared beneath a ragged tank top. His face was hard and angular, and he had a thick red beard that did little to soften his intimidating presence.

His eyes, cold and calculating, locked onto Mueller and he gave a shark-toothed smile, revealing several gold-capped teeth. He held an AK-47 rifle casually in his hands, but there was nothing casual about his stance—he was ready for a fight.

His eyes roamed Mary's body, making his intention clear, then turned his attention briefly to Mueller. "Who are you people? You ain't po-pos. You look more like the military to me."

Shouldering his rifle, aimed at the man's chest, Mueller kept his voice calm and steady. "We don't want any trouble. We're just passing through trying to get out of the city."

"This is our hood. Nobody just passing through without payment," he growled.

"We don't have much to give," Mueller said.

The gang leader leered at Mary, licking his lips. "I think you got plenty there."

Mueller nodded subtly to Smith, who was already preparing a flash-bang as a diversion. The team tensed, ready for action.

The explosion was loud and concussive. The alley filled with a thick, choking smoke that obscured their movements. Gunfire erupted, the sharp cracks echoing off the brick walls. Adrenaline coursed through Mueller's veins as he guided Mary and her children through the chaos.

The gang members fired blindly into the smoke, their shouts of confusion and anger blending with the sound of gunfire. Mueller and his team returned fire sparingly in an effort to suppress rather than kill. The priority was to get the family to safety without engaging in a prolonged firefight.

"Keep moving!" Mueller urged, his voice barely discernible over the cacophony.

They emerged from the smoke and sprinted down the street before disappearing into another narrow alley. Mueller glanced back to make sure everyone was accounted for. Mary was clutching her children, their faces pale. Nesbitt, Amos, and Smith were right behind them, covering their retreat with disciplined bursts of gunfire.

Finally, they reached a more open area, where the abandoned vehicles provided some semblance of cover. Mueller signaled for the group to take a breather, his heart pounding in his chest. He scanned the area to ensure they hadn't been followed.

"Is everyone okay?" he asked, his voice hoarse from the exertion.

Nods and murmurs of assent greeted him. They had made it past the gang, but the danger was far from over. Mueller knew they needed to keep moving, but for a brief moment, he allowed himself to feel a sliver of relief. They had survived another confrontation, and Tom's family was one step closer to safety.

"Wait! Where's Tom?" Mary asked.

They had blocks to go before reaching the garage where they'd left her deceased husband, and Mueller still needed her to be able to hold it together for her children, but he couldn't find it in himself to lie to her again.

He nodded to Amos and then chopped the air in the direction of an abandoned-looking building. Immediately, Amos and Nesbitt took off across the street and disappeared inside it. A moment later, Nesbitt stood in the doorway. "Clear."

"Ty! Where's my husband?" Mary asked again.

"Let's get your children off the street, and I'll explain," Mueller said.

Unshed tears filled her eyes.

The sight nearly wrecked him as he reached for the girl in her arms. He led Mary and her son into the vacant home and toward the center of the house where the kitchen was. He sat the young girl on the counter, keeping his hand on her arm as he turned to face Mary.

"I got him killed," Smith blurted out before Mueller could say anything. "I did it. It's my fault."

Mueller had never wanted to kill anyone as much as he wanted to end Smith at that moment.

Amos responded by tossing Smith to the ground and placing his boot on the man's chest.

Mary stood stunned, her gaze flitting between Mueller and Smith.

Mueller removed the baby from the counter and placed her on his hip before approaching Mary. "I'm so very sorry you had to hear it this way."

Mary stared back at him, unblinking. "Tom's dead?"

Mueller wrapped his arm around her shoulders. "I'm so sorry!" was all he could say.

"Tom's dead!" Mary repeated, this time as a statement.

"He was shot—on the way to get you." Mueller let his words sink in a moment before continuing. "We ran into some looters. There was this scared kid among them. I don't think the boy even intended to shoot."

Mary spun around, hunched over slightly with her hands on her hips. "Why did he say that he got Tom killed?"

Mueller recognized she wanted someone tangible to blame. Smith had placed himself in that position with his confession. Mueller half wanted to give her his pistol and let her exact her revenge, but he knew that wouldn't do anyone any good.

"I'm so sorry," Smith said, sobbing. "I taunted the guy. I belittled him, and now—"

"Your smart-ass mouth got my Tom killed?" Mary asked through gritted teeth.

Mueller felt a tiny hand take his. He glanced down, and Tom's young son slid behind him as if expecting violence to ensue at any moment. It was evident that Tom's children had already been traumatized prior to their arrival. They didn't deserve this—any of this. They'd just lost their father. What they needed was a safe place to live and heal. Mueller had to get them back to the compound where they could find comfort and peace.

"All right," Mueller said, his voice steady. "Let's keep moving. We need to get back to the compound before dark."

"Not without my husband!" Mary demanded.

"Of course. We wouldn't leave him behind. He's just a few blocks away."

Amos headed for the door. Mueller handed the baby to Mary and followed him.

"Mary, I'm so, so sorry," Smith blubbered as they exited the vacant home.

"Shut the hell up, Smith!" Nesbitt barked.

Tom's family, led by the team, pressed on, navigating the treacherous streets with caution. They made their way to the garage where they'd left Tom. Smith immediately rushed inside, gathered up Tom in a fireman's carry, and returned with him outside.

The drive back to the compound was filled with a mixture of relief and sadness. Mueller's longtime friend was dead, but the team had accomplished their mission and rescued his family. As they pulled through the gate, Mueller couldn't shake his concern about Laney. Under his breath, he recited a prayer, asking for her safety as she made her way home, just as they had planned.

Upon pulling the Suburban to a stop, the team was greeted with cheers and applause. Monica stood by, smiling. But when her eyes searched his, her smile faded.

Mueller opened the back door of the old SUV and held his hand out to assist Mary out of the vehicle. She handed him the baby and crawled out of the back seat. Her son climbed out and clung to her leg as they stood by the car. Tears streaked Mary's cheeks.

Monica, obviously sensing something dreadful was wrong, rushed to her side. She glanced up at Mueller and mouthed, "Tom?"

Mueller shook his head, and Monica wrapped her arms around Mary's shoulders. She led the mother and her children into one of the nearby cabins. After the door was closed, Mueller spun around and punched Smith in the jaw. Mueller stepped past him as he dropped to the ground. "Get the hell up and help me bury my friend!"

As Amos opened the back hatch door, Steve rushed out of the communications trailer with a huge smile across his face.

"What is it?" Mueller asked.

"Laney's in Maryland. Evergreen Camp told Crystal Springs they spoke with her!"

TWENTY

Ayden

Abandoned House
Kearneysville, West Virginia
Day Six

Elsa led them several blocks north to an abandoned house with an overgrown lawn and furniture stacked up at the curb. Inside, her son lay on the sofa, sweaty and pale. Joyce immediately set to work checking his wound. It looked angry and red. It didn't look good.

"Hi there," Clara said as Ayden lowered her down in the chair across from him. "What's your name?"

The boy just stared back at her.

Elsa placed her hand on the boy's forehead. "His name is Josiah."

"I'll be right back," Laney said, disappearing outside.

"I'll go with you," Lunch Box said, following her through the front door.

Ayden moved to the window to watch her as she kneeled in the tall grass. She withdrew her knife from its sheath and used it to dig up several plants, roots and all. When Laney and Lunch Box returned to the house, Laney headed to the kitchen. Tina and Ayden followed her there, curious. They stood in the doorway as Laney rummaged through the previous occupant's spice cabinet and selected a few bottles.

"What are those for?" Tina asked.

Laney held them up. "My mom says they can work with blood to create a scab that's antibacterial." She brushed past them and then sat next to the boy.

"I'm no expert, okay? I've watched my mom do this, but I've never applied a poultice by myself before."

The boy's eyes widened.

"Are you sure you should do it then?" Elsa asked, holding her son's hand.

"It can't hurt. It's just a little bottled water, herbs and spices with plantain and yarrow leaves. I couldn't find any calendula. My mom always used it dry leaves anyway. I don't know if fresh would work."

"Is it gonna hurt, Momma?" the boy asked.

Elsa gave Laney a questioning look.

"Some," Laney said. "Is he allergic to latex?"

"No. I don't think so."

The boy winced and squeezed his mother's hand tightly as Laney first sprinkled the red powder and then the white directly over the wound. Next, she crushed the leaves by rolling them between her fingers. She spread that over the wound as well and then used a large plantain leaf to cover it all.

"Are you sure this is going to work?" Elsa asked as Laney wrapped a self-sealing latex bandage around his leg.

"I've seen it heal animals that I thought were going to die. When I was little, my beagle went missing. When he came limping home two days later, he was covered in deep, infected wounds from a dog fight. It looked so nasty. I didn't think he'd pull through. But Mom treated him with a tincture spray, and he was fine in about a week."

"But that was on a dog," Tina said.

"Works on people, too. I've seen it many times." Laney fixed her gaze on the young mother. "I'm not guaranteeing anything. You understand that, right? I'm just saying I've seen it help before."

Elsa placed her hand on Laney's shoulder. "Anything you can do for him, I'm grateful."

Laney smiled and nodded. "So Mom would make me apply this for twelve hours, leave it off for twelve hours, and then apply a fresh poultice for twelve hours. With this, she would give me a tincture to take internally two or three times a day. After a day or so, she would spray the wound with a tincture mixed with water."

"We don't have that. Does it mean it won't work?" Elsa's tone was full of concern.

"You can keep applying the poultice, I guess. You might be able to steep it into a tea and pour it on. I don't know. My mom had a whole closet full of bottles of tinctures. She'd put a few drops of this and that into a spray bottle or into a tea." Laney frowned. "Now I wish I had paid attention when she was trying to teach me. I just thought she'd always be there to do it for me. I wasn't interested in herbal remedies. That's what pharmacies were for, right?"

"Until they were all looted out," Joyce said, her expression somber.

Dominic took both her hands in his. "Gran, do you have your medicine with you?"

She shook her head and then touched his cheek. "It's fine. I don't really need it that much."

"Don't need it?" Dominic's voice pitched higher. "It's for your heart and high blood pressure! You need them!"

"We'll keep looking," Lunch Box said. "We can check in nearby homes. Maybe someone left theirs behind."

"That's right. Maybe someone who never made it home," Tina said.

Joyce smiled, but it didn't appear genuine. "Sure. We can look. We might find something to treat your burns as well, Elsa."

"Oh, I almost forgot about them." Laney turned her attention to Elsa's burns and applied the leaves, without the powders, to her hands and then she bandaged them with gauze and tape from the medical supplies they found at the ambulance service building. "I'm sorry. I know it's painful. I wish we had something to give you for the pain and to prevent infection. The poultice is all I can offer."

"It's not nothing," Elsa said.

"Maybe we'll get lucky and find antibiotics as well," Tina said.

Ayden moved toward the door. "What medicines am I looking for?"

Laney stood. "I'll come with you."

"No! You stay." He patted his side to indicate her pistol. "I'll go. I can get in quick, have a look around, and get back here."

"I'll go as well," Dominic said.

"Me too," Lunch Box said, standing from his seat by the window.

"You two should stay and stand watch outside—alert Laney if you see or hear anything."

Dominic nodded. He moved to the window beside Lunch Box. "I can stand guard by the pickup in the neighboring driveway. It will give me a view of the street and the side yard. I'll be able to see the backyard from there as well."

Lunch Box nodded and gestured to the house across the street. "I can hide there, behind that shrub. I think I can see the other side of the house as well as the street. I can whistle if I see or hear anyone."

"Sounds good," Ayden said.

"I can go with you. My grandma took meds." Tina rushed to

Ayden's side. "I know which ones are for blood pressure." She stared up at him, waiting for his reply.

Ayden broke eye contact with her and shifted his gaze to Clara. He scanned the room, overwhelmed with the responsibility of it all. He not only had his injured sister and an elderly Joyce to look out for but now an injured child, his burned mother—and a baby. He wasn't even sure what the little boy needed. He swallowed hard. It was only a few miles to get to Elsa's sister's place. He could manage it that long.

Still lost in thought about the dangers of traveling with so many fragile people, Ayden said, "Sure, Tina, you can help me look."

TWENTY-ONE

Ayden

Abandoned House

Kearneysville, West Virginia

Day Six

While Dominic and Lunch Box headed off to their guard posts, Ayden led Tina to the house across the street. He'd wanted to check it first because the lawn looked like it had been mowed just prior to the EMP attack. Moreover, the windows and doors were still intact. Hopefully that meant it hadn't yet been looted.

As they approached the door, Ayden noticed a noxious odor coming from the home.

"What's that awful smell?" Tina said, pinching her nose between the tips of her fingers.

As Ayden and Tina stood at the threshold of the house, the pungent odor intensified. Ayden hesitated, his instincts warning him of the possibility of finding something extremely distressing inside. "It might be spoiled food or… worse. Stay behind me," he instructed.

After trying the knob and finding it locked, Ayden turned his back to the door and gave it a good backward kick. The jamb broke, and the door opened with a crack. He pushed it the rest of the way open with the toe of his boot. The smell was overwhelming and was likely the only reason the house had yet to be rifled through. Ayden covered his mouth and nose with the tail of his shirt and entered.

Inside, the house was dimly lit by the afternoon sunlight filtering through dusty windows. The living room was a time capsule of the moment everything had changed; a half-finished cup of coffee sat on a table, magazines spread across the couch. Ayden motioned for Tina to follow, and they quietly moved toward the kitchen.

The source of the smell became apparent as they entered. The refrigerator door was ajar, its contents spoiled and festering as flies fluttered about. Ayden quickly shut the refrigerator door. To their right, tucked away in a small utility-type space, was a chest freezer as well. As he neared it, his face twisted in disgust. "Yep! It's not just the fridge making such a stink."

"Yuck! It's awful. Let's look elsewhere," Tina said, pressing her body against his back.

Uncomfortable, Ayden pivoted and moved past her. "You can wait on the porch. I want to check the bathroom. This place looks promising despite the smell."

"No. I can't wait out there alone. You have the gun."

Ayden gestured to the open door. "You can wait just inside. At least you have fresher air."

She nodded and hurried in that direction. "Please make it quick. I'm about to hurl."

"I will. I just want to check the bathroom and bedrooms. The cabinets might still have something."

As he proceeded, Ayden's thoughts drifted to the fragile group they had left behind. He methodically searched the bathroom first. Under the first sink, he located a few bottles of aspirin and an unopened package of bandages before moving to the second sink on the opposite wall. He opened a drawer and let out a sigh of relief after pulling out several white prescription bottles. Ayden examined the labels, a wave of relief washing over him. "Take one tablet daily for blood pressure and heart." He unscrewed the lid and counted the pills. There were over sixty. Joyce would be good for two more months.

In a small storage caddy, he found more bottles, including one with two penicillin pills left inside. It wasn't enough, but it was something. Maybe it was enough to get the boy by until Elsa could find more.

Before leaving, Ayden noticed a photo on the dresser of a man and a beautiful young woman with their three young children—a family smiling during happier times. He paused, thinking of Mia and her three boys. When everything had first occurred, he'd taken comfort in knowing they were in Wyoming, likely far from the chaos he and Clara were experiencing. Still, with the news that Russia had invaded the West Coast, a mere thousand miles from Wyoming, he feared they, too, would soon experience the terror of war.

Shaking off the melancholy thought, Ayden returned to the living room and Tina. "I found Joyce some blood pressure meds and two antibiotic pills for the boy, but I'd like to check one more house and see if we can't get something to help Elsa, and then we'll head back."

"Anything, as long as we get out of here. I can't take that smell any longer."

Ayden left the door standing open and walked across the lawn, heading toward another house.

The second house, with its equally well-maintained facade and untouched appearance, stood quietly in the waning light. Ayden and Tina approached with caution, their steps muffled by the grass. This home, too, with its intact windows and recently mowed lawn, hinted at a sudden departure rather than prolonged neglect, raising

Ayden's hopes that they might discover more unlooted supplies within.

As they entered, the eerie silence of the house enveloped them, the kind of quiet that felt heavy with the absence of life. Together, they quickly moved from room to room, checking to ensure no one was home. Relieved that it was indeed abandoned, they decided to split up to cover more ground quickly—Ayden explored the kitchen and living room while Tina headed down the hallway toward the bedrooms.

In the kitchen, Ayden sifted through drawers and cabinets, finding little more than tiny packets of salt and pepper and a collection of utensils. The living room was no better, with its layers of dust settled on abandoned books and family photos that gazed back at him. Meanwhile, Tina treaded softly down the dimly lit hallway, and Ayden examined the drawers of the coffee table and two side tables.

Suddenly, Tina's scream shattered the silence. From the living room, the sound of a struggle reached him, a brief and horrifying clatter that ended with a gut-wrenching gasp from Tina.

As Ayden ran down the hall, the thud of her body hitting the floor propelled him into motion. His heart pounded in his chest, fear gripping him as he envisioned the worst. He rounded the corner just in time to see a figure scramble desperately through the bedroom window, the curtains fluttering as the man escaped.

Tina was on the floor, clutching her abdomen, blood seeping through her fingers. Her face contorted in shock and pain. "Help me, Ayden… oh, God, it hurts so much!"

Ayden's eyes landed upon the assailant's knife dropped beside her. "Tina!" he cried out, kneeling beside her. He grabbed a pillow from the bed, removed the slip, and pressed it against the wound to stem the flow of blood, his hands trembling as he whispered reassurances he wasn't sure he believed.

"We need to get you back to Laney and the others," Ayden said, his voice cracking with urgency. With great care, he lifted

Tina into his arms, her body limp and in shock as he retraced his steps back to the main house.

The return was a blur of motion and fear.

"Tina!" Lunch Box screamed as he spotted them.

Dominic sprinted toward them. "What happened?"

"A man stabbed me," Tina murmured softly.

"Here, get her inside," Ayden said, placing Tina carefully into Dominic's arms. "That guy is still out there, and he could have others with him." After handing off Tina, Ayden shouldered his rifle, scanning the houses across the street for movement. As Dominic carried the injured Tina through the door, Ayden surveyed the street in both directions. Seeing no one about, he backed toward the house. Inside, he locked the door and stood beside the window.

Laney and Joyce rushed to meet Dominic, their faces etched with concern. Dominic laid Tina gently on the floor while Laney, with her rudimentary medical knowledge, took charge and directed them to grab towels to put pressure on the wound.

They had ventured into the house hoping for supplies to help Elsa and her son, only to return with a life hanging precariously in the balance.

Laney glanced up at Ayden, tears streaking her cheeks. "What happened?"

"She was stabbed."

"How? How did this happen?"

"I don't know. We checked each room and didn't see anyone in there."

Tina coughed. "The house seemed deserted. Nothing about the room led me to believe anyone was hiding in there. I heard the soft rustling that drew my attention toward the closet. Then, without warning, the closet door burst open. A man lunged out, holding a kitchen knife in his hand. He was swinging wildly." She winced, and tears escaped her eyelids.

Laney bent and kissed her cheek. "I'm so sorry this happened to you, sweet friend. I wish there were something I could do to relieve your pain."

Within moments, Tina grew pale and clammy-looking. As her breaths grew shallower, the room fell silent except for the soft, grief-stricken sobs of her trail companions. Her final words, whispered with desperation, ripped Ayden's heart in two.

"I don't want to die," she murmured, her voice trailing off as her life began to slip away.

"Hold on, Proud Mary," Lunch Box said, holding her hand.

"Don't you give up," Laney said. "Just stay with us!"

Dominic stood over them, watching in silence.

Joyce slid her arm around his waist and glanced up at him with compassion as Tina drew her last breath. The moments following her death were somber. Laney, Lunch Box, and Dominic, tears streaking their faces, gathered around her. The air was heavy with sorrow.

As the initial shock subsided, the practicalities of their situation took over. Dominic and Lunch Box quietly stepped outside into the cooling evening to prepare Tina's final resting place. They chose a quiet spot in the backyard, under a gnarled, old oak tree that seemed to stand in silent witness to the solemnity of their task. The ground was tough, and their work was silent, save for the thud of shovels digging through the earth.

The sun had dipped below the horizon by the time they finished. With heavy hearts, they returned to the house, their arms and backs sore, their spirits exhausted. The group gathered once more, this time to carry Tina to her grave. Under the pale light of the moon, they laid her to rest; a few words were spoken—some tearful, some reminiscing of the times Tina had made them smile on the Appalachian Trail.

Deciding to stay the night in the house with Elsa and her children seemed the only appropriate choice. No one felt like traveling farther, and the need for proximity and mutual comfort was palpable. They arranged themselves in the living room, leaving a few candles flickering in the quiet space, casting a soft light over their sad faces.

As they settled in, the conversation was subdued. Joyce, her voice soft and steady, tried to offer some comfort, reminiscing about the resilience of the human spirit she'd witnessed throughout her life. "We endure, we survive, and we remember those we've lost not just with sorrow but with a commitment to making the most of the time we have on this earth. In doing so, we honor the memory of those who have gone before us."

Laney, Lunch Box, and Dominic shared memories of Tina, each person bringing up moments that highlighted her strength and the impact she'd had on their lives. It was a night of shared grief but also communal strength as they leaned on one another for emotional support, not just for Tina but for all those they'd lost since the lights went out.

Clara even offered fond memories of their mother—ones that Ayden had forgotten about in his bitterness toward her during his teen and young adult years. Unable to endure seeing his sister mourn their mother, Ayden quietly slipped outside to stand guard over the group in the night.

Sadness was replaced by guilt that ripped at his soul, most notably about Tina's death. He should have checked all the closets himself. His brain replayed the scene as he and Tina searched the house. He'd looked under the bed in that room as Tina had opened the closet—or at least he'd thought she had. He didn't see her do it. Maybe it was a drawer she opened. He didn't know.

Ayden paced back and forth, trying to find even a sliver of hope on which to hang on to. By some miracle, he and Clara had survived their escape from Manhattan, finding temporary refuge at Dave's mansion in New Jersey. Since then, they'd survived a carjacking. He'd made it through chemical poisoning. They'd survived the drone attack in Frederick, Maryland—the one that had likely killed the president or whoever was in his motorcade. The last six days had been as if they were living the book of Revelations from the Bible. He almost expected to see the four horsemen show up at any moment.

Around midnight, Ayden heard the door creak open. Laney exited and approached the truck Ayden was leaning against.

"I can take watch now. You go get some sleep."

"I'm good," Ayden said for the thousandth time, scanning the house where Tina had been stabbed.

"You won't be tomorrow. We'll need you sharp when we travel into Martinsburg."

Ayden knew she was right. Going into a town was dangerous, and he needed to be alert, but Ayden knew he wouldn't sleep, not with the guilt of Tina's death so heavy on his heart.

He lowered the tailgate as silently as possible and climbed into the bed. "I'll just lie here for a moment. That way, I'll be close by if you see anyone. How about that?"

"Whatever works, Cowboy!"

TWENTY-TWO

Ayden

Abandoned House
Kearneysville, West Virginia
Day Seven

Early the following day, before dawn, Ayden helped Clara onto the stretcher. Elsa's son sat between Clara's legs as the group set out toward Martinsburg. They were mostly quiet for the three hours it took to walk there. Before reaching the populated city, they took a side road that skirted the town. It added another forty-five minutes to the trip, but avoiding people was worth it in Ayden's mind.

As they arrived at the junction near Elsa's sister Kara's farm, gunshots rang out. Ayden rushed forward, grabbed Clara and Josiah from the gurney, and dragged them to the ground.

"Dominic!" Joyce screamed as they rolled into the ditch.

Ayden covered Clara and the boy with his body until the gunfire stopped.

"Dominic! Dominic!" Joyce cried over and over.

Ayden raised his head, scanning the roadway. Dominic was down. Joyce was kneeling beside him.

Laney rose from the ditch on the opposite side of the road, pistol in hand. "Lunch Box!" she shouted, rising to a crouch. "Are you hit?"

Lunch Box said nothing.

"Lunch Box!" Laney shouted, moving farther down the road.

Ayden glanced to his left and spotted a form lying thirty feet away in the same ditch as him and Clara. "Lunch Box?" he called as he moved around Clara. "Stay here, sis. I need to check on him."

As he ran toward him, a young girl emerged from the woods. "Stop! Drop your weapons!"

Ayden was about to drop her when another voice rang out.

"Elsa, I can't believe it's you!" The woman ran toward the ditch where Elsa was now hunched over her son. The baby on her back was crying, which drowned out Elsa's words to her.

"Natasha! Run and get Doc!" the woman shouted.

The young girl dropped her rifle, spun around, and disappeared into the woods.

"She shot them," Elsa said, gesturing to Dominic.

Laney arrived at Lunch Box's side first. She rolled him over just as Ayden reached them. The young man's eyes were open, but it was clear he was gone.

Ayden left Laney to check his vitals while he moved to Dominic's side. Beneath him, blood had already pooled. Ayden raised his shirt to find a bullet hole on the left side of his abdomen. Immediately, Ayden ripped off own his shirt and used it to apply pressure to the young man's wound.

Joyce and Laney cried softly while they waited for the doctor to arrive. Elsa told Kara everything she'd been through, including how she got the burns and how Ayden and his group helped her reach the farm.

Kara moved over to the gurney, where her nephew was seated. She wrapped her arms around him. "You're a hero, Josiah. You were so brave to pull your mom out of the fire and save your baby brother."

Josiah threw his arms around her and burst into tears.

"It's okay! You're safe now."

Ayden wanted to ask how she could say that with one person dead and another wounded by one of her group.

Kara examined Josiah's bandaged leg. "Don't worry," she said, kissing the top of his head. "We have a surgeon who's going to fix you right up."

Kara nodded to the stretcher. "That's smart!"

Clara chuckled. "My brother surprises me occasionally."

"You're hurt, too?" Kara asked, running over to help her to her feet.

"Shot," Clara said, leaning on Kara to stand. "But I saw a doctor a few days ago. She cleaned the wound, and I've been keeping it clean and bandaged. I don't have an infection. I just need time to heal."

"Let's have Doc look at it anyway. You can rest at the guest cabin for as long as you need."

When the doctor arrived, he pronounced Lunch Box deceased and moved to treat Dominic. "We need to get him to the clinic."

"We set up a clinic in the Smithsons' house. They never made it home. We needed a place for Doc to treat the wounded," Kara said.

"You can use this gurney. Ayden could go with you and bring it back to me," Clara said.

Without another word, the doctor directed the men with him to put Dominic on the stretcher and take him to the clinic. Joyce held her grandson's hand the whole way there. Kara led Elsa, her boys, and the rest of Ayden's group up to her farmhouse.

As they walked, the landscape unfolded around them, revealing a picturesque farmstead nestled in the rolling hills of Pennsylvania. The farmhouse itself was a charming, two-story structure with white clapboard siding and green shutters. A wide, wraparound porch adorned with wicker furniture and hanging flower baskets welcomed them. The roof, topped with weathered gray shingles, added to the rustic charm.

Beyond the house, the land stretched out in a patchwork of fertile fields, vibrant gardens, and lush pastures. Rows of corn swayed gently in the breeze, and neat rows of vegetables hinted at the farm's self-sufficiency. A large red barn stood proudly to one side, its doors slightly ajar to reveal stalls of well-cared-for livestock. Chickens roamed freely, pecking at the ground, while a few goats grazed nearby. The contrast between the scene there and the one out on the road was surreal.

The farmhouse's interior was cozy and inviting, and the air was filled with the comforting aroma of home-cooked meals. Kara guided them into the spacious kitchen, where a hearty meal was waiting.

"Our group consisted of mostly my in-laws and neighbors. We try to keep things as normal as possible," Kara said.

The table, covered with a checkered tablecloth, was laden with freshly baked bread, steaming bowls of soup, and platters of roasted vegetables.

"Please, help yourselves," Kara said with a kind smile. "You must be starving."

After they ate, Kara led them to a three-bedroom guest cabin situated a short walk from the main house. The cabin, made of sturdy logs, exuded the same rustic charm as the farmhouse. A small porch with a couple of rocking chairs overlooked a serene pond, its surface reflecting the orange hues of the setting sun.

Inside, the cabin was simply yet tastefully furnished. The living area featured a comfortable sofa and armchairs arranged around a stone fireplace. A modest kitchen with essential amenities adjoined the living space. Each of the three bedrooms was furnished with wooden beds, cozy quilts, and dressers, offering a sense of homeliness and comfort.

Laney, Clara, and Ayden gathered in the living area. No one

spoke for a long while, each lost in their own struggle to make sense of all that had occurred over the last few days. Laney sat on the floor with her back against the sofa. She drew her knees to her chest and stared at her feet. She sighed heavily a few times but said nothing.

Clara adjusted herself on the sofa and placed her hand on Laney's shoulder. "I'm so sorry about what has happened to your friends."

Laney nodded but said nothing.

Ayden leaned forward in his chair. "I'll speak with Kara about finding a place to lay Lunch Box to rest and dig his grave in the morning."

Laney glanced up with tears in her eyes. "Thank you," she said before returning her gaze to the floor. She drew in a deep breath and let it out slowly. "I had been traveling with a different group when I began my hike on the AT trail." She shifted to face them. "All they wanted to do was party. I wasn't into that. I met Tina, Christopher—Lunch Box, and Dominic at one of the hostels. They knew how to have fun without drugs and alcohol. We hit it off and traveled together after that. We got to know one another pretty well. Tina was running from overbearing parents who wanted her to become a doctor. Lunch Box was running from himself. He didn't know what he wanted to do with his life. Dominic—he just wanted to explore and enjoy nature."

"And you?" Clara asked.

Laney stared at her feet. "I think I was a little like all three of them. I was looking for my purpose, struggling with knowing how jacked up the world was and really expecting this"—she waved her hand in the air—"the end of life as we knew it."

Ayden wondered what he would have done differently had he seen this coming.

There was a long pause and then Laney broke the silence. "Dominic isn't going to be able to travel again for a long time."

Clara nodded. "And Joyce isn't going to leave him."

There was another long pause in the conversation. In the silence, the scene where Joyce's husband, Stanley, sacrificed his life to save them played in Ayden's mind. They wouldn't have made it this far without Joyce and her motorhome.

"We can't stay here indefinitely," Clara said. "We never know when the PLA will show up."

Ayden leaned back in his chair, running a hand through his hair. He was conflicted about whether to leave. He felt an obligation to Joyce after all she and her deceased husband, Stanley, had done for them. But he also had an obligation to get Laney home.

"I'm sorry for what happened to Dominic," Laney said. "He's my friend, and I love him, but I can't stay here while he heals. My father will come looking for me if I don't reach Crystal Springs and radio in. I don't want him and my mother out on the road, knowing the PLA could be anywhere. I have to warn them."

Ayden massaged the back of his neck. "I think every day we wait, the more likely it becomes that we get trapped behind enemy lines." He reached over and took Clara's hand. "They could put us in camps if they don't kill us outright."

"NO!" Clara said. "No. We can't let that happen. That would be worse than death."

Her strong reaction took Ayden aback. "Okay! All right!" He nodded at Laney. "We'll leave in the morning after we bury Lunch Box if that's okay. I'd like to poke around Martinsburg and see if I can come up with a faster mode of transportation than an ambulance stretcher."

Laney nodded. "The morning is fine. I'll go with you—watch your back, Cowboy."

That was the second time she'd called him that. He was about to ask why when there was a knock at the door.

Ayden opened it to find Kara wearing a wide smile. "I've got a gift for you—for getting my sister and nephew here safely." She stepped back and waved her hand toward a two-person three-wheeled electric tricycle parked outside.

Ayden's eyes widened. "Does it work?"

Kara frowned. "The motor doesn't. The battery is dead, and we don't have any way to charge it." She stepped over and pointed to the pedals. "But it pedals just fine, and it will carry both you and your sister, even on hills. I've done that with my disabled son—that's who I bought it for. He's sixteen and weighs more than Clara."

A wide grin formed on Ayden's lips. "It's amazing. Thank you."

"For you, Laney…" She spun to face her. "It is Laney, right?"

"Yes." Laney stepped through the doorway and down the steps.

"We have this super-duper mountain bike," Kara said, gesturing over her shoulder.

Laney ran to inspect the bicycle. "It's great! I had one like this when I was younger. That thing would go thirty-five miles per hour."

"The trike isn't going to get near that, but at least you'll all get where you're going much faster."

"We want to hit the road first thing in the morning," Laney said.

"After we bury our friend," Ayden said. "I wanted to ask if there was somewhere we could lay him to rest and if I could borrow a shovel."

Kara's expression softened. "We've already taken care of his burial place. We have an old trencher with a backhoe. A few of the guys dug the grave already. We can have a service and lay him to rest in the morning."

"Thank you," Laney said.

"It's the least we could do," Kara said. "We can plan on a sunrise service. I'm sure you'll want to get on the road as early as possible."

"That would be nice," Laney said. "I'd like to get to Crystal Springs as soon as possible."

"How far is Crystal Springs from here?" Ayden asked.

Laney shrugged. "We need a map. I'm not even sure how to get there from here."

Ayden turned to Kara.

"I'm not familiar with Crystal Springs. Is that in West Virginia?"

"Pennsylvania. Somewhere between Harrisonville, Everett, and south of Breezewood, Pennsylvania," Laney said.

Kara pivoted toward her barn. "Jackson!" she yelled.

A moment later, a man in his late sixties poked his head out the barn door. "Yeah!"

"Breezewood, Pennsylvania. About how far is that?"

He stepped out, wiping his hands on a shop towel. "Well, let me think," the man said in a thick West Virginia accent.

There was a long pause.

"Less than seventy miles, I reckon. Let me grab a map to be sure."

As he disappeared around the side of the barn, Ayden did the math in his head. Seventy miles at maybe twenty miles per hour would put them in Crystal Springs in around six or seven hours. He smiled. He felt as if a huge weight had been lifted. "How far is it to Washington County from Crystal Springs?"

"About one hundred and twenty miles to my parents' place," Laney said, still bent over, inspecting the tires on her new mountain bike.

"So three or four days," Clara said from the doorway.

Ayden smiled back at her. "Closer to four. I'm not sure I'm in shape enough to pedal more than six hours a day."

"Four days," Laney said. "My dad might decide to come get us from Crystal Springs."

"Really?" Clara asked, hopping on one foot onto the step.

"I can't guarantee that because we don't know what his situation is, but if at all possible, he'll come for me."

Jackson returned and spread the map out on the porch. "Yep,

about seventy miles." He handed the map to Laney. "You can keep it."

"Thanks," Laney said, tracing the path from Crystal Springs to Washington, Pennsylvania. "I was correct. About one hundred and twenty-five miles to the compound."

"So we theoretically could be at your parents' place tomorrow if we left now?" Ayden said.

"Riding in the dark?" Clara asked, concern in her voice.

Kara shook her head. "I wouldn't recommend that. You can't show up at someone's place at night. You have to be careful approaching people now." She lowered her head. "Hopefully, they don't have inexperienced folks on guard duty like Natasha."

"Oh, I don't think they'd allow…" Laney stopped herself.

"We wouldn't have allowed it either, but there are too few people here, and we have several people out scavenging. Natasha was all we had."

"So you gave her a gun and put her out on the road."

Kara hung her head and then looked up and shrugged. "Ain't too many good people out on the roads these days. We haven't really seen anyone for a long time. We had everyone we could spare working on the bus and getting things ready for our trip."

"Bus?" Laney asked.

Clara raised an eyebrow. "Trip?"

"We're not sticking around here. Doc has a place down in Mexico. Once we get our old bus running, we're all going to load up and head there."

Ayden and Clara shared a glance. "Smart," he said. "But dangerous. You'll attract a lot of unwanted attention. How are you going to carry enough fuel to get there?"

"We have enough between all the farms around here to get us to Texas. We'll have to scrounge for more there," Kara said.

Ayden extended his right hand to her. "I wish you all the best of luck, Kara."

"Thanks. You guys as well, and thanks again for getting my family here."

"You're welcome," Clara said.

Ayden was lost in thought, daydreaming about finding a bus and driving it to Wyoming. Yet fear gripped his gut and uncertainty about what he'd find when he reached there.

Morning brought good news about Dominic's condition. He would make it, but he wouldn't be able to travel—not on foot or by bike. Following the sunrise service for Lunch Box, Ayden, Clara, and Laney stopped in to say their goodbyes to Joyce and Dominic.

"Kara invited us to go with them to Mexico," Joyce said with a sad smile on her face. "You three could come." She took Laney's hand. "I know you want to get to your family." She smiled up at Ayden. "And Ayden and Clara will make sure you get there."

"We will, and we're happy that you'll be away from all this fighting. Mexico will be like a long vacation, especially with winter right around the corner."

"Yes," Joyce said. "I wasn't looking forward to winter cold without electricity. These old bones don't do well in that kind of weather."

They hugged and then Laney slipped inside the makeshift clinic to say her goodbyes to Dominic.

Ten minutes later, she returned, anxious to hit the road. "Dominic must be on some good drugs. He couldn't stay awake." She climbed on her mountain bike and gave everyone a wave. "Thank you for your hospitality. Good luck in Mexico!"

Clara hugged Joyce and wiped away a tear as Joyce stepped back.

Joyce spread her arms wide and embraced Ayden. "Thank you for getting me to Harpers Ferry to find my grandson. I couldn't imagine losing him too—never knowing what became of him."

Ayden's throat constricted. He understood what she meant. Not knowing the fate of Mia and the boys was torture. He had to face the fact that he might never reach them, but he couldn't bring himself to let go of the dream. "Take care of yourself, Joyce. Say our goodbyes to Dominic when he wakes."

Joyce waved goodbye as Ayden helped Clara onto the back seat of the tricycle and pushed off. His body immediately protested as he pedaled down the driveway toward the country road, feeling both exhausted already but driven to reach Crystal Springs, Pennsylvania, and the hope of a quick rescue from Laney's dad.

TWENTY-THREE

Ayden

Highway 81
Martinsburg, West Virginia
Day Seven

The interchange of Highways 81 and 9 was snarled with abandoned vehicles, making it more difficult for Ayden to maneuver the adult, two-person tricycle Kara had given them. Laney weaved through them all with ease on her mountain bike. Eventually, Ayden steered the trike up the off-ramp, entering the four-lane Highway 9 in the southbound lane. Laney rode ahead a hundred feet. As the lanes cleared of vehicles, she became so relaxed that she raised both hands in the air. Ayden recalled the time he and Mia had taken the boys to ride on the bike trails. Carter had done that exact same thing. Ayden missed those times and wished now he'd cherished them more. His mind had been preoccupied with getting stronger so he could return to climbing—and eventually, make the trek to Norway to begin training to BASE jump.

Soon, four lanes narrowed to two, and the scenery changed

from city to rural. The terrain was rather level, and Ayden settled into a steady pace. A mile later, they passed by a group of people harvesting a vast field of corn by hand. A man dressed in blue jean overalls and a white undershirt threw a hand in the air. "Howdy folks! Nice day for a ride!"

Ayden was somehow comforted by the greeting. For a moment, he could forget that their world had changed so drastically and their future was more uncertain than ever in history. From the corner of his eye, he could see Clara returning the wave.

"That corn looks so good."

"It's probably GMO," Clara said.

"Does that matter now?"

There was a pause.

"I guess not."

She grew quiet for a long moment. "How are we ever going to be able to grow enough food to survive? Where do we even begin?"

"Honestly, sis, I have no idea. We have to trust that farmers like those back there know how to grow food without all the modern technology and chemicals."

"And if they don't?"

Ayden grew quiet. After a few moments, he said, "Mia had a friend, someone in one of her mom groups. She grew things in a greenhouse. She was into all this homesteading stuff, where she grew ninety percent of her family's food. She even had a cow she milked. We need to hook up with people like that."

"I guess so," Clara said.

There was a long period of silence as Ayden pedaled northwest, skirting Hedgesville, West Virginia, and turning toward North Mountain.

"It's disheartening to think that everything we valued, all our lofty goals, they were so shallow and meaningless in the grand scheme of all things important," Clara said as they neared the town.

"There's nothing like an apocalypse to get one's priorities straight," Ayden said.

"Laney's spirits seem lifted now that we're truly on the road to her home."

"Yes, she does." He steered the trike around an abandoned school bus and followed Laney onto Allensville Road. "I sure hope she's right and her father does come get us at Crystal Springs. I'm not sure how long my butt can handle this seat."

Clara chuckled and then grew more somber. "What if he doesn't want to take us with them?"

"Why wouldn't he?"

"Because we didn't manage to get her home. Why would he want to take on two extra people who have nothing to offer?"

Ayden's gut twisted. He hadn't considered that outcome. Although he'd set out to deliver Laney home just because it was on the way and the right thing to do, he had counted on being restocked with food and supplies for the rest of their journey to Wyoming. He thought for a moment, racking his brain for something encouraging to say. "Well, if that happens, we'll just have to find food and supplies ourselves before we hit the road again."

"Sure," Clara said. "We'll be fine."

As they continued west, the terrain became more challenging. The distance between hills and curves became shorter, but Ayden was pleasantly surprised that pedaling the trike was still manageable. He knew he would be quite sore the next day, but for now, he kept his mind occupied with plans for how they'd get to western Wyoming.

They stopped for a short rest alongside the railroad tracks just east of the only bridge across the Potomac River for twenty-five miles. After a drink of water and a snack of crackers, they got back on the road, crossing the bridge into Hancock, Maryland, three hours after leaving Joyce and Dominic with Elsa at her sister's farm.

While pedaling across, Ayden pondered Kara's group's decision to head south to Mexico. The journey would be so filled with the unknown that it made Ayden's stomach sour. They could travel all that way, only to be turned away at the border. Even with the doctor owning property down there, why would the Mexican government accept American refugees? What motivation would they have?

No, it was too big of a risk to consider. Ayden had briefly considered heading to Canada. They'd be more likely to accept them, but how quickly would their own resources dwindle with the flood of people flowing across their border?

Upon arriving in Hancock, they were immediately greeted by armed guards crouched behind sandbags and stacked tires. Laney's brakes squeaked loudly as she stopped abruptly. Ayden pulled to a stop next to her.

"What now?" Clara asked.

"State your business," one of the guards shouted from behind the barricade.

"We're heading north to Pennsylvania. I'm trying to get home to Washington County," Laney called back.

"You're armed?"

"Yes, sir. It's not safe to be out here otherwise."

"Gonna have to escort you through town. You'll need to hand over your weapons temporarily."

"How do we know you'll return them?" Ayden asked.

"You don't. You have to trust us just as we have to trust you."

"Makes sense," Clara said.

"I don't like handing over our only protection," Ayden said.

"What's the alternative?" Laney asked in a hushed tone. We turn around and find another route across the river. That would add who knows how many more miles to the trip."

"True," Ayden added.

"Okay," she shouted at the guards. "I'll hand over mine until we get through your town."

"I guess that's settled." Clara shifted in her seat. "I hope this doesn't come back to bite us."

After handing over their weapons, Ayden, Clara, and Laney were escorted by armed guards to Maryland's border with Pennsylvania. There, National Guard soldiers stood by while people picked corn from a field alongside the road.

One of the soldiers stood in the roadway, munching on an ear of corn. "Where are you guys headed?"

"Crystal Springs," Laney said.

He shook his head. "I wouldn't advise that."

"Why?" Clara asked. Tension laced her tone.

The soldier glanced toward where the other soldiers were leaning against their Humvee. "There's been trouble up that way lately."

"The PLA?" Ayden asked.

The soldier raised an eyebrow. "You know about them?"

"We've run into them a time or two," Clara said.

"Where?"

"Frederick, Maryland. Their drones nearly blew us up."

"You were there?" He drew closer. "Is it true? Was the president's motorcade hit? Is he dead?"

"It was struck. I can't verify who was inside any of those vehicles, though. I don't know if the president was among them," Ayden said.

"That's the rumor. DC was leveled by a nuke. All three branches of government were wiped out in an instant. Word was that the president got out before the strike and was then blown up by PLA drones."

"I can only confirm what looked like a presidential motorcade was struck by some sort of missile. I can't say if the people inside lived or died. I was just busy trying not to get blown up myself," Ayden said.

"Understandable."

"Who's in charge of the military if the president and the Pentagon are gone?" Laney asked.

Ayden was anxious to see if DaSilva's assessment of the continuity of government was correct.

"Someone on the president's doomsday plane is what we've been told. The Designated Survivor is what they call them, though they haven't said who that is yet." The soldier took another bite of his corn and chewed for a moment before continuing. "We've just been told to follow our commanding officer's orders and trust that they are receiving theirs from someone higher up the chain."

"What's the plan?" Laney asked. "How are we going to fight back and run those commie asshats off our land?"

"Right now, the orders are to hold the bridges and secure the rail lines and our waterways. Transportation routes are key to winning ground wars. We have to be able to move troops and supplies freely." He tossed his ear of corn into the ditch. "But so does the enemy. Right now, that's their main goal as well. We're fighting their special forces units who are trying to keep us busy while they get their troops off their ships and into place. Once that happens, heaven help us."

"That's encouraging," Laney said sarcastically.

"It will take some time for their million-man army to arrive, but when they do, they'll spread out like locusts and devour the land."

"Well, aren't you a ray of sunshine and good news," Laney said, waving her hand in the air dismissively.

"If you believe that, why are you here? What's the point? Shouldn't we all be evacuating to Mexico or Canada?" Ayden asked.

The soldier grasped his belly and bent over, laughing. "Yeah. No! Those borders are closed. You'll have to sneak in, and if you do—let me put it this way—you won't be welcomed with open arms."

“Why are you still here…” Clara pointed to the roadway. “Doing your jobs?”

The soldier narrowed his gaze. “So my family eats.”

It made sense. Soldiers would be fed, and they’d want to provide for their families as well.

“My advice…” He pivoted toward the Humvee. “Go into the mountains. They’re not going to focus their attention there—not for a while.”

“Thanks.” Laney pushed off and pedaled her bike forward.

“Good luck,” the soldier said as Ayden set out after her.

Over the next two hours, as they traveled north along Interstate 70, Ayden anticipated encountering the PLA around every bend. Relief washed over him as they drew near Crystal Springs without any sign of the enemy’s troops.

At the first exit, Laney consulted her map. “Yep, this is it.”

They took the exit, crossed over the interstate, and followed the county road north along a steep elevation drop for over half a mile before making another turn onto a rural highway that eventually began to ascend the ridge until it reached a Y intersection. There, they stopped to make sure they were going the right way, and two men emerged from the woods.

Clara gasped. “Ayden. Trouble!”

Ayden spun in his seat to face them and raised the firearm from his lap.

TWENTY-FOUR

Ayden

Green Ridge Farms
Crystal Springs, Pennsylvania
Day Seven

The two men who'd emerged from the woods looked like hunters, one wearing an orange vest and the other a hunter's orange hat. Rifles dangled from slings over their shoulders. The stockier of the two raised his weapon.

"What are you doing here?" he asked, a hint of fear in his voice.

As Ayden's finger slid inside the trigger guard, he noticed the man wasn't aiming or directing his gun at them but was ready to do so. The man must have been unsure if they were a threat, but it was clear from his stiff posture he was ready for a deadly confrontation if necessary.

Laney threw her shoulders back defiantly.

"I said, what are you doing here?" the man repeated.

"None of your business," Laney snapped. She slowly lowered her right hand to the holster on her hip.

"You folks got business back here?" the other man asked. He was tall and thin but not in a way that suggested he'd missed meals. His face wasn't gaunt, and his skin didn't hang from his body. He had likely been thin before the lights went out.

Laney let her map fall to the ground and twisted her torso in their direction.

Ayden's gaze flicked between her and the two men. He studied each of their hands, fearing someone would escalate the situation with deadly consequences.

A slight, friendly smile played on Laney's lips—almost as if she'd suddenly recognized friendly faces. "Yeah. I'm looking for Green Ridge Farms."

The stockier man lowered his weapon slightly. The tension in his posture eased somewhat. "Oh yeah? What do you want there?"

Laney slid her hand from her holster to her thigh. "The owners know my dad."

The tall, thin man lowered the barrel of his rifle to the ground and straightened it slightly.

Ayden exhaled, feeling the muscles in his neck and shoulders relax. He eased his finger outside his trigger guard and lowered the barrel slightly in response.

"My dad told me I should stop by and say hi if I'm ever this way," Laney said.

"What's your daddy's name?" the stocky guy asked.

Laney lifted her chin and pulled her shoulders back proudly. "Tyson Mueller!"

The thin man stepped onto the roadway, his rifle now at his side, the barrel pointed at the ground. "You're Laney Mueller?"

The men knew her. Crisis adverted. But still, Ayden felt as if he was going to hurl what little food was in his stomach.

Laney's smile widened. "Yep. In the flesh!"

"Well, I'll be a monkey's uncle!" The stocky man stepped up beside the other and slapped him on the back. "I bet my cousin here a dollar you'd never make it this far. Your pop said you would be going through some rough territory over in Maryland. I said no way a little girl makes it all this way alone." The man's gaze shifted to Ayden and studied him as if he were sizing him up for the first time.

Ayden held his gaze until the man broke eye contact.

"You spoke to him?" Laney asked excitedly.

"We spoke to his communication guy, Steve, several times. He told us to be on the lookout for you after we relayed that you were down at Camp Evergreen."

"You spoke with DaSilva or her folks?" Ayden asked.

The stocky guy gave him a quick glance and nodded.

Returning his gaze to Laney, he said, "We tried to call out to them this morning but didn't hear anything."

"They were attacked yesterday morning—by the PLA. They had to bug out," Laney said. "Most of them didn't make it."

"Crap!" The man drew closer. "Let us grab our four-wheelers, and we'll take you up to the farm." He pointed up the ridge, but Ayden couldn't see any structures to indicate a farm.

The farm, nestled into the surrounding hillside, overlooked a vast pasture, and beyond that, Ayden could see rolling hills for miles. It was beautiful and serene. Staring at it, he couldn't imagine bombs and bullets disrupting such a peaceful place. The two-story house, with yellow-painted siding, faced the view while the red-painted, weathered-wood barn faced the house. Behind it, at the top of the hill, a huge antenna towered above them both, and along the ridge was a row of solar panels.

An older gentleman greeted them in the driveway. Ayden stopped the trike near the mailbox and scanned the area between the house and barn, watching as people poured out from behind them. Laney halted near the older man and climbed off her bike.

"Howdy!" a woman in her late seventies said, waving a tea

towel above her head. “Yinz, come on in. I got drop biscuits and sausage gravy still on the stove.”

Ayden’s stomach growled at the mention of food. It seemed he was always hungry these days, and the exertion of pedaling the trike had only exacerbated that this afternoon.

“I just picked a mess of tomatoes. There’s some bacon grease left to pour on ’em,” the old man said, licking his lips. “Sounds so good. I think I’ll join ya.”

The stocky guy climbed off his ATV and gestured to Laney. “Mom, Pop, this here is Laney.” He glanced back at Ayden and Clara. “Sorry, folks, I didn’t get your names.”

“Ayden. Ayden Miller and this is my sister, Clara.”

Clara held up her hand and smiled.

“I’m Owen Graff. That there’s my wife, Evelyn. I guess you already met my boys, Joseph and Mark.”

Laney smiled and nodded. “Pleased to make your acquaintance.”

“Well, climb on off that funny-looking bike and come on in, Ayden and Clara Miller. I’ll put on a pot of coffee, and we can hear all about your adventures,” Owen said. “I’m sure it’s been an interesting trip all the way from Harpers Ferry.”

“Interesting?” Clara said. “Terrifying is more like it.”

“I can only imagine,” Owen said as Ayden assisted Clara from the trike. He lifted her into his arms and followed the couple toward the door to the home. “Joseph, fire up the gennie so we can radio Steve and let Laney’s Pa know we got her here with us.”

Joseph climbed off his four-wheeler and disappeared around the back of the barn.

“I’m gonna head back out to the road, Pop.” He held up a handheld radio. “I’ll keep trying to reach the Snyders.”

Owen gestured toward the house, and Ayden and the others continued walking. “The Snyders are down in Mercersburg. We haven’t heard from them today. They’d reported hearing helicopters in the area and then—radio silence.”

"That's not good," Laney said as Owen opened the door and stepped back to allow everyone to enter.

Inside, the living room of the home was warm and inviting, furnished with a comfortable-looking sofa and two recliners separated by a small table. There was no television in the room. An antique mirror hung over the fireplace, and family portraits adorned the walls, depicting smiling and genuinely happy-looking families.

They were led through the room into the kitchen at the back of the house. Floor-to-ceiling windows looked out at a small garden and a chicken coop. A large wooden table filled most of the room, flanked by two long bench-style seats. To the left was the heart of the kitchen, with a large, vintage-appearing stove, an avocado green refrigerator, and a matching-colored sink. Along the back wall, between two windows, sat a desk. Atop the desk was radio equipment.

"Have a seat, and we'll get yinz fed while we get the radio set up to call your pop," Owen said, sliding into an office chair and beginning to turn knobs on the radio receiver.

Ayden and Clara ate as Laney stood beside Owen, waiting to speak to her father. The radio crackled, and a man's voice gave out a series of numbers and letters.

"The sky is purple over Philly today. Better carry an umbrella if you head to the market."

Owen sat up straighter and reached for a notebook on his desk. He flipped it open and ran his index finger down a list of words.

His wife hurried over and picked up a book from the corner of his desk. "What page?"

"Three hundred fourteen."

A concerned look passed between them.

"Is everything all right?" Clara asked.

Evelyn glanced back briefly. "They're reporting enemy jets over Philadelphia."

"That's bad," Clara said, wringing her hands.

Ayden placed his hand on her leg. “That’s two hundred miles from here.”

“And a fighter jet can fly like a thousand miles per hour. So one could reach us in minutes,” Clara said.

“Yeah, but PLA fighter jets aren’t going to be interested in this farm,” Ayden said, wanting to reassure her they were safe there. He glanced over at Owen and Evelyn to back him up, but his heart sank at their expressions. “Right, Owen?”

Owen said nothing.

A knot formed in the pit of Ayden’s stomach. “Right, Owen?”

“I don’t think they’d waste a missile to take out one farm,” Owen finally said.

“See, Clara!” Ayden said, although he wasn’t quite satisfied with Owen’s answer.

“Are you two part of some form of resistance?” Laney asked.

The elderly couple looked at one another and smiled but said nothing.

The static of the radio continued to fill the kitchen as Owen twisted the knobs, his brow creased in concentration.

Ayden and Clara watched anxiously while Laney stood by the window, peering out into the dimming light of the day.

“Anything?” Clara’s voice was a whisper, almost lost in the static that answered Owen’s attempts.

“Nothing from the repeater,” Owen muttered in frustration.

“What’s a repeater?” she asked.

“A radio device that extends the range of a portable or mobile radio system. Repeaters receive a radio signal on one frequency and simultaneously transmit the same signal on another. They’re often located on mountaintops, tall buildings, or radio towers. Our primary repeater is up on Kinton Knob, and a secondary one is on Martin Hill. I’ve tried all five repeaters in Bedford. There’s nothing.” Owen sighed. “We can’t reach Washington County without the boost from the repeater in Bedford. There’s a mountain in the way.”

Laney turned from the window, her expression tense. “Could the repeater equipment be down?”

Owen sighed, rubbing his eyes wearily. “It’s the most likely explanation. It was old to begin with, and if it’s out, we’re cut off from everyone not within shouting distance.”

The gravity of the situation settled on the group like a heavy cloak. The repeater was crucial for long-distance communication, especially in these times when the PLA’s presence was drawing ever nearer, making every transmission a lifeline.

“We need to check it out,” Owen said, standing. “If it’s down, we fix it. If it’s something else…” He didn’t finish the sentence, but they all understood the many dangers that “something else” could imply.

With the decision made, Owen sat down at the kitchen table. “Tomorrow morning, me and the boys will take a ride to Bedford and see if we can fix the repeater. If you wanna come with us, Laney, you’ll be able to radio your dad from there.”

“Yes!” Laney said. “I’ll go.”

“Should we go as well?” Clara asked. “So we can leave from there.” She turned to Owen. “If you have room in your vehicle, that is.”

“We’ll make room.”

“That’s a good idea,” Laney said. “In case we can’t contact my dad from Bedford, we’ll just keep going to the next rally point.”

“We haven’t heard a peep from Somerset or Mount Pleasant. You might want to take Highway 30 to Ligonier. We spoke with Tim a few days ago, right after he got his rig back up and running. You’ll have a better line of sight from his place, and the distance will be the same as from Somerset if you aren’t able to reach him from Kinton Knob.”

Laney smiled. “Either way, I could be home by dark.”

TWENTY-FIVE

Mueller

New Eden Compound
Somerset Township
Washington County, Pennsylvania
Day Seven

The compound was unusually quiet, the air heavy with anticipation and anxiety. Mueller paced the floor of the communications trailer, his eyes darting to Steve, who was frantically trying to reach Crystal Springs on the ham radio. The previous day's news that Laney was in Maryland had lifted their spirits, but now, as the hours ticked by with no further updates, their hope began to waver.

Steve's fingers moved rapidly over the dials, his frustration growing. "Come on, come on," he muttered.

Mueller's heart sank with every passing minute. His daughter was out there, somewhere, and he was helpless to reach her. Monica, his wife, sat in the chair next to Steve, chewing on the nails of her left hand while tapping the fingers of her right on the desk in front of her.

Steve finally looked up, shaking his head. "No luck, Ty. I can't get through to Crystal Springs."

Mueller's stomach churned. "We'll have to be patient. She's on the move, and we don't know her exact location. If we head out now, we could miss her completely."

Monica shot to her feet, sending the rolling office chair flying across the room and crashing into the opposite wall. "How can you say that? She needs us!" Her eyes flashed with rage. She shook her fist at Mueller. "We should be out there looking for her right now!"

Mueller felt a pang of guilt. "I know, Monica. But if we leave without knowing where she is, we could end up searching blindly and waste precious time."

Monica's lips trembled, and she turned away, wiping at her eyes. "I can't just sit here and do nothing."

Mueller reached out to her, his voice soft. "We'll find her. I promise. But we have to be smart about this. She's not alone, and she's in a vehicle. She'll make her way to one of our contacts. We could hear from her any moment."

The sun climbed higher, and time dragged on without a word; Mueller tried to keep busy, overseeing various tasks and ensuring everything ran smoothly. It was a futile attempt to distract himself from the gnawing worry about Laney.

Suddenly, Steve came running from the communications trailer, his face pale. "Ty, I've got bad news. Camp Evergreen's been attacked."

Mueller's blood ran cold. "What? By who?"

"Reports say it's the PLA. They're crawling all over Crystal Springs, too."

Monica, who was nearby, overheard the conversation and rushed over, her eyes wide with fear. "We have to go, Ty. Now!"

Mueller clenched his fists, torn between his duty to the compound and his desperate need to find Laney. "Monica, I—"

She grabbed his arm, her grip tight. "She's our daughter! We can't just leave her out there!"

His heart ached to see her so distressed, but he knew he had to stay rational. "If we go now without knowing where she is, we could miss her entirely. We have to wait for her to contact us first."

Monica's face crumpled, and she stepped back, tears streaming down her cheeks. "You're just going to let her die out there?"

Her words were like daggers to his heart. He would do absolutely anything to eliminate Monica's pain, but he couldn't do what she was asking. He had to hold strong—and wait. Mueller's voice broke. "No, never. I'll do everything in my power to bring her back. But we can't go yet."

If looks could kill, he would have dropped where he stood as she glared back at him. She shook her head and wiped her tears before turning her back and walking away from him.

Mueller forced himself to focus as he entered the meeting hall. The council members were already seated, discussing the new rules of conduct and appropriate punishments for wrongdoings within the camp.

Frank started, his voice steady. "We need to decide on a system that combines fairness with strict discipline. We can't afford any more lapses."

Mueller nodded, but his mind was elsewhere. "Agreed. Let's start with the sentry who fell asleep. How's he doing with his new duties?"

Nesbitt, who had been overseeing the punishment, spoke up. "He's been doing extra shifts in the kitchen and helping the team dig the new latrines in the southern section of the compound. He's shown remorse and is taking his duties more seriously now."

Mueller rubbed his temples, trying to stay engaged. "Good. We need to set clear examples. What about more serious offenses?"

Amos leaned forward. "For major breaches, we've selected Herb Jones, Miles Ganser, and Ken Isberg due to their prior military service and familiarity with court-martial procedures."

Mueller's thoughts drifted back to Laney. The anxiety of not knowing her fate made it hard to concentrate. He knew the council's decisions were important, but all he could think about was his daughter and the news about Camp Evergreen and Crystal Springs.

After the meeting ended, Mueller found a quiet spot and sank down, his head in his hands. He replayed the events of the day over and over, guilt and worry gnawing at him. His rescue mission had gone horribly wrong, his friend had died, and now his daughter's life hung in the balance. He sat there second-guessing himself. Was he even the right person to lead this group?

Monica found him there, her eyes red from crying. She sat beside him, silent for a long moment before speaking. "I'm sorry, Ty. I know you're trying your best. I just… I can't stand not knowing if she's safe."

Mueller lifted his head, his eyes meeting hers. He wrapped his arm around her shoulders. She rested her head on his chest. "I'm scared too, Monica. Every minute feels like an eternity." He stroked her hair. "But we have to trust that she'll find a way to contact us."

Monica nodded, staring up at him. A tear slipped down her cheek. "We need to be ready to leave as soon as we hear from her."

"We will be," Mueller said. "The moment we get her location, we'll go. Together. I promise."

They sat there, leaning on each other for strength as the sun began to set. Soon, the stars twinkled in the night sky. Mueller held his wife close, praying for Laney's safety in a world gone completely mad.

TWENTY-SIX

Ayden

Green Ridge Farms
Crystal Springs, Pennsylvania
Day Eight

As Ayden ate the best breakfast of his life, the radio, left on in a faint hope of catching stray transmissions, crackled to life. An urgent, breathless voice, relayed the chilling message: "PLA is tracking signals. They're raiding the homes of ham operators. Don't transmit. Take down your towers, hide your equipment. Stay safe."

Evelyn, who was standing at the sink, spun around. "Is that Eugene?"

Owen stood, his eyes wide. "It is."

"What does that mean?" Clara asked, her voice cracking.

Owen hurried to the desk and slid into his chair. In seconds, he was turning knobs, and then the message repeated. "Raiding homes… Don't transmit… Stay safe."

Evelyn moved to Owen's side. "He's still transmitting. Do you think it's a trick?"

Owen stood and touched her face. "I think it's Eugene being Eugene. He must know it's too late for him, and he's trying to warn the rest of us."

"What does that mean?" Clara asked again. "Are they coming here?"

Owen ignored her and headed toward the back door. "I have to get the boys and get them busy taking down the tower."

Ayden followed Owen outside. "Level with me, Owen," he said as they headed toward a carport where several ATVs sat waiting. "What's really going on? Why is the PLA targeting ham operators?"

"We've been relaying coded information to our military and…" He paused, and then a slight smile played on his lips. "And to the resistance network. We're reporting PLA activities. The Chinese have been using barrage jamming, which spreads power across multiple frequencies simultaneously, in the cities to interfere with radio transmissions." Owen climbed onto his four-wheeler. "I was in a conversation with an operator in Maryland when the frequency was suddenly disrupted by interference. I moved to another frequency to reach him, and it was also jammed."

Ayden stopped beside him. "Can they find you just by you transmitting?"

"Yes."

Ayden glanced back at the house, his thoughts racing. He needed to grab his sister and Laney and get away from there before the PLA showed up at Owen's doorstep.

"We'll take down the tower and go mobile. We'll be fine. They won't be able to locate us."

"Go mobile?"

"Load everything into my trailer and hit the roads. We'll drive around, set up the antennae, and then listen for a while. We'll only transmit if we hear a transmission that requires us to relay a message," Owen said.

"So that means Laney won't be able to contact her father?"

"We'll have to wait and see. Ty and I worked out a coded system to relay information about Laney to one another, but we'll have to see whether we'll be able to transmit it."

Under the cloak of night, they worked with hurried precision. Owen supervised his two sons, Joseph and Mark, in lowering the antenna tower in his backyard while Ayden and Laney helped Evelyn dismantle the radio equipment, packing it away in a small cargo trailer, along with an array of solar panels, batteries, and telescoping antennae. The tower came down piece by piece until the final pieces were stowed away.

Owen poked his head inside the cargo trailer. "Good job, guys! Now let's take this show on the road. I want to go over to Bedford and check on the repeater. I need to take it offline so they can't track it. We'll leave the tower. We'd need equipment to disassemble that."

"You think it's safe to be out on the roads after that warning?" Evelyn asked with concern etched on her face.

"We're not going to transmit. Just listen. We'll have a better signal up on Kinton Knob."

"We're still joining you, right?" Laney asked. "And leaving from there?"

"Sure thing," Owen said, gesturing toward an older model pickup truck. "We'll leave as soon as you're loaded up."

After Owen's oldest son backed the truck up to the mobile radio trailer, Ayden loaded the bicycle and adult trike into the back of Owen's 1970 crew cab Ford pickup truck, tossed in their heavy backpacks, fishing poles, and tackle box, and assisted Clara into the back seat behind Joseph. Owen's other son, Mark, climbed into the bed of the truck and sat next to the back window.

"Thank you for your hospitality, Evelyn." Laney climbed in and slid across the bench seat beside Clara.

"My pleasure, dear," Evelyn said. She approached Ayden and handed him a bundle wrapped in a tea towel. "For the road."

Ayden unwrapped the towel and took in the heavenly scent of buttermilk biscuits. "Wow! Thank you so much."

"You have to share those, brother." Clara chuckled.

Ayden tucked the bundle behind his back. "What biscuits. I don't see any biscuits."

"Funny!" Clara said. "Hand them over. You can't be trusted with food," she said with her hand outstretched.

Ayden leaned into the truck, and Laney took the bundle from him. She held it up to her nose and closed her eyes. "I can't wait to get home and have some of my dad's sourdough cinnamon rolls."

Owen opened the truck's passenger side door. "You know, he promised to give me that recipe at our last meetup and never did send it."

Laney laughed. "He probably wouldn't have given you the correct one anyway. That's a family secret, supposedly handed down from my great-grandmother."

"Those are always the best ones," Evelyn said as Ayden climbed into the back seat behind Owen.

Ayden rolled down the window and rested his arm in the opening. "Thanks again for everything."

Evelyn placed her hand on his. "I'll keep you young'uns in my prayers. Safe travels."

Ayden nodded.

"We'll be home by dark, my dear," Owen said as she stepped over to his door.

"I'll keep the light on for you." She leaned slightly to meet Joseph's gaze. "You take care of your pop. He forgets he's not a spring chicken anymore."

Joseph put the truck into gear. "Yes, ma'am."

"We'll look out for each other," Owen said.

Evelyn leaned into the truck and kissed his cheek. "I know you will."

In minutes, they were turning onto Interstate 70, heading west. The drive to Bedford, Pennsylvania, was quiet and uneventful, each mile stretching out as the landscape moved past.

Twenty minutes later, Joseph steered the truck down the off-ramp and onto a rural highway toward Bedford. From there, they continued west, approaching the town of Everett, Pennsylvania. On the outskirts of the city, a man in shorts and a T-shirt, with a fishing pole in his hand, flagged them down. Clara's eyes were wide as Joseph pulled to a stop next to the man.

"Hey, Harry, are the fish biting today?" Owen called to him from the passenger seat.

"Not even a nibble," Harry said. He lifted his ball cap and ran a hand threw his shoulder length hair. "What brings yinz this way?"

"Came over to check on the Kinton Knob repeaters."

"They're down again?" Harry asked.

"I'm assuming. I couldn't get through yesterday or this morning."

Harry settled the hat on his head, angled it a fraction and then dropped his chin slightly. "Might have something to do with the military over that way."

Owen's eyebrows arched in a question. "Military? Ours?"

"That's what I heard. Troops have been running up and down the interstate from Pittsburgh to Philly."

"Philly?" Clara asked, leaning forward in her seat. She glanced back at Ayden. "Maybe the military jets reported there are ours."

"Military jets?" Harry asked. "Over Philadelphia?"

"They did say they were the enemy's," Owen said. "Gerry would know the difference."

Harry grimaced. "Well, that kinda sucks."

"Don't it!" Owen nodded.

"Any reports about how many of our troops are in the area?" Harry asked.

“A battalion from 2nd Infantry out of Washington, Pennsylvania,” Owen said.

Laney scooted forward in her seat. “The 2nd?” Laney asked. “I have an uncle with 2nd Infantry.”

“Not sure what they’re doing in these parts, but I heard they’re joining troops out of Philly to secure the bridges across the rivers at Pittsburgh.”

“I could see that,” Owen said. “Bridges are usually critical for movement, and the enemy would need to cross either the Allegheny, Monongahela, or the Ohio rivers to push into the Midwest from here.”

“Let’s hope they never reach this far,” Harry said.

“Fingers crossed,” Owen said.

“I’ll let yinz get on your way. I just wanted to say hi.”

“Take care, Harry,” Owen said as Joseph put the truck in gear.

When they arrived at Bedford, the streets were ominously deserted. Ayden noted the lack of signs of looting and rioting he’d seen in other places.

“Roadblock!” Joseph suddenly yelled as they rounded the curve before the bridge spanning the Raystown Branch of the Juniata River.

“Military?” Laney asked, leaning forward.

“Looks civilian. What do you want me to do, Pops?”

“Pull on up there. Let’s see what they know about military activity in the area,” Owen said.

TWENTY-SEVEN

Mia

Christiansen Ranch
Farson, Wyoming
Day Eight

The buzz of activity had continued for days as the Christiansens prepared for the possibility of armed conflict reaching them. After breakfast that morning, her father had laid out the plan to make a safe room in the house and one for the wranglers in the bunkhouse. They started by designating her parents' bedroom walk-in closet as the primary safe room. It was centrally located and had no windows, making it easier to fortify. With a plan in mind, Neil enlisted the help of her mother, Melody, and the boys to begin transforming the room.

"Carter, Luke, and Xavy, I need you to help clear out all the shoes," Mia instructed, her voice calm but firm. The boys immediately set to work, removing them and clearing space for the supplies they would soon bring in.

Next, her mom removed all the clothes and placed them in the closet of the guest room. Once the closet was cleared, Neil and Melody began fortifying it. They used a heavy-duty steel plate to cover the door, leaving a small slot at the bottom for air circulation.

Mia and the boys hauled in air mattresses, sheets, blankets, and pillows, and then the boys helped her parents bring in food, water, weapons, and ammunition.

Mia and Melody had already begun gathering supplies earlier, but now it was time to move everything into the safe room. They started with the essentials: food and water. Mia had the boys form a chain from the pantry to Xavy's little red wagon, passing cans of food, bottled water, and dried goods down the line and placing them inside until they were full and ready to be unloaded into the makeshift safe room.

"Make sure we have a good variety," Mia instructed as she handed a box of canned vegetables to Carter. "We don't know how long we might need to stay in here."

Next, they brought in medical supplies. Mia carefully packed a first-aid kit with bandages, antiseptics, pain relievers, and any prescription medications they had on hand. She also included blankets, warm clothing, and sleeping bags, knowing they needed to be prepared for the possibility of spending nights in the safe room.

"Luke, grab the flashlights and batteries from the kitchen drawer," Melody said. "And don't forget the radio."

Melody worked alongside Mia, ensuring that nothing was overlooked. They included a covered bucket with the necessary deodorizing supplies for use as a toilet, along with hygiene items, such as soap, toothpaste, and toilet paper, knowing that comfort and cleanliness would be important for maintaining morale.

"We should also bring in some books and games for the boys," Melody suggested, and Mia agreed. Keeping the children occupied and calm would be crucial.

As the last of the supplies were moved into the safe room, Mia took a moment to review their work. The room was now a well-stocked sanctuary, ready to provide shelter and sustenance in the event of an emergency. She felt a sense of relief, knowing they had taken significant steps to protect themselves.

"Mom, is there anything else we need?" Carter asked.

"I think we're about set," Mia said, placing a reassuring hand on his shoulder. "You've all done a great job. Now let's make sure we're ready for anything."

Carter and his brothers nodded, their expressions mirroring Mia's resolve. She felt a surge of pride at their bravery and willingness to help.

"I can't wait to show Ayden," he said.

Mia forced a smile and nodded. "He'll think it's pretty cool."

As the day progressed, Neil gathered his family in the living room. Dirk joined them, his weathered face showing signs of concern.

"We've done everything we can in here for now," Neil said calmly. "We're as ready as we can be." He turned to Dirk. "How are you doing in the bunkhouse?"

"Good. We turned that old cellar into our panic room. We stocked it with food, water, and plenty of weapons and ammo."

"Good. That's great!" Neil said. "Hopefully, we'll never have to use it, but I think we should start doing drills so it's automatic should the alarm be sounded."

"How much time do you think we'd have?" Mia asked.

"Five minutes—maybe."

"That's not long," Melody said.

"I've thought about talking to the Ridgeways about setting up an observation outpost up their way. If we could have a rider alert us the moment they see anything suspicious from there, we'd have more time to get to safety."

"I could ride over there tomorrow," Dirk said.

"I'd want to go with you. There's a lot to discuss. It would be good if we could all work together out here."

Neil looked at each of them in turn. "Everyone knows what to do if there's an emergency. Stay close, stay safe, and look out for each other."

TWENTY-EIGHT

Ayden

Checkpoint Neon Unicorn
Bedford, Pennsylvania
Day Eight

Bedford, Pennsylvania, located one hundred miles southeast of Pittsburgh, appeared to have been a welcoming little town tucked away in the Allegheny Mountains before the EMP attack and subsequent invasion. Now the residents were walking around armed to the teeth, clearly on high alert.

Joseph rolled to a stop one hundred feet from the Bedford roadblock guarded by four armed men and women.

"Turn off the engine!" a man shouted at them.

Owen poked his head out the passenger side window. "Owen Graff here with my boys and three friends. Is Sheriff Chaney around today?"

The geeky-looking man lowered his rifle and walked toward the truck. "He's at Overwatch." He unclipped a handheld radio from his belt and spoke into it. "Sheriff, I got Owen Graff here at Checkpoint Neon Unicorn."

His radio crackled. "Owen Graff?"

"Yes, sir."

"You're sure?"

Owen leaned forward and fished in his back pocket, retrieving a wallet. He pulled out his driver's license.

"That's who he says he is," the guard said into his radio.

"Ask for ID."

The guard turned toward the truck. "Sheriff wants—"

"I know!" Owen held out his license.

The guard took it and backed away, staring at it, and then glanced up at Owen. He pulled his radio to his mouth. "It's him. The license confirms it. What do you want me to do with him?"

"Arrest his ass and take him to the station."

The guard's eyes widened. "Say again, sir."

Owen snickered. "Tell that old coot if he wants me to come get me himself."

The guard looked confused. So was Ayden.

"Give the radio to Owen," the sheriff said.

The man walked over, held out the handheld, and then backed away.

Owen keyed the mic. "Evelyn sends her love."

Joseph chuckled. "I won't tell Mom you said that."

"I bet she did," the sheriff said through the radio. There was a long pause. "What can I do for you, Owen?"

"Well, Colt, I've had to take my show on the road and hoped you'd have a place for me."

Another long pause.

"Crap, Owen. Hand the radio back to the doofus standing by your truck."

Owen handed the guard the radio. "I guess you're Doofus?"

The guard frowned. "I guess so."

"What'd you do to earn that title?"

"Married his daughter."

Owen nodded. "I see."

Doofus walked away and then spoke into his radio. Ayden couldn't make out what was being said, but a moment later, Doofus returned and instructed them to follow him. He led them through town to the Sheriff's Department.

Joseph pulled the truck and trailer into a spot indicated for county vehicles only.

Owen opened the truck's door. "I won't be but a moment."

Five minutes later, Owen returned with a large key ring dangling from his hand. "We're in business!" he said, climbing into the truck.

"Where to, Pop?" Joseph asked.

"Your aunt Darcy's cabin," Owen said.

The truck climbed a winding road, and ten minutes later, they pulled down the drive and stopped in front of a small white cabin situated on the Raystown Branch of the Juniata River. Owen tossed the keys to the cabin to his son, Mark. "Unlock the door and then unhook the trailer. We'll leave it here. Park the truck behind the cabin near that old logging road in case we have to bug out quickly." Owen turned to Ayden. "You're all welcome to wait inside while I get everything set up."

Laney opted to stay with Owen as Ayden helped Clara onto the cabin's front porch.

The soft crunch of gravel under tires heralded Sheriff Chaney's arrival. His dusty older model SUV with a faded county logo pulled up alongside the quaint cabin. Owen, who had been setting up the mobile antenna for the ham radio, straightened up and wiped the sweat from his brow as the vehicle came to a stop.

The door creaked open, and the sheriff stepped out, his weathered face breaking into a scowl as he caught sight of Owen. "It takes the world going to shit before you come around?" he called out, his voice echoing across the vast lawn.

Owen huffed and walked over to shake the sheriff's hand. "Road runs both ways, Colt."

"What are you doing?" the sheriff asked, gesturing to the radio antenna.

"We needed a safe spot to listen."

The sheriff's smile faded as his eyes swept over the area, his gaze sharp and assessing. "Don't know that there is a safe spot for all this. Especially with the PLA running around with bizarre-looking vehicles with radar, huge antennae, and domed roofs."

Owen nodded, his expression serious. "We knew they'd do that. They don't want us reporting their activities to the military and the resistance."

The sheriff shrugged. "Yeah, but it's one thing to talk about it in theory and quite the other to be living it." He sighed, leaning against his vehicle. "It's not good, Owen. The PLA is making moves on all major communication hubs. They're not just disrupting; they're taking control. And there's talk—they're targeting ham operators like yourself. Jay Olsen's farm was burned to the ground. Neighbors say they heard vehicles and then gunfire. My deputies scoured the debris and didn't find any evidence that Jay or his family were in the house or barn at the time."

"You think they took them?"

"For interrogation, I'm assuming," the sheriff said.

"Why not do it there at the farm? And where would they take them?" Laney asked, approaching them.

"They wouldn't want to attract unwanted attention by staying too long," the sheriff said. "That kind of thing can take a while sometimes."

"How many ham operators are in this part of the country?" Ayden asked, moving up alongside Laney.

Both Owen and the sheriff gave him a look.

"Not enough now," Owen said.

"You think the PLA damaged the repeaters as well?" Laney asked. "Is that why we couldn't get a call out to my dad?"

"Could be." Owen pivoted toward the sheriff. "Any news about Lovato or Bauman?"

"Their vehicles were seen up there yesterday," the sheriff said.

Owen sighed. "I sure would like to get up there and see for myself."

"I wouldn't advise that, especially with that rig of yours. That thing puts a huge bull's-eye on you."

"We're dead in the water without those repeaters," Owen said.

"You're willing to risk your life for it?"

Owen glanced back at his sons, who were continuing to set up the antenna. "Don't have much choice. We have a mission to accomplish."

Ayden pulled Laney aside. "As much as I would like to contact your dad and wait for him to come and get us, I don't think that is wise—or safe to hang around here considering the situation."

Laney stepped back and glanced over her shoulder. "You're right. I know that my dad would agree with you. It's just a part of me wants to stay and help Owen alert everyone and still be able to transmit information valuable to the military and the resistance."

"I get that." He nodded toward his sister, who was seated in a chair on the porch of the cabin. "If I didn't need to get her somewhere safe, I'd join the resistance—wherever they are. I haven't seen them yet, but I'd be right in there, ready to push the enemy back to the Atlantic Ocean."

"I'm sure my dad will join as well—if he hasn't already," Laney said. "Give me a minute. I want to explain to Owen and say goodbye."

Ayden removed their trike and bicycle from the bed of the pickup and joined Clara on the porch as Laney spoke to Owen and his sons. "We're going to head out as soon as Laney speaks to Owen," he told Clara.

"I'm not looking forward to it—I feel so bad just sitting there listening to you huff and puff up the steep inclines."

Ayden chuckled. "I'm not huffing and puffing."

"Right!" Clara said.

Owen glanced their way and waved. "Good luck!"

"Thanks—for everything," Clara said.

Laney hugged Owen and moved toward her bike as Owen returned to where he'd set up the antenna one hundred feet away.

"Ready, Ayden and Clara?" Laney asked, climbing onto her bike and turning it toward the driveway.

"Lead the way," Ayden said, helping Clara to her feet. He slid his arm around her waist and carried her down the porch steps. They were ten feet from the trike when an ear-splitting explosion knocked him to the ground.

The terrifying whistling of incoming mortar fire abruptly shattered the air. The ground vibrated underfoot, sending them scattering for cover among the trees.

"Mortars! Move!" Owen's voice was a sharp command as explosions erupted around them, spewing dirt and debris into the air. "Dad!" Joseph cried out as he and his brother ran toward the communications trailer where their father had taken cover.

Automatic gunfire ripped across the lawn, tearing into them and dropping them to the ground before they could reach him. Owen was struck next as the PLA fired round after round into the trailer as they advanced.

The sheriff ran toward his SUV and climbed in as Ayden and Clara dove for cover. A second later, the SUV was hit and burst into flames. Ayden grabbed Clara and ran around the side of the cabin. Laney ran in front of them. "We need to get to the truck," she said.

"And go where?" Clara asked, her voice shrill as Ayden carried her.

His chest heaved in and out as he reached the vehicle. Clara opened the passenger door, and Ayden placed his sister inside. By the time he made it around to the driver's side, she'd slid over to the middle, and Laney was climbing in beside her.

"Take that dirt road," Laney said as Ayden fired up the engine.

Ayden put the truck into gear and stomped on the gas. "Where does it go?"

"Hell if I know. Just go! Go! Go!"

TWENTY-NINE

Ayden

Checkpoint Neon Unicorn
Bedford, Pennsylvania
Day Eight

The dirt road behind the cabin was rutted, and each bump sent waves of fresh pain through Ayden's battered body. As he navigated the dirt trail through the woods, he glanced into the rearview mirror every few seconds, expecting to see fighters coming for them, leaving behind the smoke and the sound of warfare. His hands trembled on the wheel as he white-knuckled his way along the rugged track, barely visible under the overgrowth. Soon, the trail branched off right and left. Ayden chose the path on the left and was relieved to find it led to a blacktop road. But his relief was short-lived as seconds later, PLA military vehicles sped around a curve in the asphalt road.

"Oh crap!" Ayden shouted, throwing the truck into Reverse. As he sped backward, the convoy raced past.

"Did they see us?" Clara asked.

"I don't think so, or they would have stopped."

"Maybe," Ayden said. "They might not have been looking for the truck—yet."

"What are we going to do now?" Clara asked.

"Wait," Ayden said.

"Here? We're just going to stay here in the woods?"

"For now."

They were hidden from view of the road, surrounded by dense trees, but he knew that if the PLA was looking for them, they had all types of location technology at their disposal. He steered the truck down the dirt path, pushing branches aside until it was too narrow to go farther. They found a clearing just big enough to conceal the vehicle.

"This is it!"

"This is what?" Clara said, scanning the clearing.

"We'll hang out here for a while and let them clear out of the area."

"And what if they don't clear out?"

"We'll make camp here until they do," Laney said.

"Make camp?" Clara asked as Laney opened the truck's door and climbed out.

"Make a shelter, sleep, try to slip away later."

"How are we going to know if they're gone?" Clara asked.

Ayden pondered that for a moment as he exited the vehicle and moved around to help Clara get out. "We can't be sure. I could ride Laney's bike into town and ask if they've seen PLA troops."

"Sounds dangerous."

"Everything is now," Laney said.

Ayden strung a piece of rope from one tree to another, and then Laney tossed the plastic sheeting they'd found at the lawn and garden center back in Kearneysville over top of it. Ayden couldn't help but think of Tina and what had happened to her there. A fresh wave of guilt washed over him.

This led him to remember how the young female guard had cut down Lunch Box and injured Dominic. That young girl would have that on her conscience as well. So many traumatic things had occurred in such a short period. There hadn't been time to process all the death and violence he'd witnessed and partaken in since the lights went out. Unfortunately, he knew he'd likely experience even more before they reached Wyoming. After that, there could still be foreign invaders to fight and a world to rebuild. It could be years before life slowed down, and he was sure it'd never return to normal. At some point, he'd be forced to confront all the things he'd witnessed after the lights went out—but today was not the time. Pushing it aside, he helped Laney pick up rocks to place around the bottom of the plastic and hold it down along the edge so that any potential rain that might fall in the night would run off and away from where they'd be sleeping.

After securing the edges, they gathered leaves and moss to help soften the floor of their makeshift shelter. Clara helped as best as she could, cutting a section of the plastic sheeting to cover the leaves and protect them from the moisture that might seep up from the ground.

"This is so going to suck," Clara said, curling the edges up along the sides.

"I've slept in worse." Ayden recalled all the times he'd slept on the narrow ledge of a rock face a thousand feet above a valley floor, strapped in lest he roll over and fall to his death.

"So have I." Laney chuckled. "My dad sent me out into the woods to make a primitive shelter out of sticks and leaves. Of course my skills sucked, and it rained so hard I woke up in the middle of the night soaking wet. I was so afraid of getting struck by lightning that I lay there until morning. I walked out of there with my skin all puckered up like a prune. It took days before I felt warm again."

"Crap!" Clara said. "I hope it doesn't rain tonight."

"Me too," Laney said, shivering.

Clara's stomach growled loudly, and she placed a hand on her abdomen. "Do we have any of Evelyn's biscuits left?"

Ayden gave her a sheepish grin. "Sorry, no." He reached into the back of Owen's truck and retrieved the fishing poles and tackle box. "I saw a pond about a quarter mile back down the trail. I'll see if I can catch us some dinner."

"You know how to use those things?" Clara asked sarcastically.

"I've fished. I'm not sure what species lives in the ponds of Pennsylvania, but I'll do my best." A memory flashed into his mind of him and Mia taking the boys fishing for brown trout at Big Sandy Reservoir near their ranch in Wyoming. It was where Xavier caught his first fish. Ayden's heart ached from missing the little guy's laughter. Not being able to call them and know that they were safe was a form of torture Ayden could never have imagined.

"If you have a lighter, I'll see if I can start a fire so we can boil water and cook the fish you're going to catch," Clara said.

"I don't think it's a good idea to make a fire," Laney said.

"You're probably right," Ayden said. He removed the portable propane torch from the duffle bag. "You think we could just hold the fish over this?"

Laney scrunched her face. "I'm not sure. It's worth a try, I guess."

"What about boiling water?" Clara asked.

Ayden glanced over at Laney. "It would only take five minutes or so to boil water."

"Yeah, but that's after you have a good bed of coals. That's going to take twenty or thirty minutes."

"What about a rocket-type stove?" Ayden asked. He'd never built one himself, but he'd seen one another camper had made once.

Laney chewed her bottom lip and stared off at a nearby pile of rocks. "If we do it right, it would burn really hot very quickly. We could boil the water and cook the fish in just a few minutes. It's not totally smokeless but a lot less than a traditional campfire." She smiled, nodding. "It's doable. I'll see what I can do while you fish." She handed him the duffle bag filled with empty sports water bottles. "Fill these too?"

"Good idea," Ayden said. "If you have time after you build the rocket stove, would you mind going over the maps again and tracing several different routes from here to your parents' place? I want to study them and commit them to memory so that if we encounter trouble after we leave here, I can adjust on the fly if we encounter trouble later."

"Maybe I should drive," Laney said.

"Do you know this area well?" Clara asked.

"No, but—"

"I think it would be more beneficial for you to navigate so you'll be free to use the rifle or pistol to cover our escape if necessary," Ayden said.

"You're right. I'll go over the map and trace out some back roads we can take. We can talk about it after you get back from catching our dinner."

"Let's hope there's fish in that pond—ravenous ones because I haven't fished since I was twelve. I'm not sure I remember how."

Ayden slung his rifle over his back, gathered his fishing gear and duffle bag, and headed back down the trail.

THIRTY

Ayden

Bedford, Pennsylvania
Day Eight

The walk to the pond was quiet. Ayden's mind wandered, replaying the scene at the cabin with Owen and the others. The PLA must have known they were there. They'd tracked them somehow. He should have known how dangerous it was to travel with Owen. He should have trusted his instincts, but due to fatigue, he'd ignored common sense, wanting to reduce the miles he had to pedal that trike up the hills of central Pennsylvania as he could.

He told himself he'd be smarter next time, but deep down, he knew that both his physical and mental conditions were impairing his judgment. What he needed was a day or two of rest—days when he wasn't fighting for his life and witnessing the people around him getting ripped to shreds by violence.

The sight of the pond ahead filled his mind with peace. Its calm waters beckoned him. It was as if he'd found a little slice of normalcy in the midst of a chaotic world. As he drew nearer, he discovered the edge of the pond was overgrown with vegetation, making it difficult to fish from the shore. Ayden would have to clear a small area or find a way to fish from a more accessible spot, like a fallen log or large rock. He scanned the water's edge and located just the spot. A large log had fallen into the water.

As Ayden approached the pond, he spotted a group of deer drinking at the water's edge. He stopped, grateful for the chance to watch them. Curious, he inched closer, trying to get a view of a mother and her fawn, inadvertently stepping on a branch in the process. The loud cracking noise spooked them, causing the whole herd to bolt into the surrounding woods.

"What the hell, dude? That was my deer you ran off," a woman in her forties yelled, stepping out from behind a tree and lowering her crossbow. "Don't you know how to walk in the woods without sounding like a herd of elephants?"

"Um—I'm sorry. I didn't know you were hunting them."

"Your apology ain't going to feed my kids."

"I'm sorry about that," Ayden said, unsure what else he could say.

"What are you doing out here anyways?" the woman asked, approaching him.

"Um—well, we..." He paused, scanning the wood line, wondering if the woman was alone out there.

"You're with others?" the woman asked.

"Are you?"

"I live near here. I've hunted these woods most of my life." She looked him up and down. "Ain't never seen you around before."

Ayden dropped his gaze to the ground, unsure what story he could give her other than the truth.

"We pulled down a dirt trail to avoid the PLA."

"The what?"

"The PLA?"

She stared back at him with a blank expression.

"People's Liberation Army? The armed wing of the Chinese Communist Party?"

She looked at him like he was crazy. "The Chinese? Here?"

"You haven't seen them?"

"No!" Her hand came up to cover her throat. "They're the ones who caused the blackout?"

"Yes."

"And now they're here? In Pennsylvania?"

"Yes."

"What in the flying spaghetti monster?" She rubbed the back of her neck and kicked a rock with the toe of her brown leather boot. "Um… Well, that really sucks!"

"I'm sorry to just spring that kind of news on you like that," Ayden said.

Sweat beaded on her brow. "How do you know? How can you be so sure that you saw the Chinese army and not ours?"

"It's a long story, but we encountered them first in Maryland while in a US Army convoy for refugees."

"Maryland? Does that mean DC has fallen?"

"Nuked is what I heard."

She shook her head. "We're good and truly screwed then, huh?"

Ayden said nothing. It was something he was struggling with himself. It was difficult to hold on to hope when all he saw was chaos.

A single tear slid down the woman's cheek.

Ayden felt the need to at least attempt to find the words to offer her hope. "We're a resilient people. They may have an advantage now, but the resistance has already begun, and once our military is able to fully deploy, I'm sure they will gain the upper hand and defeat the enemy."

"Eventually, but at what cost? Will it drag on long enough that I'll be sending my barely teen sons out to defend the homeland?"

Ayden hadn't given that much thought. He'd been preoccupied with keeping himself and Clara alive.

The woman pivoted toward the pond and then gestured to the fishing gear Ayden had dropped near his feet. "Here to catch dinner?"

"I am," Ayden said.

"Got many mouths to feed?"

Ayden hesitated. He decided to be truthful. "Just three."

"Well, you're not going to catch anything here. It was fished out years ago and was never restocked after Aunt Darcy died. The land has been vacant for twenty years." She shifted from one foot to the other and turned toward the trail leading back toward the cabin where the PLA had attacked Owen and the others. "You'll have better luck about half a mile that way at the creek."

"Thanks," Ayden said. "I appreciate that. I would have sat here half the day thinking my fishing skills were lacking before giving up and going back empty-handed." He chuckled. "And would have had to face my sister's ridicule."

"You're traveling with your sister?"

"And a friend."

"Where ya headed?"

"West." He hung his head. Wyoming felt a million miles away. "Toward Washington, Pennsylvania…" He glanced up. "And then hopefully to Wyoming."

"Wyoming? That's going to be a long trip."

Ayden ran a hand through his messy hair. "For sure."

"Well, thanks for the information, and good luck with getting to Wyoming," she said. "I better get home and figure out how my boys and I are going to survive this mess."

"We've encountered a few people heading south to Mexico."

The woman laughed. "Isn't that some twist!" She shrugged. "I've always wanted to winter in the south. Maybe we'll load up the truck and see how far we get."

"Good luck, and thanks for the tip about the pond."

She turned and walked back into the woods. At the edge, she turned and waved before disappearing into the foliage.

Ayden returned to the pond, filled the sports bottles, and then placed them all back into the duffle bag. After carrying it over and placing it beside the trail, he turned west and set out to find the creek the woman spoke about. He glanced skyward, unsure how many hours of daylight he had left. He hoped to quickly catch a few fish—enough to feed the three of them for the day—and then make their way back to the highway.

He assumed that taking back roads would be their best option for avoiding any more PLA vehicles. It would take longer, but at least they'd get there in one piece.

After walking the bank of the creek and trying several spots over the next few hours, Ayden finally managed to catch two brown trout and one yellow perch. The sun was going down as he returned to the trail leading to where he'd left Clara and Laney. It was getting dark by the time he reached the pond and retrieved the duffle bag filled with water bottles. He hefted the heavy bag over one shoulder and used the light on his rifle's scope to illuminate the path ahead.

As he approached the truck, he didn't see his sister or Laney. He dropped the duffle onto the tailgate and called out to them.

"Hey, where are you two?"

"Ayden," Clara muttered.

"Clara? Where are you?"

"Over here. Lower your voice and turn out that light. There are people in the woods."

THIRTY-ONE

Ayden

Bedford, Pennsylvania
Day Eight

Upon returning to the truck, Ayden had found Clara and Laney concealed behind a boulder to avoid a small group of hunters who had bagged a deer and decided to dress it out in a clearing nearby. Their voices carried through the woods, and the tone of their conversations suggested they, like the woman Ayden had encountered at the pond, knew nothing of the foreign invaders or the dangers the region was in.

"I caught three fish," Ayden whispered proudly.

"Too bad we can't light the fire in the rocket stove Laney built and eat them. I'm starving."

"You could eat it raw. You like sushi," Ayden said.

"I love sushi, but that's not the right kind of fish," Clara said.

Laney scooted closer. "You can eat it raw. It's called sashimi. However, to kill the parasites, it should be frozen first."

"Yuck! No, thank you."

"You'll eat it when you get hungry enough."

"Nope! I'll never be hungry enough to eat something filled with worms."

"They'll leave soon. They won't want to walk out in complete darkness," Ayden said. "We'll light the fire then, cook the fish—thoroughly—and then boil the water. In the morning, I'd like to hit one of the back roads and get away from here."

Laney nodded. "I've mapped a few routes, including back roads."

They sat listening to the hunters' banter for another thirty minutes before Ayden spotted the beams of their flashlights bouncing through the woods. They came within fifty feet of the truck but didn't seem to notice it parked there. After their voices faded into the night, Ayden helped Clara back to the pickup, and Laney used the propane torch to light the stacked stone stove she'd constructed in his absence.

Ayden gazed into the firelight. She'd stacked the flat stones in a square, leaving the middle open with an air gap at the bottom where she'd stuffed twigs and branches. The fire burned hot, with flames shooting nearly to the top of the two-foot-tall structure. Ayden stuck a stick through the sides of the fish and held them over the fire, allowing the rising heat to cook them.

After eating, Ayden climbed into the truck's bed and retrieved the four-way tire iron. He returned to the stove and placed it on top of the opening. Laney sat the clay pot from the lawn and garden center upon it. She poured a small amount of water into it and let it boil.

"That should sterilize it some," she said.

"Um—how are we going to remove the hot pot from the heat?" Clara asked.

"We may have to scoop the water out and then let it cool off before removing it," Laney said.

"Do we still have that thin wire we found?" Ayden asked.

Laney raised her eyebrows. "Yeah."

"You'll see," Ayden said.

He scrounged around inside Laney's pack and retrieved a three-foot section of thin wire. He returned to the fire and, starting in the middle of the wire, wrapped it around the pot a couple of times, leaving long tails of wire to loop above it. He ran a stick through the loops, lifted the pot, and then sat it back on top of the tire iron.

"Awesome, little brother! Good thinking!" Clara said.

Once the water had boiled and cooled, they each filled a sports bottle and placed it in their individual packs. The rest were put into the duffle for later. After the pot cooled, Laney returned it to the market bag she'd carried it in, and they sat in front of the stacked stone stove, talking until the last embers of the fire died.

Clara yawned, which also set Ayden and Laney off.

"You two get some sleep. I'll take the first watch."

"I'll take you up on that, little brother. I don't think I could keep my eyes open. I'd probably fall asleep standing up," Clara said.

"I wouldn't fall asleep on watch no matter how tired I am. My dad taught me that the hard way," Laney said.

"You trained in taking watch?" Ayden asked.

"Yep! I was about fourteen, I'd say. I volunteered because this boy I liked was also on watch duty, and I thought we'd have a chance to talk—alone. Well, that didn't happen. I waited for him to walk the perimeter like he was supposed to, but I fell asleep sitting against a tree. My dad was so disappointed. He didn't need to say a word. The look on his face broke my heart. My mom was pissed. She yelled a lot, and then I got all the crappy jobs after that."

"It sounds like you have great parents who love you enough to teach you how to survive," Clara said.

Laney nodded. "I didn't use to see it that way, but now I do."

"I can't wait to meet them," Ayden said as Laney and Clara crawled into the makeshift shelter for the night.

Ayden's watch proceeded without incident. He somehow managed to stay awake, and the only noises he heard were from nature. Laney relieved him four hours later, and he fell asleep almost immediately.

His dreams were fitful, and so were Clara's. Ayden awoke to his sister crying out. He crawled over to her and placed his hand on her foot. "Clara! Are you okay?" he said in the dark.

"What?" she asked, lifting her head.

"You were crying. Were you having a bad dream?"

She exhaled loudly. "Yes!"

"You're safe now!"

"That's a lie. I'm sleeping in a homemade shelter in the middle of the woods, running from Chinese soldiers who've tried to blow me up or shoot me dead across three states."

Ayden chuckled. He couldn't help himself. The way she'd said it just struck him as funny. "I'm sorry. I don't mean to make light of things. It's just…" He laughed so hard he snorted, which caused Clara to start laughing.

"Your levity is good," Laney called from beside the truck. "It relieves tension and the fear of death."

Clara slapped her good leg and laughed until she, too, snorted.

"At least we're not running from a T-X."

"A what?" Clara said, attempting to get herself under control.

"T-X. The female terminatrix?" Laney said.

"You're a Terminator fan?" Ayden said.

"Had to be. I watched it like a hundred times with my dad."

She grew quiet as she took a seat near the stone stove she'd built.

"Tell us again about this compound he built," Clara said.

"Not just him, but a group of people—some he met in survival schools and others at prepper meetups around the state."

"Prepper meetups?" Clara asked. "Like some kind of club?"

"More like at conventions and conferences. They'd talk on social media and arrange to have dinner after one of the homesteading conferences or something. I used to have to go with them when I was little, but I haven't been in years."

"So they planned this compound at these conferences?"

"Not exactly. After my parents had known them for a few years, they decided to invite them to our family property to train together. The compound idea grew from there. A few years back, my dad started ranting about the news and the state of the country. Soon, he and some of the guys started putting up buildings and, two years ago, they built the first of the dirt walls."

"You said they trained together. For what?" Ayden asked.

"For this," Laney said. "For anarchy or invasion."

THIRTY-TWO

Ayden

Bedford County, Pennsylvania
Day Nine

None of them slept much that night, and they were all tired by the time they loaded up and drove the truck back down the trail toward the blacktop road. Ayden steered the pickup north and was about to cross over a major divided four-lane highway when from the passenger seat, Laney spotted a large convoy of military vehicles below them.

"Go! Go!" Laney said, chopping the air with her hand.

Ayden floored it, and the old truck took off across the bridge.

Laney screamed and pointed. "Stop! Stop! Stop!"

Ahead, more military vehicles appeared, heading straight toward them.

Laney jabbed the air with her thumb. "Turn here," she said, indicating the two-lane road to their left. Ayden cut the steering wheel and made the turn, barely slowing. The vehicle bumped over rough asphalt, and Ayden punched the gas, racing south, hoping to find somewhere to hide out of sight. They sped past a few houses, and then the road dead-ended at a pipe gate overhung with low tree branches and overgrown with knee-high grass.

Ayden glanced into his rearview mirror, preparing to back up and turn around, when two helicopters appeared in the sky to the north of them.

Laney threw open her door, sprinted to the gate, and flung it open. "Hurry!" she yelled, beckoning him with her hands.

Ayden rolled the truck forward, and they waited under the cover of the trees for the helos to pass overhead and disappear before Laney climbed back inside and they pulled on through and up the driveway. He stopped the truck in front of an old, weathered barn missing half of its roof. Beyond it was the rubble of a home. To the right of the barn was a carport. Ayden backed the truck under it, and the trio sat in silence for several minutes.

"This whole area is crawling with the enemy," Clara said. "How are we ever going to get away from here? Even the back roads are dangerous."

"Let's just pray they're just passing through," Ayden said. "We'll have to wait them out."

"This sucks. We have no food, very little water, and I have to pee." Clara bounced her left knee up and down.

"I'll check around and see if there's a pond to fish in and fill our water bottles while you go pee behind the barn there," Ayden said.

"Seriously? How am I going to squat behind a barn with my leg?"

Ayden shrugged.

"I'll help her. You go investigate this place and see what resources are available. I'll see what we have that I can fashion into a stove for another fire."

"With those helos in the air, I don't think we can do a fire today."

Laney glanced skyward. "Probably not. I'll think of something. You just concentrate on food and water."

Ayden patted his hip. "If I hear shooting, I'll come running."

Laney smiled. "Good to know!"

Half an hour later, Ayden returned with bad news. They'd managed to land on likely the only farm in the area with no water source, which meant no fish for dinner, and they wouldn't be able to refill their water bottles.

Laney had spread the plastic sheeting across a bed of hay inside the standing side of the barn, so they had a relatively soft bed that night. Ayden thought he might have even been able to sleep if it hadn't been for the gnawing hunger in his gut.

The following day, as sunlight filtered through the gaps between the weathered boards of the barn's walls, Ayden, Clara, and Laney each sipped their water. Without another water source, Ayden knew it was only a matter of time before dehydration became an issue for them.

However, as they prepared to leave, the sound of helicopter blades sliced through the air above them. Ayden peeked through a small crack in the barn wall, watching a PLA convoy roll down the nearby road. He turned back to Clara and Laney, his face grim. "We can't move. They've got this area locked down tight."

Clara, sitting on a bale of hay with her bad leg propped up, nodded. "We're almost out of everything. Water, food… we can't last much longer like this."

Laney, who had been quiet, finally spoke up. "How long do you think they'll stay? They can't search every farm, right?"

Ayden shook his head. "Honestly, I don't know. But we can't take the risk of being seen. If we get caught, it's over."

Clara's eyes were wide with worry. "They'll go soon. They have to, right?"

Ayden nodded.

Laney sighed, leaning against the barn wall. "We've got enough water for maybe another day if we ration it strictly. Food's another story. We've got some crackers. That's it."

Ayden clenched his fists, frustration boiling over. A siege could kill them without a single bullet fired.

Clara reached out, placing a hand on his arm. "We'll think of something. We always do."

Laney nodded in agreement. "Maybe we can find a way to sneak out at night, see if there's any place nearby we can scavenge for supplies."

Ayden looked at the two women, their resolve steady despite the dire situation. "All right, we'll stay put for now. But if things don't change soon, we'll have to take that risk. We can't just sit here and starve."

The sound of another helicopter passing overhead sent a shiver down Ayden's spine. His eyes met Laney's and Clara's. He forced a smile. "They'll be gone soon."

THIRTY-THREE

Mueller

New Eden Compound
Somerset Township
Washington County, Pennsylvania
Day Eleven

The meeting room in New Eden's main lodge was warm as the midafternoon sun streamed through the windows. Tyson Mueller sat at the head of a large wooden table, his wife Monica at his side, along with council members Jack, Linda, Frank, and David. The discussion was tense and centered around the recent skirmishes in Bowers Township.

"There's too much instability over there," Jack said, shaking his head. "If it spills over, we could be dealing with an influx of desperate people."

Frank nodded. "And we know what desperate people are capable of."

"But we can't just shut ourselves off from the world," Linda said. "We need allies, especially those who can contribute."

Before the debate could escalate further, a knock at the door interrupted them. A gate guard, out of breath and visibly anxious, stepped inside. "Sir, there's a group at one of our roadblocks. They say they know you and are asking to speak with you."

Mueller's eyes narrowed. "Who's their leader?"

"He says his name is Walt Cayman. He mentioned something about Jefferson's Survival and Tactical Training Center."

Mueller's expression shifted to one of cautious interest. "Walt Cayman?" he muttered, mostly to himself. He stood up and addressed the room. "I need to see this for myself. Excuse me."

Mueller slung his AR-15 rifle over his back and rode a four-wheeler through the compound's thick steel gate. The tires kicked up gravel and left a cloud of dust behind him as he approached the roadblock. There, on the opposite side of the dirt-filled stack of tires, stood a weary group of individuals. Mueller immediately recognized Walt Cayman, who was at the forefront, looking both relieved and wary. His clothes were torn and dirty, his face marked with fresh bruises. Behind him, his team appeared battered and exhausted, their eyes hollow with fatigue.

Mueller stopped the four-wheeler and dismounted, approaching the group with caution and suspicion. "Walt," he said, shouldering his rifle and pointing the barrel at the ground. "What brings you here?"

Walt stepped forward, attempting to maintain an air of confidence despite his condition. "Tyson, it's been a while. How have—"

"Cut to the chase, Walt. I don't have time for small talk," Mueller said, cutting him off.

"We were minding our own business when another group ambushed our compound. We had taken in folks from West Dentonville. They were inexperienced and panicked. To avoid unnecessary loss of life, we gave up our compound—at least for now."

Mueller's eyes scanned the group, assessing their condition and numbers. "You fled?" he asked, skepticism evident in his voice. "Instead of fighting back?"

Walt nodded, frustration clear on his face. "Yes, but not out of cowardice. Craig Hall's people were so green that staying and fighting would have been a slaughter. We just didn't have the numbers to defend against the mob who descended upon us. I took the ones I could save, but they turned on me, blamed me for the attack, and chose Hall as their new leader."

Mueller crossed his arms, scrutinizing Walt. "So you're here now. What do you expect from me?"

"We'd like to join your group."

Mueller kept his expression neutral, choosing to keep his thoughts close to his vest.

"We're willing to do whatever it takes to prove ourselves an asset to New Eden. We have skills, and we can contribute."

Mueller considered this, his tactical mind weighing the risks and benefits. Walt did have training and skills. He'd been to most of the same schools as Mueller had, but he'd held some strange ideas about what it would take to survive and rebuild after an apocalyptic event. He was prone to believe every conspiracy theory out there, no matter how outlandish. But, on the other hand, he was a very hard worker and, from what Mueller had heard, had gathered a group of people who were as well. "It's not solely my decision. I need to take this to the council."

"Thank you, Ty. Thank you. My guys are beat. We just want a chance to be a part of a group that knows what they're doing."

"I'll relay that to the council. You stay here, and I'll let you know our decision soon."

Back in the meeting room, Mueller told them about the encounter. "Walt Cayman and his group are at the gate. He claims they were attacked and had to flee, and now they're asking for sanctuary."

Jake was immediately opposed. "We can't just let anyone in. Especially not someone who abandoned their own compound."

Frank agreed. "This could be a ploy. We don't know their true intentions."

Linda spoke up, her voice steady and calm. "We need people. Trained individuals who can work and contribute to our community. We can't afford to turn away potential assets."

"We can always keep them under strict surveillance," David said. "We could deny them access to sensitive areas like our war room or this meeting room. Sure, it would take manpower we are in short supply of, but if these folks turn out to be genuine, this could be a game-changer. We could then implement phase two of our plan and really start building and growing crops."

Linda nodded. "And helping our neighbors."

After a heated debate, Jack shook his head. "If this goes wrong, it's on all of us. Remember that."

Mueller folded his hands on the table and let out a harsh breath. "We'll put it to a vote. All in favor of allowing them in under a probationary basis, raise your hand."

The vote passed with a majority, and Mueller instructed the guard to escort Walt and his group to the pavilion.

Monica was unusually quiet on the walk over to the pavilion. Mueller wasn't sure he wanted to know why. As they reached the simple but sturdy structure, he asked her what she thought anyway.

"I don't know. I can't recall who Walt is. I want to see and hear them for myself."

Walt and his team were led over to where Mueller and Monica stood waiting.

"Walt," Mueller began, his tone firm, "you and your men will be allowed in under strict conditions. You'll be on probation. You'll be assigned duties and must follow orders without questions. If any one of you doesn't comply, you'll all be asked to leave."

Walt nodded, his expression serious. "Understood. We're grateful for the opportunity."

Mueller motioned to a burly man standing nearby. "This is Larry. He'll be your sponsor and guide. He'll also be watching your every move."

Larry stepped forward, nodding curtly at Walt and his team.

As they were led away, Monica approached Mueller, her expression worried. "I remember him now and I don't trust him, Tyson."

Mueller placed a reassuring hand on her shoulder. "Don't worry, love. I won't let them cause any trouble. We'll keep a close eye on them."

The night deepened around the compound, the air thick with tension, and Jake and Frank were still debating whether to allow this group into the compound. "Look at it this way. We'll get some labor out of them, at least. We need that west wall completed before we can start plowing the fields over there."

"As long as they know that one wrong move, and we'll put them down."

"That's a little harsh," Linda said.

"We can't let them walk away now. They'll have too much information about our compound," Frank said.

"What are you saying, Frank?" Linda asked.

"I'm saying that if they mess up here, they need to understand it will cost them their lives. Plain and simple."

The next morning, during the briefing in the chow hall, Mueller outlined the day's tasks, focusing on expanding the compound's footprint to accommodate more personnel and facilities. He assigned Walt and his team to fortify the outer perimeter by constructing dirt-filled defensive walls. After a few hours, Larry, their team leader, approached, his rifle resting across his forearms, scrutinizing their work. "You let the burlap slip below the top. Dirt's spilling out. We need these filled all the way and dirt packed down tight for the second layer to sit correctly."

Mueller waited to see their response to the critique. A good attitude was important for working efficiently together.

Kelter adjusted the liner, muttering under his breath as the team leader walked away.

Mueller could tell from his body language that the man wasn't a team player. He climbed down from the wall and approached Larry. "Assign someone to listen to their conversations today. I don't like that guy's attitude."

Larry had reported other murmurings. Mueller wasn't too concerned. It was natural for there to be criticisms. Walt had been a leader at his own compound, and making comparisons was natural. However, could he accept his new role and become a productive member of the team?

Later that day, Mueller went out to inspect their work. He stood upon the finished section of the western wall and surveyed the scene with a critical eye. Mueller prided himself on the design, which mirrored military outposts he'd studied, complete with defensive perimeters and strategic placement of resources. However, the compound was far from impregnable. His recent observations, coupled with reports from his security team, painted a picture of a looming threat. The surrounding area was filled with desperate people fleeing Pittsburgh and surrounding towns in search of life-saving resources, and Mueller had yet to address the possibility of these people turning hostile.

That afternoon, Larry reported that Kelter, a senior member of Walt's team, had whispered about hearing rumors about the size of the armory and asked whether they had robbed a military installation. Walt had told him that they had had a high-roller backer who'd financed the compound's extensive arsenal. This wasn't true, but maybe it wasn't a bad thing for people to believe the compound had the means to defend itself against major threats. Mueller knew that was a double-edged sword. It could act as a deterrent or enticement for attack by a group aiming to acquire the weapons for themselves.

Mueller decided he needed to be sure where Walt's loyalties lay before letting his guard down with him. He requested a special detail from the security team he tasked with monitoring Walt and his companions closely. Within hours, they reported back with valuable intelligence.

One of his top security members, Daniels, stepped forward. "Sir, we've been keeping a close watch. Hutson was seen talking to Jimmy from Craig Hall's group."

Mueller raised an eyebrow. "Interesting. About what?"

"Jimmy mentioned they're staying at a subdivision on a golf course. Seems Hall has managed to secure a pretty cushy setup," Daniels reported.

Mueller nodded thoughtfully. "Anything else?"

"Yes, sir. They discussed a possible false-flag operation. Hall wants Hutson to make it look like Walt's crew is attacking the local farmers. He believes this will push the farmers to seek his protection," Daniels said.

Mueller's eyes narrowed. "So Hall is trying to play both sides. What does Walt think about this?"

"From what we overheard, Walt sees it as an opportunity. He plans to use the distraction to retake their former compound," Daniels replied.

At first, the news was disturbing. Mueller had begun to question his decision to allow Walt and his team inside the compound. Still, with the report that this Hall guy was setting up shop at the golf course in Bowers Township, an area already plagued by problems, any information he could glean from Walt and his team was helpful.

Mueller leaned forward, his expression serious. "We need to

stay one step ahead. Keep monitoring their conversations. I want to know every detail."

Walt's reaction to Hutson's report revealed his own ambitions to retake his former compound. Clearly, Walt intended to use Hall's distraction as a cover to reclaim what he considered his. Mueller wasn't sure how that might affect New Eden, but he knew Frank and Jake would never allow it.

THIRTY-FOUR

Mia

Christiansen Ranch
Farson, Wyoming
Day Eleven

Over the last few days, much had been accomplished, not just on the Christiansen Ranch but in the Farson, Wyoming, area as a whole.

Mid-morning, Neil and Dirk gathered everyone in the kitchen to discuss the next critical steps in their preparation.

"We need to establish a reliable way to communicate with our neighbors," Neil began, addressing the group. "If something happens, we've got to be able to warn each other and coordinate our efforts."

"Mr. Simmons's ham radio is our best bet for outside information," Dirk added. "It's got the range. He's already been in touch with people on both the East and West Coasts."

Dirk nodded. "I'll go over there for regular check-ins."

"As far as communication between ranches, we'll have to have messengers riding out and delivering notes."

"Like Paul Revere and his midnight ride," Carter asked.

"Exactly, son."

"I could do that," Luke said. "I'm a good rider."

"You are, but midnight is past your bedtime." Mia chuckled.

"I'll assign one of the wranglers and talk to the cowboys on the other ranches about doing the same," Dirk said, jotting down a note on a pad of paper in front of him.

"We need eyes on the main routes in and out of here," Neil explained. "If we see anything unusual, we can warn everyone in time."

Dirk pointed to a map spread out on the kitchen table. "We've identified a few strategic spots for outposts—high ground with clear views of the roads and valleys."

"Each ranch has volunteered personnel to man the outposts. They set up small, well-hidden observation points equipped with binoculars, radios, and basic supplies. Volunteers will take turns in shifts, ensuring constant vigilance without exhausting anyone," Neil said.

With the communication network and outposts in place, the community could now turn its attention to sharing resources.

Just after lunch, several of the nearby ranchers gathered at the cabin to discuss how to help one another with needed food and supplies.

"We need to make sure everyone has what they need," Melody said, her voice firm. "Food, medical supplies, fuel—whatever it takes to keep us all going."

They created a central inventory list and established a system for trade. Each ranch established a list of necessities and what they had for trade. The sense of unity and cooperation was palpable as everyone understood the importance of supporting one another.

The next day, Neil, Mia, and Dirk gathered with their community once more to finalize their evacuation plan and begin training sessions.

"All right, everyone," Neil said, addressing the assembled

group. "We've done a lot to prepare, but we need to be ready for the worst-case scenario."

Dirk stepped forward and unfurled a large map. "We've identified two main evacuation routes: one heading west into the mountains and another north to Pinedale. Each family should know these routes by heart."

They spent the morning reviewing the routes, discussing landmarks, and planning meeting points. Each family packed evacuation kits with essentials to ensure they could leave at a moment's notice.

In the afternoon, Dirk led the first training session. "We need to know how to defend ourselves and provide first aid," he explained. "Today, we'll start with basic firearm safety and handling."

Mia watched as Dirk demonstrated how to load and fire a rifle safely. The older children, including Carter and Luke, listened intently, their young faces serious. After the demonstration, everyone had a chance to practice under Dirk's supervision.

"What about me, Mommy?" Xavier asked.

Mia stared down at him. "Um—" she said, searching for an answer.

Neil walked over and handed him a whistle on a rope. "Here you go, Xavy. I'm giving you a critical job to protect us. Put this around your neck, and if you see anything, you blow it, and then we'll have time to get everyone someplace safe."

Xavy smiled, and his eyes twinkled with pride. "I can do that!"

Next, Melody and Mia led a first aid workshop. "We need to be able to handle injuries and illnesses," she said, showing the group how to treat wounds and administer basic medical care.

The training sessions continued into the evening, with everyone taking turns practicing and asking questions.

As the sun set on their training day, the ranchers gathered around a campfire. The air was filled with the scent of wood smoke and the murmur of quiet conversations. Despite the gravity of their situation, a sense of camaraderie and mutual support brought a measure of comfort.

Mia sat beside her father, with Xavy in her lap. As she stared into the fire, she thought of Ayden. She closed her eyes and murmured a prayer, asking that he make it safely home to her.

“We’ve done everything we can to prepare,” Neil said softly, his eyes reflecting the firelight.

Melody nodded and placed a hand on his. “Yes, we have. I feel pretty good about what we’ve accomplished. We’ve come together, and we’re stronger that way.”

THIRTY-FIVE

Mueller

New Eden Compound
Somerset Township
Washington County, Pennsylvania
Day Thirteen

Two days later, Mueller received another report from his security team stating that Fox Team had disappeared from their patrol.

Furious, Mueller jumped to his feet. "Do an after-action review. I want to know if our team was outmaneuvered or if there's something else at play!"

"We'll get right on it, sir," Daniels assured him.

"Good. And, Daniels, make sure everyone knows we're all on the same team here. Any sign of disloyalty, and I want to hear about it immediately," Mueller said, his voice cold.

"Yes, sir. We'll keep a close watch," Daniels affirmed before leaving the room.

Mueller stared at the closed door, deep in thought. The complexities of leadership in a survivalist compound were becoming increasingly apparent. Trust was paramount, and Mueller's grip on his community needed to be as solid as the defenses he had painstakingly constructed.

Jake walked in and sat down across from him. Mueller was relieved that he didn't start with an *I told you so.*

"What are we going to do about Walt and his men?" he asked.

"Use him to find out what's going on over in Bowers Township first of all, and then—"

"You know what we're going to have to do, Ty," Jake said. "Frank was right."

And there it was—the *I told you so.*

Mueller had returned to the wall to oversee the team expanding their perimeter. He glanced up from the construction as one of the security team members came running toward him. "What's up?" he asked as the stocky man stopped beside him.

"We just got word that Craig Hall and his folks attacked a group over in Bowers Township. Hall's been killed. Apparently, someone from here was working with him on the attack. That group might show up here seeking revenge."

Mueller's gut tightened. "Who was working with Hall?"

"Hutson. Kenny Hutson."

"Cayman's guy?" Walt Cayman had indeed betrayed him. Most of his team felt that Cayman or his men should be executed rather than released if they crossed the line.

"Kelter and his team never returned from patrol," the guard continued. "Hutson said he and another of Cayman's guys were searching for them. We heard radio chatter that they were involved in planning an attack on the roadblocks in Bowers Township."

"Why would they do that?"

"Maybe retribution for the attack on Cayman's compound," the guard said.

"Where's Cayman now?"

"At his post."

"Send a team to apprehend him. Lock him up in the cellar. I'm going to talk to Steve and then have a chat with Cayman. I need to know who might show up here seeking revenge."

"And then?"

"We hand him and the rest of his group over to them."

"And if that doesn't satisfy them?"

"We defend the compound by any means necessary."

Mueller entered the commandeered Commonwealth of Pennsylvania's Mobile Communications trailer. Steve Jackson, the communications specialist, was seated at one of the workstations before a bank of amateur radio equipment.

"Tell me about this group that Cayman's folks attacked," Mueller said.

"I have no direct evidence Cayman was involved. Hutson planned and executed the attack on the Bowers Township roadblocks at Craig Hall's request," Steve replied.

"Why?"

"Hall wanted to scare the farmers into a cooperative security agreement where the subdivision residents provided security and the farmers supplied food."

"What fool would think anyone would agree to that?"

"Apparently, Craig Hall," Steve said. "It doesn't make sense why Cayman's men would risk their lives for Hall. Maybe Hall promised to help Cayman attack us?"

"What do you know about these farmers? Why wouldn't Hall and Bowers Township just take what they want?"

"The farmers don't have a formal leader, but Hugh Meecham's name comes up a lot. He led the raid on Cayman's compound."

Mueller considered the implications. "They're not just regular farmers. They successfully penetrated a guarded compound."

"They had to know Cayman's security was a joke to attempt the attack. That took tactical knowledge," Steve noted.

"We have two potential problem areas: the Bowers Township residents and these farmers. If Walt's guys worked with Hall, they know about us. They'll come looking for a handout or to take over."

"We knew people might find us. We're prepared for such scenarios, but we haven't faced them yet. We don't know how our folks will react," Steve said.

"We'll deal with them before they reach us," Mueller said. That's why he'd pushed the patrols out to a five-mile radius for advanced warning.

Steve shoved his hands into his pockets. "The flood of refugees has died down. The city of Washington imploded when refugees broke through their roadblocks. Conflict is coming; it's just a matter of from which direction."

"We'll step up patrols and finish the new section of the wall," Mueller decided.

"I have some other news," Steve said, his tone shifting.

Mueller's thoughts shot to his daughter. "About Laney?"

"No, not her. Not yet."

Mueller felt a mix of relief and disappointment. No news wasn't always good news. "What about Dahlgren, Virginia?"

"The Chinese Navy controls the naval base."

"Crap!" Mueller sat down heavily. "That probably means ground troops."

"Russians and now the Chinese," Steve said.

"We need to inform the compound. Maybe the Chinese won't make it this far."

"This is our country, Steve. If we have any hope of surviving, we must fight to keep it."

"How? We have twenty fighters against thousands. We were defeated when they nuked Washington and set off the EMP."

"I refuse to see it that way," Mueller said, more determined to bring his daughter to safety. "Try again to contact Pete in Greencastle. See if they've heard anything from Williamsport."

"I'll keep trying," Steve said.

"If you hear anything about Laney—"

"I'll tell you right away," Steve promised.

THIRTY-SIX

Ayden

Abandoned Farm
Bedford County, Pennsylvania
Day Thirteen

The next few days stretched into an agonizing wait, each moment filled with the oppressive hum of enemy aircraft and the looming threat of discovery. Ayden remained on high alert, his mind cycling through plans and contingencies. As the sun set on yet another day of confinement, the three of them clung to their hope, their strength, and each other, determined to endure.

Ayden's constant vigilance left him unable to rest for most of that time. Eventually, his body gave way to exhaustion, and he fell asleep. He woke in the middle of the night with his head pounding and his mouth so dry his tongue clung to the roof of his mouth. He knew he had to find water, or they weren't going to survive long enough for the PLA to leave the area. He slid his boots on, flung his rifle over one shoulder and the duffle of water bottles over the other, and stepped outside the barn into the moonlight, aiming to walk across the overgrown pasture until he located a farmhouse with a pond or well.

"Where are you going?" Laney whispered, stepping out from beside the truck.

"To find water."

"Go south. I already looked north. There's nothing but a few houses. They looked occupied, so I avoided them."

"When did you do this?"

"While you were sleeping," Laney said. "Clara was on watch."

"Maybe I should take your bike and ride around. I can travel farther and cover more ground."

"True, but you'd have to take the road."

"I doubt they move much at night," Ayden said.

"Maybe." She was quiet for a moment. "Maybe we should take off now and drive only at night then."

"I don't know. The problem with that is we might not be able to see them coming until it's too late."

"We'd see their headlights from far off."

Ayden thought for a moment. "Let me ride around for a bit. If I can't find food or water nearby, we'll load back into the truck and head out again."

Ayden pedaled for an hour, first south and then back east along one of the back roads. It was too difficult to spot ponds in the dark, and from the road, he was unable to tell which homes were occupied and which might be abandoned. Again, he returned empty-handed. Feeling defeated, he tossed the bike back into the bed of the truck and helped Laney load everything for the trip.

Back at the gate, Ayden swallowed hard and stuck his head out the window, listening for the sound of helicopters or of PLA's heavy military vehicles.

"Hear anything?" Clara asked.

"Nothing but crickets," he said, pulling forward through the gate.

"That's a good sign. Maybe they've all left the area."

"Hopefully," Ayden said. "Because we have to get to water regardless."

They took several back roads but ended up getting lost twice and backtracking a few times, and they still didn't find a water source. Ayden tried his best to fight through the dizziness and headache, but dehydration was affecting his judgment and ability to drive.

"I can't believe there's not a stream or creek in sight and no one around here has a pond," Clara said.

"We'll find something soon," Ayden said, straining to scan every field they passed. He stopped the truck near a small concrete bridge. "It looks like a small stream or creek down below. I'm going to check it out. Keep alert. Call out if you see or hear anything."

He could tell almost immediately that the stream bed was dry, but he hoped it would contain a small pool farther up or downstream. He was only able to walk a short distance due to his physical condition, but it was clear that it was only a wet weather creek, and it hadn't rained in a while.

"Nothing," he said as he climbed back into the truck.

Soon, they reached the intersection with Highway 30. Ayden stopped the pickup, rolled down his window, and listened. "No aircraft, and I don't hear any armored vehicle traffic." In fact, he heard nothing but the sound of the ticking engine and their breathing.

"I think we're going to have to risk it."

"There has to be a water source out here somewhere," Laney said.

"Check the map," Ayden said. "Let's try to figure out where exactly we are and see if it shows a river or lake nearby."

Laney pulled the map from a side pocket on the door and

spread it out on her lap. She pointed to a spot with her finger. "I think we're here. See that little jog we made back there."

"You're right," Clara said. She traced the line that indicated Highway 30.

"Is that a lake?" she asked, pointing to an area shaded in blue.

"Says it is. Indian Lake. Looks fairly big."

"Works for me." Ayden turned over the engine and steered the pickup onto the highway heading west.

Moments later, he turned down a road leading to the lake and pulled to a stop on the boat ramp of a marina. "Wait here, sis. I'll fill your bottle and bring it to you."

Ayden grabbed the duffle bag and hurried to the water's edge with Laney on his heels. He tossed a bottle to her and began filling one for Clara. While it filled, he dunked a second bottle in, filled it partially, and took a long drink.

"It doesn't look too dirty." Laney wiped water from her lips with the back of her hand.

They both knew that if they weren't literally dying of thirst, they'd never drink untreated water.

"We should only drink enough to wet our tongues until we boil it."

"Good idea. I'll get started on a fire while you fill the bottles."

While Ayden took a water bottle to Clara, Laney set out in search of wood to burn.

"Just take a few sips for now," he said, handing it to Clara. "We're going to start a fire and boil the rest."

"You think that's wise?" Clara asked between sips.

"I think in our physical condition, we shouldn't risk waterborne diseases. It could kill us."

Clara yanked the bottle away from her lips. "How much dirty water is enough to do that?"

"I'd stop there. I wouldn't drink more than you have already."

Clara glanced down at the bottle. "It's crazy that something vital to sustaining life could also be the thing that ends it."

"There are trillions of microorganisms on Earth that can take a person down. We just have to be as careful as we can to avoid them."

Laney emerged from the woods with a bundle of branches. Thirty minutes later, they were drinking purified water.

"Too bad boiling it does nothing for the taste," Laney said, tipping up her bottle.

Clara grimaced. "Or remove the stuff floating in it."

"At least we don't have to worry about diarrhea, giardia, dysentery, typhoid fever, E. coli infection, and salmonella," Ayden said.

"That's true, and my tongue is no longer stuck on the roof of my mouth. I couldn't even make enough saliva to spit," Clara said.

"What do you say, ladies? Should we stay here tonight or push on?"

"That water sure does look inviting," Laney said. She raised her arm and sniffed her armpit. "I could use a bath in the worst way."

"Oh, that would be lovely. What I wouldn't give for a hot shower and a bottle of shampoo." Clara ran a hand down her ponytail. "Disgusting."

"We have shampoo." Laney fished around in the duffle and pulled out the hygiene bag.

"Let's do it," Clara said, pointing to the lake.

While they swam, Ayden tried his luck fishing from the dock, catching several small bluegills and a couple of sunfish for dinner.

After their swim, they ate their fish and then found a secluded spot under the trees and pitched their makeshift shelters. The ladies were asleep before sunset. While they slept, Ayden sat on the dock, staring up at the stars. He forced himself to stay in the present and not ruminate on how impossible it seemed that he'd ever make it back to Wyoming. He knew he should try to face the fact that he may never see Mia and the boys again. He might never know whether all this had affected them—if they were safe or even alive.

The dock squeaked, and he jumped to his feet and spun around, aiming his rifle directly at Laney.

"Sorry to startle you. It's just me. Let me stand watch for a while, and you get some rest."

"Okay. I'll take you up on that," he said, even though he doubted he'd sleep. His body needed the rest, and if he was going to be in any condition to fight, he had to listen to it.

THIRTY-SEVEN

Ayden

Highway 30
Indian Lake, Pennsylvania
Day Sixteen

When morning came, Ayden, Clara, and Laney climbed back into the truck and returned to the highway. A few minutes later, they were passing the Flight 93 National Memorial. Ayden slowed and then pulled onto the road leading to the memorial. The memorial stretched out with solemn dignity, the marble wall etched with the names of the forty passengers and crew who had heroically thwarted a terrorist attack on September 11, 2001. The morning light cast long shadows across the wall, giving the site a reverent and almost sacred aura.

"My parents brought me here once," Laney said softly, her voice tinged with emotion. "It was one of the few times I've ever seen my dad cry. He read aloud each of the names written on the wall. He called them true heroes." Laney wiped tears from her cheeks. She cleared her throat. "Dad said he prayed I never encountered a situation like those brave souls had, but if I did, he knew that I, too, would face it with as much bravery and self-sacrifice."

Clara put her arm around Laney's shoulders, offering comfort. "You've lived up to his expectations. He is going to be so proud of the way you've handled yourself through this crisis, Laney. Truly! Sometimes I forget that you're only eighteen years old. You are one of the bravest people I've ever known, and you've put yourself on the line for us more times than I can count already."

"Thank you, Clara. I'm so glad I met the two of you," Laney replied, her voice steadying.

Ayden glanced south in the direction of the memorial. "I was in elementary school in Manhattan that morning. Both of my parents were working down near the towers. I recall the fear on Nanny's face when she came to the school to pick Clara and me up. During the walk home, I asked her what was wrong, but she wouldn't tell me. I knew something was up because all the grown-ups looked terrified or sad."

Clara nodded, her eyes distant with memory. "Me too. I remember a girl from my class crying when her grandmother came to pick her up. Her father worked in the north tower. She never returned to that school. I learned later that he'd died that day, and she'd moved away."

"I wasn't born yet," Laney said. "But we watched the news report in school and learned about that day. I love how the nation pulled together after such a tragic event."

"And we will again after this one," Clara said with conviction.

"It'll be harder without technology," Laney said, voicing a concern that hung heavily in the air.

Ayden was deep in thought about the comparison as he steered the truck back onto Highway 30 and headed west. Although he agreed with Clara that Americans pulled together in times of crisis, he wondered whether it would be enough to save their nation this time. The weight of the current turmoil felt different, more impossible, without the aid of technology and infrastructure they had always relied upon.

As they drove away from the memorial, the silence was filled with the shared burden of the past and the uncertain future. The heroes of Flight 93 had shown incredible bravery in the face of insurmountable odds, and their legacy was a reminder of the resilience and strength that lay within them. Ayden hoped the same spirit would guide them through the challenges ahead as they faced their own moments of crisis and decision.

Near Stoystown, Pennsylvania, Ayden spotted a convoy of four PLA vehicles. He quickly decided to veer left and take Highway 281 south. They skirted Friedens, Pennsylvania, and turned west again onto Interstate 76 north of Somerset. Thirty minutes later, disaster struck again.

The sun was in his eyes now as he drove west on Interstate 76. Ayden's thoughts still lingered on the Flight 93 Memorial and the stories they had shared. Suddenly, the serene moment was shattered by a loud bang, and the truck lurched violently to the right.

Ayden's heart pounded as he fought to keep the vehicle under control. The steering wheel wrenched in his hands as the blown tire threw the truck into a wild swerve. He swerved right, nearly dropping off the edge of the road, then jerked the wheel left, overcorrecting and veering hard right again. He tried to slow the vehicle by pumping the brakes, resisting the instinct to stomp on them.

The thought flashed through Ayden's mind. His father had always been too busy running their financial company, leaving a friend's dad to teach him the skills he needed now. Ayden remembered the calm, steady advice. "Stay relaxed, don't panic, pump the brakes, and steer into the skid."

Clara's scream pierced the chaos, a high, terrified sound that cut through Ayden's concentration. "Hold on!" he yelled, his knuckles white as he gripped the wheel. The truck fishtailed, the back end swinging out as he fought for control.

After what felt like an eternity, Ayden managed to bring the truck to a slow, grinding stop on the shoulder of the road. The vehicle shuddered to a halt, and the silence that followed was deafening.

Laney let out a harsh breath. "Nice driving, Cowboy," she said, her voice trembling slightly but laced with admiration.

Ayden exhaled slowly, his heart still racing. "Thanks. I didn't think we were going to make it there for a second." He glanced past his sister, and his eyes met Laney's. "Why do you keep calling me cowboy?"

Laney shrugged. "I thought Wyoming was full of cowboys. Didn't you say your girlfriend had a ranch there?"

The image of Mia's ranch ran through his mind. He'd never known peace like he had there. The crystal-clear water of the stream that ran through it. The grass fields that stretched as far as the eye could see. And Mia's intoxicating smile. Pain gripped his heart, and he pushed the images away.

Clara was pale and gripping the seat hard. "That was… that was terrifying."

"Yeah, it was," Ayden agreed as he climbed out of the truck to assess the damage. The tire was completely shredded, and pieces of rubber were scattered across the road. He ran a hand through his hair, grateful they had avoided a more serious accident. He'd come close to flipping the truck. If that had happened, they might all have died—or worse, been so severely injured they would have lain there and suffered before death.

Laney joined him, her eyes scanning the surroundings. "Let's get this tire changed fast. We're too exposed out here."

As he glanced in the bed of the truck, his face fell. "Damn it. Owen didn't have a spare tire."

"It was in the trailer he was hauling," Clara said, frustration evident in her voice.

Ayden sighed. "You two stay here with the truck. I'll ride

Laney's bike ahead and see if I can find an abandoned vehicle with a tire to match the truck."

He removed the bike, placed one of the sports bottles in the holder, and pedaled down the road.

THIRTY-EIGHT

Mueller

New Eden Compound
Somerset Township
Washington County, Pennsylvania
Day Sixteen

The compound had been on high alert ever since learning about Walt Cayman's involvement in the attack on Bowers Township.

"What time will you be back?" Monica asked, rolling over and getting out of bed.

Mueller explained to his wife that he was taking a ride to Bowers Township to hopefully meet Hugh Meecham, the de facto leader of the farmers there.

"If this goes well, I'm going to put together a team and—"

"I want on that team!" she interrupted.

"I don't think it's a good idea."

"I don't give a crap what you think, Ty." Monica glared at him as she pulled on her bathrobe. "Laney is my baby, and I'm going."

Mueller blinked rapidly for a moment. "Okay."

Monica placed her hands on her curvy hips. "I'll be ready to go when you get back."

"Okay," was all he could say.

The 1970 Chevrolet Suburban's roof rack was loaded down with essential survival gear, and the hitch-mounted cargo carrier was full of extra fuel cans. He intended to siphon gasoline from abandoned vehicles to fill them so they'd have enough gas for their trip to eastern Pennsylvania to find Laney.

After filling a duffle bag with weapons, ammunition, tactical gear, and two-way radios they could use to communicate, Mueller met the guards at the compound's root cellar—a relic from the old farm that had been in his family for over one hundred and fifty years. "Open the door," he said. Mueller stepped back from the root cellar with his right hand resting comfortably on the holstered pistol at his side. After three days in the dark hole, without food or water, Walt Cayman was no longer a threat, but Mueller didn't take chances.

The guard removed the lock from the hasp, grasped the handle, and slowly pulled the door open. The guards zip-tied Walt's hands behind his back, stood him up, and brought him out to stand before Mueller. "We're going to take a drive over to Bowers Township."

After steering the Suburban through the gate and onto the roadway, Mueller cocked his head at a disturbing sound. He stomped the brakes, stopping the SUV.

"What is it, Mueller?" Amos asked, leaning forward in his seat.

"Sounds like helos," Smith said.

"Helicopters?" Amos's voice pitched.

Smith leaned out the passenger window and pointed skyward. "And those aren't American!"

Mueller pulled to a stop at a Bowers Township roadblock. A chubby man in dockers and a polo approached the car with a pistol in his hand but pointed at the ground. Mueller explained who he was and the purpose of his visit. The chubby man waved to a man behind the barricade, and the piece of lumber blocking the lane was lifted, allowing him to pass through.

"They do know that wouldn't stop a car, right?" Amos asked from the passenger seat.

"I'm not sure what they're thinking there," Mueller said.

Mueller carried the weapons into the municipal center while Amos and Smith led Walt inside behind him. They were taken into the chairman's office, where they were in the process of asking for his assistance with scheduling a meeting with Meecham when the man himself walked in.

Meecham took one look at Walt, who was seated on the floor at Amos's feet and stopped in his tracks.

"What is this?" he said, pulling his sidearm from the holster on his hip.

Smith pulled his and aimed it at the man.

"Hold on. Smith, put that away. We're just here to talk. That's all. Just a friendly conversation," Mueller said, stepping in front of Smith.

An instant later, a teenage girl burst into the office. She stopped in her tracks and raised her pistol, aiming directly at Walt Cayman.

Amos and Smith whirled around and pointed guns of their own back at the girl.

"Serenity!" Meecham shouted. "Lower your weapon!"

"Me! They're the ones who need to lower their guns." Her gaze bored into Walt. "What's going on here?" she asked, lowering her firearm slightly.

Meecham moved to stand next to her. "That's what I was just asking."

The chairman spoke up. "This is Tyson Mueller. He has a community in Somerset Township. It seems Mr. Cayman has been a guest there."

"You zip-tie all your guests?" Serenity asked.

Mueller lowered his gun and gestured for Smith and Amos to do the same. "Not usually." He addressed Meecham with an outstretched hand. "Tyson Mueller. We have a community over in Somerset Township called New Eden. We had nothing to do with what Walt and his people did to you folks." Mueller gauged his reaction. "As soon as we learned about it, we locked him up, ready to hand him over to you."

"And we're supposed to just take your word for that?" Hugh said.

Mueller stepped aside. "No! We didn't think you would. That's why we brought these." He gestured toward the rifles and boxes of ammunition piled on the chairman's desk.

Serenity frowned. "What's this?"

"An offering!" Mueller said. "Amos and I were just about to ask the chairman to escort us to your place, Hugh, to tell you that we'd like to work together to rebuild this community. Once you hear what I have to say, you'll want to work with us."

"Well, say it then." Hugh glanced down at Walt.

"If we can just step outside," Mueller said. "Time is of the essence here. I'm sure you'll agree once I fill you in."

Hugh brushed past the chairman. "Follow me."

"What about him?" Amos asked.

Mueller turned to the girl. "Up to her. He's her prisoner now."

Serenity pressed the barrel of her pistol against Walt's forehead.

"You're not going to execute him in here, are you?" Wendall asked from behind her.

Meecham rushed to her side. "You don't have to do it, Serenity." He ran his hand down on her arm and lowered the pistol toward the floor.

"We should have a trial," the chairman said. "Like a civilized society."

"I agree!" Serenity said. "All the young girls he abducted should be able to have their say in his punishment—not just me."

"Okay," Meecham said. "We'll take him back and hold him in his own jail at his old compound. We'll schedule a trial, and everyone who wants to participate can come and testify."

In Walt Cayman's old command center, Mueller and Hugh Meecham stood before a backdrop of wall maps of the United States and Pennsylvania. Serenity seemed distracted as she sat at the table, taking notes for her group.

"It's important for us all to work as a team. Especially in light of what I'm about to reveal to you." Mueller cleared his throat and began to explain. "The Russians are on our West Coast!" His voice rose slightly. "Today, on our way here, we saw Chinese helicopters."

"So did we," Meecham said. "I wasn't sure if my eyes were playing tricks on me or what. It's the worst-case scenario—our worst nightmare. A two-war construct!"

"I'm afraid so," Mueller said. "The sheer scale of China's and Russia's military modernization should have been a wake-up call. Their integration of cyber warfare, electronic jamming, and advanced missile systems was designed to counter our strengths directly," Mueller said.

Meecham leaned forward in his chair. "Exactly!"

For several minutes, they discussed the implications and how the government had failed to prevent the current scenario. Mueller stood and walked to the map pinned on the wall, tracing lines that once symbolized secure borders now rendered porous. "We go back to basics. Guerrilla tactics, local intelligence gathering, and, above all, community defense. We have to be swift, silent, and efficient."

Meecham agreed.

Mueller stabbed the table with his finger. “We’re going to have to be the resistance to their occupation. We have to make it too costly for them to stay here. We’ll be the resistance on the ground. We’ll hold the line here while the bigger gears turn.”

“So we take them from the enemy!” Meecham said.

Mueller nodded. “It’ll come to that—if and when we encounter enemy forces.”

They talked about strategy for another hour. “I was thinking if we were able to round up enough diesel, I would know where we could find an old eighteen-wheel semi-truck.”

“If you have access to the semi-truck, what about going after steel beams?” Mueller asked.

“What are we going to do with steel beams?” Serenity asked.

“Make hedgehogs,” Mueller said.

“Yeah, anti-tank obstacle defense made of metal angle beams or I-beams welded into a three-armed cross.”

“Where would we find them?” Serenity asked.

Meecham smiled. “I know a couple of places. There’s a semi-truck loaded with beams for the new church that was being built in Jefferson Hills for one.”

“That’s a start,” Mueller said. “If you can get the big rig running, I’ll find you the diesel to fuel it. You should pick up all the cattle fence panels and barbed wire you can find on your trip to the fence company in Clairton.”

Mueller felt good about the meeting as he, Amos, and Smith returned to the compound. He liked Hugh Meecham and thought he had a level head and he found it hard to believe that Serenity was only sixteen years old. She seemed wise beyond her years—much like Laney.

~

Hours later, Meecham and two other men appeared at Mueller's checkpoint.

Mueller radioed to the guard at the checkpoint to escort them to the compound, and Mueller welcomed them as they entered the gate.

"Mueller, this is Serenity's dad, Keith, and Joe Mansell, a member of their group," Meecham said, introducing them.

Mueller nodded a greeting and then led them along a well-trodden path to the compound's chow hall. Once seated, the trio of visitors delved into the urgent matters that had brought them to Mueller's doorstep.

"We've stumbled upon some intel that could be pivotal," Meecham said. "There are railcars full of fertilizer between here and Clairton, and potentially some construction equipment marked with orange placards—meaning explosives."

Mueller leaned in. "Explosives, you say? That could be a game-changer. How solid is this lead?"

"It's firsthand. Serenity spotted them," Keith said. "She's certain of what she saw. The problem is, she's the only one who knows the exact location."

Mueller rubbed his chin thoughtfully. "Retrieving that could significantly boost our defensive capabilities. Fertilizer for improvised explosives, construction explosives for more controlled demolitions… both are crucial."

As the discussion progressed, they delved deeper into the application of guerrilla warfare tactics against the superior forces of the invaders, specifically homing in on sabotage operations designed to undermine the enemy's logistical capabilities.

Mueller laid out the strategy. "Let's prepare detailed plans for each target. We'll need recon teams to gather intel and demolition experts to handle the explosives." Mueller stood and extended his hand. "Let's make it happen. I'd like to get eyes on these explosives and see how much fertilizer we're talking about. I'll pick you all up first thing in the morning. I have a Suburban and a truck with a trailer so that you can haul back the cattle panels and barbed wire you're going after. I won't be returning with you. You'll be coming back with Nesbitt and White."

"You're not coming back with us?" Keith asked.

"No. Something's come up. I'm leaving from there to find my daughter."

THIRTY-NINE

Ayden

Highway 76
North of Donegal, Pennsylvania
Day Seventeen

Ayden had scanned the landscape for any sign of an abandoned vehicle but found nothing. As the sun had dipped below the horizon, frustrated, he returned. They camped for the night in a clearing beside the road. Huddled around a small, crackling fire, they shared the last of their rations.

The next morning, Ayden set out again, determined to find a spare tire. He took a side road this time, the path winding through dense woods and open fields.

Late in the afternoon, Ayden stumbled upon a farm with several older trucks scattered around. He left the bike in the brush beside the road and snuck across a field to inspect the tires. When he found the right size, he almost shouted with relief. It took another fifteen minutes to locate a tire iron and remove the lug nuts. Thirty minutes later, he was still struggling to loosen them.

Exhausted, Ayden leaned against the fender and drank the last of his water before trying again. As the minutes passed, he feared he just didn't have the strength to loosen them. He thought of Clara and Laney back at the truck, relying on him to do this and get them to the safety of Laney's compound. Gritting his teeth, he tried one last time and finally managed to loosen the last one.

After wrestling the tire off the vehicle, he rolled it across the uneven field and back to the bike. There, he faced another problem: how to carry it and pedal the bike.

With no better option, Ayden tied the tire to the bike rack with some rope he had found, balancing it as best as he could. The added weight made the ride back slow and treacherous, but he pressed on, his determination fueling each pedal stroke.

When Ayden finally returned to the truck, sweat-drenched and exhausted, Clara and Laney rushed to meet him.

"You did it!" Clara exclaimed, her eyes wide with relief.

"Barely," Ayden said hoarsely. "But we've got the tire. Let's get it on and get moving."

With Laney's and Clara's help, they quickly replaced the blown tire. Ayden's hands were shaking from fatigue, but he managed to secure the lug nuts and lower the truck back to the ground.

They climbed back into the truck, Ayden behind the wheel. As he started the engine and steered back onto the highway, he glanced at Laney and Clara. "We're going to be okay. We've got each other, and we're not giving up."

Laney smiled. "Damn right, Cowboy. Let's keep moving."

They continued along Interstate 76 from Donegal but were detoured again east of Yukon due to a roadblock and wound their way around the town to Highway 31 at Turkeytown.

Ayden stopped across from a fire station to check their direction. "Where does this highway lead?"

Laney glanced up from reading the map in the passenger seat. "You're going to make a right here, and then we'll cross Youghiogheny River at West Newton."

"In the town?" Ayden asked.

"Yes."

He'd been trying his best to avoid populated areas. "Is there another place to cross away from towns?"

"Interstate 70."

Ayden wanted to avoid the interstates as well. They'd seen increased military traffic there. He wanted to stick to the back roads where there was less of a chance of running into them. He glanced down at the fuel gauge. They had a quarter tank of gas left and couldn't afford many more detours. They didn't have a gas can or hose to siphon fuel, and it would take precious time to search for them. "How many more miles to the compound?"

"About forty or so," Laney said, a slight smile forming on her lips.

Ayden knew how anxious she was to reach home and be reunited with her parents. It felt good to know that something good could come during this crisis. "We'll have to risk it and cross in West Newton."

The quaint town appeared deserted as they passed through, heading for the bridge. It was as if the whole community had just vanished. The stores and businesses sat empty, and there were no signs of life anywhere. They passed over the two-lane bridge to the other side of the river and continued past residential homes, heading west.

"Okay, now we'll want to stay on this road. I'll tell you where to turn to cross the Dentonville bridge to cross the Monongahela River, and from there, we'll take various back roads to avoid the interstate."

"You're the navigator. I'll turn where you say turn," Ayden said, steering the pickup along the winding and rolling hills of central Pennsylvania.

Up ahead, Ayden spotted movement to his right on the lawn outside a trailer home. The man turned and, as he did, raised a rifle in the truck's direction. Clara shouted as Ayden braked and then threw the pickup into Reverse.

"Turn on the next road on your right!" Laney shouted as more men appeared from their homes. Ayden passed the road, stopped, shifted into Drive, and took the turn as fast as the truck could handle.

Laney, with the map spread across her lap, went to work recalculating their route. "This road will take us to Clairton. We can cross the river there, hit the turnpike, and take it south to connect to Highway 136. That will take us to my parents' compound."

The two-lane road they'd turned onto wound its way through the countryside. Ayden's whole body was on high alert. They were so close, but it seemed as if everything was conspiring against them.

Thirty minutes later, Laney directed them onto a road that ran north and paralleled the river south of the borough of Glassport, Pennsylvania.

Ayden began noticing cars pushed off into the ditches on both sides of the two-lane road.

The midafternoon sun nearly blinded him as he began to make the turn onto the bridge. As he turned, Ayden glanced left and spotted what looked to be US military vehicles on the hill near a water tower. From there, they would have a clear view of the bridge.

"Oh no!" Clara shouted, gesturing toward them.

"Those are ours!" Laney yelled. "They're American!"

Suddenly, a cloud of smoke rose into the sky near the Humvees. An instant later, an explosion reverberated through the river valley. "I think they're firing at someone behind us!" Laney yelled. "We're caught in the middle. Get us out of here, Ayden!"

Ayden punched the gas and raced westward across the bridge in an attempt to escape the fighting.

"PLA vehicles are behind us. Hurry!" Laney shouted.

The lead PLA vehicle opened fire from the road behind them. Their rounds peppered the rear of Owen's pickup, causing Laney and Clara to duck down for cover. As Ayden maneuvered the vehicle into the northbound lanes, the invaders' bullets punched through the back window between Ayden and Clara and exited out the windshield in multiple places. Fragments of bullets and glass grazed Ayden's right shoulder and bicep. Adrenaline coursed through his body, shielding him from the pain. He didn't have time to examine the damage; he had to get them out of there.

Laney popped her head back up and attempted to return fire, but the enemy was undeterred. In seconds, they were across the bridge. Ayden punched it and sped toward the cross street and through a residential area in Clairton. On the next road, he took a left turn a little too fast and clipped the side of a mid-sized sedan parked at the curb. They were rolling down toward an intersection with two-story brick buildings on either side and hit at a fast rate of speed, when a massive explosion shook the ground. Windows in the buildings shattered, and brick and concrete flew into the air and rained down on the cab of the truck. A massive piece of a fire escape dropped onto the roadway in front of them. Ayden yanked the wheel hard to the right, bounced onto the sidewalk, and veered around it just as several eight-wheeled armored vehicles came into view, crossing a set of railroad tracks. PLA soldiers carrying AK machine guns walked beside them. The turret on the lead IFV swiveled toward them. It fired, and the facade of the building to their left exploded in a shower of bricks, wood, metal, and glass.

Ayden yanked the wheel to the right and took the alley. They bumped across the cross street and down the next alleyway, turned onto a side street, and raced south for several blocks, weaving in and out between abandoned cars. As they bumped across the railroad tracks, Ayden spotted a US military Humvee.

"We're in a freaking war zone. We have to stop and find cover," Ayden said, following the current street east, looking for a safe place to hunker down.

"There!" Laney said, pointing ahead to an open bay door of a printing business across from a truck service shop. "In there!"

Ayden pulled the truck into the open bay door and shut off the engine. The sound of sporadic gunfire echoed outside as US forces battled the PLA. He tried to calm his thoughts and assess their next move.

"Laney, come around and get behind the wheel. I'm going to check out this business and find us somewhere to lie low until this fighting stops," Ayden said before opening the driver's door.

"Be careful, Ayden. They could be anywhere," Clara said, her voice filled with concern.

He nodded and tried to offer her a comforting smile. "I'll be right back."

As Ayden approached the door into the office of the building, Laney climbed into the driver's seat. Ayden stopped and turned to face the truck. "Laney, if shit goes down, get the hell out of here."

"We're not leaving you behind," Clara called out through the open window.

"Laney!"

"Just hurry back, brother. I love you!"

"You have to look out for one another if things go south."

"We will!" Laney said. "Just clear the office and hurry back."

Ayden nodded and turned back toward the door, peering through its window. He hesitated a moment, took a deep breath, and attempted to slow his pounding heart. It was beating so loud in his ears that he worried he wouldn't be able to hear if someone was inside. Finally, he reached down and held his breath as he turned the knob. The door squeaked loudly as he opened it. Ayden hesitated in the threshold, listening, expecting to hear the sound of a gun being racked or heavy footfalls running toward him. However, he heard nothing but the roar in his ears.

FORTY

Mia

Christiansen Ranch
Farson, Wyoming
Day Seventeen

Over the next few days, the ranch remained in a tense but productive state of readiness. Training sessions continued, supplies were traded and shared, and a sense of uneasy calm settled over the community. Mia and her family worked tirelessly, honing their skills and reinforcing their bonds with neighbors. The nights were spent keeping watch, the days in preparation.

It was a clear, crisp morning on the seventeenth day when the first signs of trouble emerged. Mia was out on the porch, sipping her coffee, when she saw a rider galloping toward the ranch at breakneck speed. The sight made her heart leap into her throat. She set her cup down and rushed to meet him.

"What's happened?" she asked as the rider, out of breath and covered in dust, pulled his horse to a stop.

"Convoy spotted," he managed between gasps. "Heading this way on Highway 28. Could be here within the hour."

Mia's stomach twisted. This was the moment they had all been dreading.

Neil immediately called a meeting. The kitchen, now the nerve center of their operations, buzzed with anxious energy as Mia and her family gathered.

"We've got a convoy coming," Neil announced, his voice steady but urgent. "We don't know their intentions, but we have to assume the worst."

The room fell silent, the gravity of the situation settling in.

"We need to be ready to follow our evacuation plan," Dirk said, spreading the map on the table. The wranglers and I will stay behind to delay them and buy you some time."

Mia's heart pounded as she gathered her boys and directed them to pack their evacuation kits. "Remember what we practiced," she told Carter, Luke, and Xavier, her voice calm but firm. "Stick together and follow the plan."

Melody and Mia worked quickly, distributing the remaining supplies and ensuring everyone knew their roles. The wranglers, including Dirk, prepared to join the ambush that had been set up along the main routes to slow the convoy.

Time seemed to slow as Dirk and the wranglers moved out to set up their ambush.

"Stay safe." Mia's eyes filled with worry.

"We will," Dirk replied. "We'll catch up with you later."

Soon, the neighboring families gathered with their evacuation kits and prepared to leave. Mia made one last sweep of the cabin to ensure nothing essential was left behind. She looked around the home she had known all her life, a mix of nostalgia and fear gripping her heart.

Just as they were about to leave, a rider rushed down the drive. "They're close," he said, stopping in front of the porch. "Convoy spotted less than five miles out. Everyone needs to hunker down and get armed!"

Panic surged, but Mia fought to keep calm. She herded the

boys and the other children into the safe room. The children, wide-eyed and frightened, clung to their mothers.

“You have to stay here.” Mia turned to the oldest, a girl no more than thirteen. “Keep them in here—no matter what.”

Mothers peeled their crying children off, and Mia closed the door. “Lock it!” she called to the girl. She stood there until she heard it click. “I love you, boys!” she called through the thick steel door.

Mia and the other mothers gathered in the living room as the convoy drew nearer. The sound of engines grew louder as Mia’s parents and her neighbors spread out to their defensive positions, prepared to protect their children.

At the door, Mia listened intently for the ambush Dirk and the others had prepared for the Russian convoy. But the explosion never went off. Suddenly, the ear-splitting roar of fighter jets streaked overhead. Mia rushed to the window and stared out through the slits in the plywood. A moment later, an enormous explosion rattled the whole house.

Mia hurried to the door and flung it open just in time to see a massive ball of fire in the distance. The ground shook with the force of the blast, and the sky lit up with the fiery aftermath. Heart pounding, Mia turned to see one of the wranglers emerging from a foxhole, binoculars in hand.

“They’re American fighter jets!” he yelled, his voice filled with relief and disbelief.

The realization sent a wave of hope through Mia. Moments later, a rider galloped up to the house, his face flushed with excitement.

“The convoy’s been destroyed!” he shouted. “The jets took them out completely. We’re safe for now!”

The relief was palpable as Mia and the others processed the news. Tears of relief streamed down her face as she hugged Melody tightly.

“Thank God,” Melody whispered, her voice breaking.

Mia took a deep breath, her thoughts turning to Dirk and the others out on the defensive lines.

But the threat wasn't entirely over. They still needed to remain vigilant and prepared for whatever might come next.

FORTY-ONE

Mueller

New Life Church
Bowers Township
Washington County, Pennsylvania
Day 17

The vehicles stopped in front of the mansion, and the doors flew open. Mueller stepped out, dressed in his tactical vest and body armor. They spoke for a moment about gear and guns, and then Mueller gestured for Serenity, Keith, and Joe to get into his Suburban. The sun was cresting over the horizon when they met up with Meecham and his son, Cody, at the church north of the equestrian center.

A short time later, Serenity called out, "That's it!"

Mueller stopped the Suburban parallel to one of the trucks. "Yep, they have the orange explosives placards. Get me the bolt cutters, White."

White ran up with the tool and stood beside Mueller as he cut the locks off the boxes in the construction truck's bed. Inside was a red box. Mueller carefully continued to pull it out and placed it on the ground near his feet. Amos flipped back the lid and whooped with delight. "The detonators are still here. That means the explosive will be, too."

"Okay, here's the plan," Mueller said, placing the box of detonators back into the compartment. "First, we're going to pull that placard off the truck. Then we're going to push the vehicle down the road and to that gravel drive very carefully. White, head on down there and cut the lock on the gate. I want to be able to push both of these trucks inside the fence and hide them behind the tree line. We'll stop back by here on our way home and check on the contents, then bring the horse trailer back to transport it all."

Everyone piled out of their vehicles and took up positions around the backs of the two trucks. They pushed as Mueller and Amos steered the pickups toward the open gate. Once they were inside the fence and concealed behind thick underbrush, they headed back to their own waiting vehicles. "We don't have a lot of time. We should get going," Mueller said, glancing at his watch. "Where's that boxcar you saw with fertilizer in it?"

Two miles from Clairton, Serenity instructed Mueller to pull over at a roadside turnout with access to both the creek and the railroad tracks. On the track sat a long train filled with covered hopper cars, just as Serenity had described. Even before crossing the small concrete bridge, he could tell they had found what they were looking for.

"Sweet!" Amos said. "We can do a heck of a lot of damage with this much ammonium nitrate."

"Just one of these contains over two hundred thousand pounds. So yes, we're going to blow a lot of stuff up."

"Hopefully, not one or all of us," Keith said.

Mueller made a fist and held it out toward Serenity. "Great job, kid!"

She bristled.

"Sorry! I know you're not a child. I'm just older than dirt, and everyone's a kid to me."

Serenity smiled.

As they headed into Clairton, Hugh gestured to the east. "The fence supply company is near the river, but I'd really like to stop at this truck service shop to see if I can find parts for my Peterbilt," Hugh said.

Moments later, they were pulling into the parking lot of the semi-truck service center. One of the tall bay doors was up, revealing a big rig with its hood up. Oversized tools and mechanical parts were arrayed neatly beside it, left as if the mechanic who'd been working on them had only stepped away momentarily. Mueller pulled the Suburban to a stop in front of the open bay.

Mueller and Amos were sitting in the Suburban, mapping their route and discussing where they'd begin their search for Laney when Smith and another crew member Mueller had stationed as a sentry near the street sprinted toward them. Before he spoke, the distinctive growl of an engine cut through the air.

"Four Chinese IFVs heading our way," Smith shouted.

An instant later, Nesbitt, another sentry, unleashed a barrage of gunfire at the advancing convoy.

Mueller and Amos exited the Suburban, shouldering their rifles as they approached the semi-truck parked outside one of the bay doors. Mueller ran around to the opposite side and moved along the vehicle toward the rear of the cab, stopping to acquire a target as the first of the eight-wheeled armored vehicles came into view. Behind and in front of each infantry fighting vehicle (IFV) Type 19s were PLA soldiers carrying AK machine guns. The turret on the lead IFV swiveled menacingly, and its 30mm caliber automatic cannon roared to life, spewing death. Across the street from the repair shop, the building's facade exploded in a shower of bricks, wood, metal, and glass.

"Fall back! Get to the building!" Mueller shouted. A round caught Mueller in the arm as he ran toward the shop. Meecham pulled Mueller inside just before another one struck the frame of the bay door. "Is there a back door?" Mueller shouted, rushing toward the rear of the shop.

"Back here!" someone said.

Light flooded in, temporarily blinding Mueller. "Everyone! This way!" he shouted. He stopped short of the doorway, shielding his eyes from the sun. He waved everyone over as he waited for his vision to adjust to the light. Shoving Meecham's son, Cody, out of the way, Mueller peered outside, scanning from left to right, searching for any enemy soldiers. Seeing none, he stepped outside. He surveyed the back of the shop. Across an alley was an old warehouse. "There!" he said, gesturing to it. "Amos!" he called. Amos rushed to his side. "Take Smith and Nesbitt and check out that warehouse."

The men double-timed it across the one-lane alley and stacked it up just outside the man-sized entrance. Amos stepped back, landed a kick to the center of the door, and then rushed inside. The two other men hurried in behind him.

A moment later, Amos reappeared, waving them over. "It's clear."

Gunfire faded away as Mueller led everyone toward the warehouse.

"What are we doing here, boss?" Smith asked, pointing the beam of his scope's light at the floor by Mueller's feet.

"Waiting, Smith."

"Waiting for what? We should be out there sending those commie bastards straight to hell!"

Mueller clenched his jaw. "You got an army with you I don't know about, Smith?"

Smith said something smart-ass, and Amos backhanded him, sending Smith stumbling backward into the wall.

"So what's the plan now?" Amos asked. "We still going to try to hit the fence supply store?"

"That's what we came here for," Mueller said. "They need those cattle panels and barbed wire more now than ever. We'll wait until the convoy leaves the area and then run over there, slip in, load up the supplies, and then they can hightail it out of town and back to Bowers Township."

"And you guys?" Hugh asked. "What if they've blocked the bridge?"

"Then we'll drop south and try the bridge in West Elizabeth," Mueller said, pacing and planning his next move.

He was heading toward the door when Smith's voice rang out.

"The good guys are here!"

The door burst open, and US soldiers rushed inside. Their leader barked orders as the others fanned out, weapons shouldered.

"Weapons down!" Mueller said. "Friendlies," Mueller shouted. "Americans!"

Everyone lowered their weapons and stepped back, allowing the soldiers to run past.

"Friendlies!" one of the soldiers barked.

"I got nine friendlies," another said into a handheld radio.

"We're damn glad to see you guys," Mueller said.

The lead soldier said nothing as he, too, moved past them deeper into the warehouse.

"Sarge, most of the floor is gone," one of the soldiers called down from the second floor.

"Can you get to that window?" the sergeant asked.

"Maybe," he said, disappearing from view.

"Made it, Sarge. I've got eyes on the intersection. I can see the bridge from here."

"Alpha Two. SITREP!" the sergeant barked into the radio.

"Alpha One. This is Alpha Two. We need another five minutes," crackled through the radio.

"Copy that. Five more minutes, Alpha Two."

"Schmidt. You got eyes on the east side of the river?"

"Roger that," Schmidt yelled down. "I've got ten Tango vehicles, four mikes out."

The sergeant relayed that information to whoever was on the other end of the radio.

"Copy that. Alpha One. Wait one."

There was a long pause.

"Alpha One. Ramirez is setting the last charge now."

"Charge?" Serenity asked.

The sergeant glanced back at her like he'd just noticed they were there but said nothing. "Copy, Alpha Two. Set the charge and return to the ORP."

"Copy, Alpha One. Setting charge and returning to ORP."

Mueller spun around, heading for the door. "Smith, Nesbitt. Get these folks home. Tell Steve I'll radio when I find Laney!" he said as he slipped out the door.

Amos was on his heels. "Nesbitt, feed my cat!" he called over his shoulder.

Mueller and Amos navigated side streets west through Clairton and then south toward West Elizabeth along Ridge Road. After weaving through dead cars along the side streets of the town, they encountered an impenetrable obstacle: a wall of US military vehicles blocking their path to the bridge.

"Turn back. No unauthorized crossings allowed," the lead soldier barked, his rifle pointed at the truck.

Mueller's hands tightened on the steering wheel as he fought back a surge of frustration. "Please," he pleaded, his voice edged with desperation. "My daughter is out there. I need to get across that bridge to find her."

The soldier's expression softened slightly, but he remained firm. "I'm sorry, sir. Orders are orders. Now I'm going to have to order you out of the truck."

Mueller's jaw clenched. "You don't understand. This isn't just about me. My daughter's life is at stake. I've got to get to her. Please."

The soldier shook his head. "We're under strict orders to prevent any unauthorized crossings. We have to ensure the safety of everyone in the area. I can't make exceptions."

Amos leaned forward, trying to bolster Mueller's argument. "We've come a long way. We've faced hell to get here. Just give us a chance to explain."

The soldier raised a hand, signaling for calm. "I sympathize with your situation, but my hands are tied. Step out of the vehicle now."

Desperation twisted Mueller's features. "If you won't let us through, at least let us keep the truck. We can find another way around."

The soldier's eyes hardened. "No can do. We need every vehicle we can get. Now, step out of the truck, or we'll be forced to remove you."

Mueller's heart pounded. He knew arguing further was futile. With a heavy sigh, he opened the door and stepped out with his hands raised in surrender. Amos followed, glaring at the soldiers.

As they were escorted away from the truck, Mueller turned to the soldier one last time. "If you have children, you must understand what I'm going through. Please, think about that."

The soldier's eyes flickered with something like empathy, but he remained silent, signaling them to move along.

Mueller and Amos limped away from the military blockade, their steps heavy with frustration and defeat, but Mueller's resolve to find his daughter only grew stronger.

"We'll find another way," Amos said in a firm voice. "We can't give up now."

Dejected, Mueller and Amos turned back. As Mueller walked away, his jaw clenched in frustration. "There has to be an alternative. We can't just give up," he muttered.

Amos nodded. "Let's head to the river. Maybe we can find a boat or a place to cross unseen."

They skirted the riverbank, avoiding both PLA and US patrols. Exhaustion tugged at their limbs, but their determination kept them moving and searching for a rickety rowboat or some other means across the river—but they found nothing.

"We could head back to the warehouse and grab the Suburban," Amos said.

Mueller shook his head. "I can't strand those people in a war zone."

They made their way through the chaotic streets, managing to avoid both military and PLA patrols. It was an arduous journey, each step a battle against their exhaustion and the lingering threat of discovery.

As they approached the area near the warehouse where he'd left Meecham and the others, the signs of recent fighting were evident. Burnt-out vehicles shattered, window glass and debris littered the streets. The PLA now occupied the truck repair shop where they'd left the Suburban.

"Maybe they headed to the fence supply store," Amos said.

Mueller nodded. "We'll try there."

Navigating through the chaotic streets, they kept to the shadows, avoiding both enemy and allied forces. They moved with a sense of urgency, knowing that every minute spent in the open was a risk.

Finally, they spotted a familiar face. Mueller called out to her in a hushed tone. "Serenity?"

She spun around, lifting her rifle.

Amos stepped out of the shadows with his hands raised. "Don't shoot! It's Tyson Mueller and Amos Harper."

"Mueller?"

She looked shocked to see them.

"Where are the others?" Mueller asked, guiding her back toward the donation box.

Serenity recounted what had happened at the warehouse after they'd left. Smith and Meecham's son had been killed.

"I'm so sorry," Mueller said. "What about Nesbitt, Meecham, and Joe?"

"I don't know. We got separated from Hugh and Joe when we went for the Suburban. Nesbitt followed us between the buildings and stayed behind to cover my father and me as we got away."

"They could still be in that area," Amos said.

"I'm headed back there. I need to get to your SUV. My dad's been shot. He's lost a lot of blood. I need to get him home."

"The warehouse and that area are crawling with the PLA," Mueller said in a low voice. "We made it to West Elizabeth, but the US forces have control of the bridge there, and they wouldn't let us cross."

"And they took our truck," Amos said.

"More of a reason to get the heck out of here," Serenity said, tugging on his arm.

"We can't. I still have to get across the river and find my daughter. We came back for the Suburban, but we can't even get close to it."

Amos raked a hand through his hair. "We keep getting pushed farther and farther away from it."

"My dad doesn't have much time. I have to try," Serenity said. "Can't we somehow draw them away from the warehouse?"

Amos and Mueller looked at one another for a moment.

"If we could cause some type of diversion, she might be able to slip in and get the Suburban. We could meet up back where Keith is holed up. We grab our gear and cover them as they head out of town," Amos said.

Amos gestured toward the river. "I still have some firecrackers. If we set them on a long detonation cord, we'll draw the PLA in that direction. They'll do a search. That would give her long enough to make it to the warehouse to get the Suburban."

"You still have the bottle rockets?" Mueller said.

"A few," Amos said. "We can split up. You set the firecrackers inside one of the railcars. I'll launch the bottle rockets into the window of one of the buildings down the street—we'll make it look more like a spread-out attack. They have to come to investigate."

"Where's your dad now?" Mueller asked.

Serenity explained where to find him.

"After we set off the fireworks, we'll head straight to your dad. We'll have him ready to go as soon as you pull up."

Mueller placed a hand on her shoulder. "You can do this, kid. Keep to the alleys, make it to the Suburban, and then back to your dad."

"Got it! Thanks," she said.

As Mueller and Amos turned toward the river, Serenity took off in a sprint across the street toward the alley. Mueller's injured arm dangled at his side as he and Amos ran toward the boxcars to set up the fireworks diversion. Once they reached the tracks, Mueller laid out the firecrackers, linking the fuses of each together with the detonator cord and stringing the whole thing out the door of the boxcar and around the back, where he waited until Amos had climbed the stairs of the two-story building halfway down the block. As the first of the bottle rockets were fired, Mueller lit his fuse. The sound coming from the boxcar was deafening.

Mueller and Amos took off running. "This way," Mueller shouted, turning west on a side street. As they approached a dilapidated house on the corner, PLA soldiers immediately cut them off, separating him from Amos.

"There!" Mueller gestured to the house. The words had barely left his mouth when one of the PLA's tracked vehicles turned the corner. "Keith! Get out! Get out!" Mueller screamed, running toward him as the turret turned toward the abandoned house. Mueller flung open the door and yanked Keith out, dragging him away from the building and diving on top of him seconds before the house exploded, raining firing fiery debris down upon them.

FORTY-TWO

Ayden

Clairton Printing
Clairton, Pennsylvania
Day Seventeen

Ayden stepped inside the print shop's office, leaving the door open for a quick escape, and moved through a small storage room before entering the break room. The place looked abandoned. There was nothing on the counters—no coffee pot, no paper cups, not even a roll of paper towels. He felt a chill as he observed the scene.

To the left, Ayden found a small office. Instead of a desk or conference table, it contained a bare mattress in the corner surrounded by beer cans and an ashtray overflowing with cigarette butts as if the homeless had been squatting there. The smell coming from the bathroom to his right was putrid. He quickly poked his head inside, just long enough to confirm no one hid behind the door. Nearly gagging from the smell, he closed it, hoping to block some of the odor, and then raced back through the office and stepped out into the garage—grateful for the fresh air. He held up his thumb to indicate the place was clear. Taking several more deep breaths, he moved to the passenger side of the pickup and assisted his sister from the vehicle.

After settling Clara inside on the floor near a small window in the back office overlooking the street, Ayden returned to the garage. He waited in the doorway near the road, listening to the sound of explosions and gunfire for a moment before pulling down the garage door and joining both Clara and Laney inside.

Ayden crouched near the window, his rifle in his hands, listening to the chaos outside. The sounds of gunfire and explosions echoed through the streets, creating a cacophony of violence. He peered out the small window and scanned the area for any signs of movement.

"Four Chinese IFVs heading our way," someone shouted from across the street.

An instant later, men in the service station parking lot unleashed a barrage of gunfire at the advancing convoy. Ayden saw two men dressed in tactical gear, but they didn't look military. They exited a Suburban, shouldering their rifles as they approached a semi-truck parked outside one of the bay doors. One of the men ran around to the opposite side and moved along the vehicle toward the rear of the cab, stopping to acquire a target as the first of the eight-wheeled armored vehicles came into view.

Behind and in front of each PLA vehicle were enemy soldiers carrying machine guns. The turret on the lead PLA vehicle spun, and its weapon roared to life, spitting out round after round, striking the print shop where Ayden and the ladies were hiding. The building's facade exploded, raining down bricks, wood, metal, and glass.

Ayden's heart raced as he realized they were directly in the line of fire. The PLA was targeting them. Sheetrock and wood fragments rained down around them, and he instinctively ducked, shielding Clara with his body.

Gunfire echoed down the stairs at the end of the corridor. Someone was on the roof, firing down on the enemy soldiers.

There was a momentary pause in the fighting. Ayden glanced up, ready to grab Clara and flee deeper into the building, away from the street and the soldier. The big man in the parking lot across the street shouted orders to his men before opening fire upon the unmounted PLA soldiers as he retreated toward the repair shop.

An instant later, a pickup filled with civilians came under heavy automatic rifle fire, sending them spilling out of the truck in search of cover.

"Fall back! Get to the building!" the big man shouted as another appeared at the bay doors.

As the PLA turned their attention to the repair shop, Ayden took the opportunity to get Clara and Laney somewhere safer. He scooped his sister into his arms and ran down a long corridor toward the back of the print shop, past giant printing machines and stacks of paper products. Along one wall were several doors. Laney ran ahead and tried the one closest to them. "Locked!" She tried the next two, and they were the same. The third door on the left opened, and Laney ran inside, pistol in hand. "Clear!"

Ayden carried Clara in behind her, and Laney slammed the door shut. Ayden sat Clara down on the floor in the corner and flicked on the light on his rifle scope, illuminating a paper storage closet. The walls were concrete cinder blocks, and there were no windows. Ayden wasn't sure how well the space would hold up to military bombs and gunfire, but it seemed like the safest place they could be under the circumstances.

The sporadic gunfire outside continued, each shot a reminder of the danger they were in. Ayden knew they couldn't stay here forever, but for now, they had to ride out the storm. He checked his rifle, making sure it was ready, and then positioned himself near the door and listened, hoping the gunfire would eventually fade so they could be on their way.

During an intense battle, the PLA soldiers infiltrated the print shop, fanning out and shouting as they moved from room to room.

Ayden knew that at any moment, they would make their way to the print shop floor and find them hiding there. He had to do something to draw them away from Laney and his sister. He had to cause a diversion so they could get away.

Ayden cracked the door open a few inches and peered through the opening. "I have to draw them away. Once they move back to the front, Laney, help my sister up and the two of you escape through that side door. I think it leads to the alley."

"No, Ayden. We don't split up!" Clara said. "You'll die if you go out there."

"They're going to find us here if I do nothing, Clara!"

"Ayden!"

"I'll draw them away and then meet you…" They didn't have a rallying point. He didn't know the town or how to make it to Laney's compound.

"Follow the tracks. There's a construction company just past the turnpike. We'll meet you there," Laney said, standing.

Ayden nodded and flicked off his light. "I love you, Clara!" he called, flinging open the door.

"Ayden, no!" she cried out. "I love you, too!" she said as Laney closed the door behind him.

Ayden met the PLA in the corridor and ducked into one of the rooms. As they rushed toward him, he fired, using up all his ammunition before diving out the broken window and landing on the glass-strewn sidewalk. He rolled, feeling the pain shoot through him before jumping to his feet and taking off across the street toward the truck repair shop.

He glanced back to discover that the PLA wasn't following him. Soldiers were hiding behind vehicles, firing up at the upper floors and roof of the print shop. When Ayden reached the repair shop where he'd seen civilians before, they were gone. He ran through the repair bays to a back door that led into an alley. From there, he saw a dilapidated warehouse, but nothing he could use to attract the PLA soldiers away from the print shop. He returned to the front of the building and ran toward the parked Suburban. As he reached the driver's door, the sounds of battle intensified, the PLA pushing harder against the US forces.

An explosion echoed through the streets, and the building at the end of the block went up in flames. Ayden was forced to take cover between the vintage SUV and a concrete wall. Round after round rained down upon the street. As PLA soldiers ran into the repair shop for cover, Ayden took a deep breath and steeled himself for what was to come. He was pinned down, caught between whoever was on the roof and enemy fighters.

Every time Ayden made any attempt to move from his spot, he was fired upon. Soon, the sound of tracked military vehicles echoed off the buildings, followed by thunderous explosions and an intense gunfight. US soldiers poured from the front of the printing business, sending automatic gunfire into the truck repair shop mere feet from the SUV where Ayden was seeking cover.

They ran across the street and down the side of the shop, disappearing from sight.

Ayden waited briefly before sprinting back to where he'd left his sister and Laney. He flung open the storage room door and let out a sigh of relief. They weren't there. They'd done as he'd instructed and fled as the battle moved across the street.

He stepped into the alley where a tall US soldier, his head covered with a mass of dark, curly hair, barked orders as the others fanned out, weapons shouldered, and disappeared around the side of the building.

Ayden turned west on the next street, unsure which direction to go to find the railroad tracks they'd passed earlier. At the sound of military vehicles, Ayden ducked between two brick buildings. The heavy machines slowed as if searching for someone. Ayden dropped to the ground in the tall grass and held his breath. He could hear them speaking to one another in a foreign language that he presumed was Mandarin, Cantonese, or one of the many dialects of China. Two PLA soldiers walked within fifteen feet of

Ayden but fortunately didn't see him in the overgrown lot between the buildings. Seconds after they passed by, an ear-splitting explosion reverberated through the streets, knocking out windows in storefronts and automobiles. The PLA soldiers loaded back into the military vehicles and sped away.

Ayden shot to his feet and ran toward the street. When he reached it, two PLA soldiers stepped out the door of a building across the street. A surprised look crossed their faces as Ayden raised his. He squeezed the trigger, the shot hitting the first squarely in the chest. The soldier dropped his rifle and it clattered to the ground.

Ayden immediately ducked behind a nearby sedan as the second PLA soldier peppered the vehicle with rifle fire. Crouched beside the front tire, Ayden knew he had to move.

He spotted an SUV ten feet away and decided to make a break for it. As soon as he stepped out, the PLA soldier fired upon him. Ayden spun around and returned fire, managing to graze the soldier's arm just as eight more PLA soldiers arrived. He was outnumbered and outgunned.

Ayden dove for cover behind the SUV, the sound of a tracked vehicle moving toward them growing louder. Suddenly, the building where the PLA soldiers had been standing exploded, and the PLA soldiers scattered. Seconds later, US soldiers came into view, and the battle intensified between them.

Ayden took advantage of the chaos, darting down a side alley and running back the way he'd come, ending up three buildings away from where he'd parked Owen's truck. He was surrounded by fighting, and the only thing he could do was pray it ended soon. The battle had stretched on for hours, and the inside of the flower shop he'd taken cover in grew darker as the sun began to set. There was nothing he could do. He was out of ammunition and cut off from his sister.

FORTY-THREE

Ayden

Pansies Flower Shop
Clairton, Pennsylvania
Day Eighteen

After a long night of fighting, by midmorning the next day, it was over. As the sun rose, Ayden left the flower shop, returned to the print shop, and retrieved Owen's pickup. He studied Laney's map and found what he thought might be the construction company where she'd told him to meet them. He prayed they had made it there. It was a long way for his sister to walk with her injury. They could have stopped somewhere. Ayden brushed away the fear he'd never find them as he climbed into the truck and backed out of the garage.

As he drove through town, he spotted two men—civilians by their clothing—walking near the railroad tracks. One was supporting the other's weight as if he were severely injured. As they recognized the sound of the truck's engine, both men turned to face it. They were badly bloodied and battered. Ayden studied their features, trying to determine whether they were friend or foe—

American or enemy invaders. American, he determined—likely caught up in the fight just like him. Ayden's heart went out to them.

"Please!" the bigger of the men pleaded. "Please, help us."

Ayden stopped the truck and ran over to them. "Are you two soldiers?" he asked, assisting them into the cab of the truck.

"Not officially," the big man said. "We fought like hell, though, as you can tell." He nodded toward his friend. "He needs a doctor. We have one at my place. It's not that far, only about twenty-five miles. We can pay you—in food or…" He hesitated a moment. "Or gold."

Gold?

Ayden wasn't sure it had any value under the circumstances. Where would you spend it? Food, on the other hand, was needed. Ayden nodded. "Food sounds good, but I have to stop up ahead. I'm looking for someone. I'm supposed to meet them at a construction company by the railroad tracks west of town."

"I know the place. Turn right just ahead."

The big man's companion slumped in the seat, unconscious, as they drove west. The moment Ayden pulled into the parking lot, Laney stepped out of the building.

The big man gasped and then burst into tears. "Laney?" He threw open his door before they came to a complete stop. "My baby! My baby girl!"

"Laney's your daughter?" Ayden asked, stunned.

"Yes," he said, leaping from the vehicle.

"Daddy!" Laney shouted, running toward him.

Ayden watched the reunion with profound joy. By some miracle, he'd found Laney's father.

The man hugged Laney tightly with his uninjured arm, tears streaming down his face.

Ayden stepped from the pickup and turned to see Clara emerging from the building, limping toward him. Her face lit up when she saw Ayden. "Clara!" Ayden called out, rushing to her and enveloping her in a tight embrace. "I was so worried about you."

"I'm okay," Clara whispered, her voice thick with emotion. "Thanks to Laney." She nodded toward the trike. "She got us here in one piece and, unlike you, didn't manage to hit every single pothole." Ayden chuckled and squeezed her tighter.

She released him and gestured to the truck. "Who's that?"

"Oh, crap. We have to go," Ayden said. "He needs a doctor, like now!"

Ayden helped Clara into the back of the pickup with Laney and her father, then returned to the front.

The man in the seat next to him moaned and then muttered a name. "Serenity?"

"What's that?" Ayden asked him.

The man groaned as Ayden turned out of the parking lot. "Just hold on. We're going to get you to a doctor."

Ayden took Peters Creek Road, too leery to take the turnpike, unwilling to risk running into more PLA convoys. The road wound through the serene Pennsylvania countryside, offering a brief respite from the constant tension. Approaching Finleyville, the truck sputtered and came to a stop. Ayden glanced at the fuel gauge, cursing under his breath.

Laney climbed out of the bed of the truck and appeared at his driver's window. "What's wrong? Why'd you stop?"

"We're out of gas."

Laney sighed. "We'll have to go on foot to find some."

"What's going on, Laney?" her dad asked.

"The truck's out of fuel. We're going to have to go into town and find more. We'll be as quick as we can," she said to her father.

Ayden and Laney set out for town, the road stretching out before them. Every rustle and distant noise made Ayden jumpy. He found a fuel can in the back of a newer model truck that had been abandoned in the roadway into town. Once they reached the houses, he saw a garden hose spread out across one of the lawns.

With his knife, Ayden cut the length he needed, and several doors down, in the driveway of a small house, he managed to siphon gas from an older model car. With the filled fuel can in hand, they began the trek back toward the truck.

As they walked along the railroad tracks, Ayden and Laney talked about how lucky they all were to escape the fighting in Clairton and how crazy it was that he had run across her father.

"Did he say what they were doing there in the first place?" Ayden asked.

"Looking for supplies to fortify the injured man's home and beef up our compound's defenses after learning about the invasion."

"They weren't prepared for the battle they encountered, I bet," Ayden said.

"They weren't aware the PLA were in the area. Long-range communications have been down the last few days," Laney said.

"Like they were at Owen's? Are they here as well, hunting down ham operators?"

Laney's eyes widened. "Possibly. Or they could be jamming radio waves to prevent our army from communicating with one another."

"It was good to see our military engaged with them," Ayden said.

"They blew up the bridge over the Monongahela with those commies on it."

Ayden smiled. "That's what that explosion was?"

"Dad said they stopped their advance. We control the only bridges across now. Dad says it should slow the PLA down long enough for the US military to get into place to form a front line and defend it."

Ayden knew nothing about military tactics, but it was comforting to know that the military was successful in slowing their advance. Even so, Ayden was strongly considering depositing Laney, her father, and the injured man at their compound, and then racing west as fast as possible with Clara in hopes of staying ahead of the fighting. "Your dad looks to be in pretty rough shape," Ayden began. "But if possible, I'd load up everything you can and get away from here, Laney. It's only a matter of time before that fighting reaches your doorstep."

Laney was quiet for a moment. "I agree, but that will be up to my parents. Honestly, I don't know if we can outrun them. We may be better off fighting them on our own turf."

"I understand, but Clara and I are going to push on and try to make it to Wyoming."

"Won't you at least stay the night and get resupplied? I'm sure my parents will want to help you out with food and stuff."

It was tempting, but Ayden wasn't sure how much time they had before the fighting began pushing west across the Monongahela River. He was weighing the risk of such a delay as they rounded the bend in the tracks when he spotted a young woman in the distance. She was walking unsteadily, her steps faltering. He was just about to call out to her when she tumbled down the embankment into the tall grass.

Ayden scanned the tree line and the houses ahead for signs that someone was with her but saw no one. "Laney, wait here," he said, dropping the fuel can and running toward the woman.

As Ayden took off toward her, Laney called out a warning, "Be careful! It could be a trick. She might be armed, or there could be others waiting to ambush us like last time."

Nodding, Ayden pulled his pistol and cautiously scanned the surrounding buildings and tree line again. Seeing no signs of threat, he moved toward the young woman with deliberate caution, keeping alert for any sign of an ambush. Approaching slowly, Ayden reached out and touched her.

"Are you okay?" It was a stupid question. Of course she wasn't all right. "Are you hurt?" was what he'd meant to say. He was so exhausted and dehydrated that he wasn't thinking clearly.

The young woman, clearly disoriented, swung out weakly in

defense. Ayden's firm grip steadied her as he calmly reassured her, "Whoa! We're here to help!"

For a moment, Ayden thought she might have confused him for someone else—someone who had hurt her.

Her dazed eyes tried to focus on him.

That was when he realized she wasn't a woman—just a girl. A little younger than Laney. Perhaps only fifteen or sixteen. She had long, dark blond hair tied back in a ponytail. The knees of her dark-colored jeans were ripped. He could see fresh blood where she'd scraped them as she fell. Ayden eased back the flap of her jacket.

She held up a bloody hand as if to ward off a blow.

"It's okay. We're here to help!"

Ayden scanned the woods adjacent to the railroad tracks. Had the girl been running away from someone? Was that how she'd tripped? Her face was covered in bruises and cuts in various stages of healing, much like his and Clara's. She'd definitely fought for her life at some point. Her appearance reinforced his theory that she could have escaped somewhere after being held against her will. "Are you injured?" he asked. "Did someone hurt you?"

Laney came up behind him. "She's bleeding!" Laney dropped to her knees beside her.

"Were you shot?" Ayden asked, his voice laced with urgency.

The girl simply nodded, her eyes closing.

Quickly but gently, Laney lifted the young woman's shirt to assess the wound. "She needs a doctor, or she's not going to make it," she said. "Let's get her to the truck. My dad will know what to do to help her!"

"We're going to move you off the tracks to our truck," Ayden began to explain as he bent over her.

She moaned and tried to speak, but Ayden couldn't make out her words.

"We're going to take you somewhere to get your wounds treated. I'm going to lift you now. It might hurt."

She said nothing.

As he lifted her from the ground, her head lolled back. Her eyes opened wide for a moment and then closed. She was totally helpless and vulnerable out there alone. He cast another glance at the houses up ahead. She could live in one of them. She could have a family—a mom and dad, maybe some siblings waiting for her there. He hesitated, standing there with the wounded girl in his arms, conflicted about what to do. Ayden glanced back at Laney. He had a responsibility to them. Knocking on doors was risky—he'd learned that the hard way. He glanced down at her. "Do you live around here?" he asked.

She said nothing.

He jostled her awake. "Hey!"

Her eyes fluttered open, but only for a moment.

"Hey! Do you live around here? Do you have family nearby?"

He couldn't imagine why a young girl her age would be out wandering around alone. Ayden imagined all sorts of reasons. Her parents could have been killed, and she was out trying to find food and supplies for her siblings. Or she could have been kidnapped and somehow escaped and was making her way home. That could explain her injuries. There were so many possibilities, and only she had the answers. Unfortunately, she was unable to give them to him. His only option was to take Laney's suggestion. Take her with them to Laney's compound.

Ayden picked her up and cradled her in his arms, careful not to jostle her too much.

Laney retrieved the fuel can, and they carefully carried the girl back down the tracks to their hidden vehicle. Ayden felt her weight with every step. Although she probably weighed only a little over one hundred and ten pounds, his energy was so low that it felt greater. She moaned as Ayden shifted her in his arms.

Laney walked alongside them, holding the fuel can. "Just hang in there. We'll be there in a few minutes. It's not that far."

Ayden carried the girl back to the truck, where Clara and the two injured men waited.

"We found someone who needs help," Ayden explained to Laney's father as they approached the truck.

"Get her in the back," he said, moving to make room. "We'll take her with us."

As Ayden placed her into the bed of the pickup, Laney's father gasped.

"Serenity?"

"You know her, Dad?" Laney asked, placing the fuel can down beside the back tire.

"She's his daughter!" He gestured to the unconscious man inside the cab of the truck.

Laney's mouth dropped open. "What? How is that possible?"

"Someone upstairs must be smiling down on us—that's what your grandma would say anyway."

With Serenity in the back, Ayden poured the gas into the truck's tank while Laney climbed into the bed of the truck, retrieved a medical kit from her pack, and then began to dress the girl's wound.

Ayden climbed into the cab of the pickup and turned to the young girl's father as he cranked the engine. "We found your little girl. She's in the bed of the truck. We're going to get medical help for you both. You're all going to be fine."

The man stirred and muttered something unintelligible.

Ayden called out the driver's window. "Hold on, back there. It could get a little rough, but we need to get out of here before someone hears us."

He sped away, returning to the highway, heading west along the route Laney had said would lead to her father's compound in Somerset Township, Pennsylvania. Ayden carefully maneuvered the truck through the winding roads. The young woman they had found was resting in the back, Laney's father keeping an eye on her condition.

As they rounded a curve, they encountered another roadblock. Ayden stopped the truck. Laney called out to someone behind the barricade and then ran over to it. A few moments later, one of the vehicles blocking the lanes rolled out of the way, and Laney returned to the pickup.

"It's one of ours. Drive on through. We're almost there," she said.

They drove on, escorted by two older-model SUVs. Headlights illuminated the road ahead. Ayden followed as they finally turned down a gravel driveway, the headlights briefly illuminating a sign that read, "New Eden." He stopped the truck in front of a thick steel gate, where a figure emerged from the shadows, holding a flashlight. The gate opened, and they drove through, the truck rumbling to a stop in front of a large farmhouse. Laney's mother rushed out and enveloped her in hugs and tears.

Her mother turned toward the truck. "Tyson! Oh my. How bad are you hurt?"

"I'll live. Keith and Serenity are in pretty bad shape, though."

"My sister needs medical attention as well," Ayden said.

A man in pajamas carrying a medical satchel rushed toward the truck. "Get them down to the clinic," he shouted before climbing into a utility vehicle.

"Climb out. We'll take it from here," the guard from the gate said.

Ayden opened the truck's door and stepped out. "I'll come see you in a moment," he said, squeezing Clara's hand. He joined Laney and her mother by the front porch and watched as the pick-up's headlights disappeared around a curve in the gravel lane.

Laney's mother climbed into a second four-seat utility vehicle. "You coming?" she asked him, stopping beside Ayden.

Ayden felt the weight of their journey suddenly lift off his shoulders as he climbed into the seat behind Laney. He'd done it. He'd delivered Laney back to her family.

"Doc will patch them up," her mother said.

Laney turned and glanced over her shoulder, her eyes shining with gratitude. "We made it. We're safe here."

Ayden smiled, nodding. It felt comforting to see how well-fortified the compound was, but he wasn't sure it would be enough after what he'd witnessed the night before.

As they settled into the safety of the compound, Ayden knew their journey wasn't over, but for now, they had found a refuge. Tomorrow, he'd find out what they knew about troop movements in the area and decide how quickly he and Clara needed to hit the road again. Witnessing two miracle reunions, Ayden was feeling hopeful that, somehow, someway, there was one waiting for him and Mia.

Thank you for reading ***Carnage***, the third installment of the gripping *Conquer the Dark* series. The journey of Ayden, Clara, and Mia continues in ***Desolation***, book four of the series, slated for release in August 2024. Pre-order your copy today!

As you eagerly anticipate the next chapter in their saga, immerse yourself in the captivating world of Endure the Dark, the inaugural novel of the companion series ***Reign of Darkness***. This foundational book lays the groundwork for the epic adventures to come, introducing you to characters whose destinies have intertwined with Ayden and Clara in unforeseen ways.

Keep scrolling to read sample chapters of Endure the Dark below, or order your copy today to embark on the thrilling tale of Serenity, Mueller, and others before they come to meet Ayden, Clara, and Laney.

Don't forget to sign up for my spam-free newsletter to receive a FREE ebook copy of Last Light: A Reign of Darkness Novella **and be the first to know of my new releases, giveaways, and special offers.**

If you enjoyed *Carnage*, I'd love to hear from you. Please

consider leaving a review on Amazon. Doing so helps me find new readers who might enjoy the book.

Carnage has gone through several layers of editing. If you found a typographical, grammatical, or other error that impacted your enjoyment of the book, I offer my apologies and ask that you let me know so I can fix it for future readers. To do so, CLICK HERE or email me at contact@tlpayne.com. In appreciation, I would like to offer you a free electronic copy of my next new release.

Sample of Endure the Dark

REIGN OF DARKNESS SERIES BOOK ONE

CHAPTER ONE
SERENITY JONES

Main Street
Dentonville, Pennsylvania
One Week before Event

From the corner of her eye, Serenity Jones noticed two male silhouettes advancing parallel to her on the other side of Main Street. An icy shiver ran down her spine as she clenched the straps of her backpack and picked up her pace. Instead of risking a direct glance at the men, she flicked her eyes toward the reflective surface of a storefront window she was passing. It gave her the opportunity to scrutinize the figures trailing her, under the pretense of casual window shopping.

As soon as she saw their faces, she recognized her pursuers. It was them. It was the two men from the corner where she'd spent the afternoon panhandling. They'd argued with her over the spot she'd claimed as her own for the last two years, ever since she had first come to live on the streets at the age of fourteen.

A knot of dread twisted in her stomach. Had they followed her? They were like predators on the prowl, mirroring her steps across the street.

One of them glanced in her direction before pointing toward an alleyway on her side of the street. Then, like they were in sync, they both walked toward her, their intent apparent in their intimidating strides. Were they plotting to corner her in that deserted alley?

As soon as the men vanished around the building's corner, Serenity seized her chance. She darted across the street and slipped into the comforting refuge of Harrington's Bistro. Shrugging off her backpack, she let it thud onto a booth seat by the window and slid in after it. In a swift motion, she picked up a menu from the table rack and used it as a veil to blend into the restaurant's ambiance while keeping her eyes peeled on the street outside.

Instinctively, she reached into her pocket, expecting to feel the ironwood handle of her pocketknife, and then remembered it was still tucked securely beneath her sleeping pad back at her tent. An uncomfortable vulnerability gnawed at her as she registered its absence. She had left the knife behind that morning, knowing that carrying weapons was strictly forbidden at the youth shelter she frequented for an occasional, much-needed shower and to get clean clothes.

The knife had been a gift from her father, a relic from a time when safety wasn't a daily struggle. It had been her constant companion since she'd been living on the streets, and now, more than ever, she felt vulnerable and exposed without it.

Serenity chanced a peek over the top of the menu, her gaze trained on the alley from where she expected the pair to emerge. And emerge they did. The taller figure cast wary glances into the store windows as if hunting for her, while the shorter one ripped open the door of the neighboring hair salon.

Every nerve in Serenity's body was on high alert. As usual, she was already strategizing and plotting her next two moves to maneuver out of this dangerous predicament. They were looking for her. That was obvious. It was a deadly game of hide and seek, and they'd aimed to make her their prey—their mistake!

"Are you going to order something?" The question hurled at her sliced through the tense silence with a sharp-edged hostility. The voice belonged to the waitress, a woman who had long since abandoned any pretense of hospitality. Her deep-set eyes, with deep crow's-feet webbing from the corners, were filled with fatigue and frustration. She wore her blonde hair pulled back into a taut ponytail, the severe style exacerbating her perpetual scowl. Her impatience and disinterest seemed as ingrained as the coffee stains on her apron.

Harrington's bistro had a tired appearance, just like the people in it. Tucked away in a quieter corner of the city, its once-polished mahogany furniture now looked muted and scratched. Faded tapestries lined the walls, their lack of color testifying to many a day spent under the harsh sunlight. There was some great jazz playing on a crappy stereo in the restaurant, but you could barely hear it over the sounds of people talking. It was a haven for the likes of Serenity—a little run-down, somewhat invisible, but still enduring.

Serenity gave the waitress a side-on look, trying to play it cool. "Just a water, please."

"You gotta order food or pay for a drink," she said firmly.

The delicious aroma wafting from the kitchen taunted Serenity's empty stomach. She cast a longing glance at the menu and the mouth-watering images of juicy hamburgers, cheesy pizzas—even the golden-brown grilled cheese sandwich stirred a visceral hunger. If only she could…

"Water is a drink."

"We charge for it," the waitress fired back, scowling.

Serenity shrugged. She rose from the booth, the worn vinyl squeaking in protest, and passed the menu back. "Fine." Her voice dropped into a conspiratorial whisper. "You got a back door here?"

The waitress's sharp eyes followed her gaze across the bustling street. Her tone softened. "Those guys giving you trouble?"

Serenity offered a slight nod in response without taking her eyes off the men, who seemed increasingly agitated.

"Through the kitchen." The waitress gestured with a nod toward the back of the bistro. "There's a door that leads straight to the alley."

Serenity's eyes flickered with gratitude. "Appreciate it," she replied, her voice barely more than a whisper.

Serenity's sneakers scraped against the checkerboard floor as she navigated through the bistro toward the kitchen, a ripple of attention following in her wake. The hum of chitchat among white-collar workers on their lunch break stuttered, their gazes slicing through the air to land on her. City shoppers with their nice clothes and polished shoes gave her the once over and then wrinkled their noses as if they'd caught a whiff of something unpleasant. Those looks—a mix of disdain and poorly concealed pity—felt like cold daggers scraping against the thin walls of her pride. She could almost hear the whispers behind manicured hands, their pointed fingers masked behind expensive designer bags. Yet Serenity bore it all with a hardened exterior, an armor forged on the unforgiving streets. No matter what they thought, they were no better than her. Her eyes, lit by the fire of gritty resolve, remained locked ahead. Such glances were the price for staying alive and being free. And no one could rob her of that freedom.

The kitchen was a cacophony of smells and sounds. The sizzle and spit of meat on hot grills, the rhythmic chop-chop of sharp knives against wooden boards, and the symphony of clanging pots and pans all merged into a chaotic harmony. The air was heavy with the aroma of grilled meat, simmering sauces, and the pungent scent of spices, creating a sensory tapestry that was both overwhelming and oddly comforting.

The cook, a burly man with a generous belly spilling over his apron and sweat glistening on his brow, halted mid-stir as he noticed her. His bushy eyebrows shot up in surprise, a wooden spoon dripping with thick red sauce suspended in midair. His graying hair and weary, weathered face spoke of a hectic life lived in the unforgiving crucible of kitchen heat.

Serenity caught the faint traces of worry etched into the lines of his face as if he were a man hanging onto the fringes of stability, treading the thin line between a warm bed and the unrelenting hardness of the sidewalk. It was a reality she knew only too well; the city was littered with stories of lives that had derailed, of people who were only one missed paycheck away from where she was now.

She offered him a curt nod, an unspoken acknowledgment of the shared understanding that existed between them. Their lives might have been worlds apart, but in the grand scheme of things, they were both just survivors, fighting to make it another day in the ruthless jungle of urban life.

Once outside, the back alley greeted her in stark contrast to the frenzy of the kitchen. The smell of stale garbage and cigarettes hung heavy in the air, an unsavory mix that was a far cry from the rich and tempting aromas she'd just left behind. A figure appeared within the darkness, the glowing end of a cigarette briefly showing his gaunt face. She locked eyes with the kitchen worker as he threw away his cigarette, the embers fizzling out on the wet ground.

Turning from her, he pulled a bulging garbage bag from the bin, the metallic scrape echoing through the alley. Serenity tightened the straps of her backpack and then twisted her long, blonde hair into a ponytail and secured it with a hair tie. As he tossed the bag into the dumpster, Serenity bolted. Her sneakers pounded against the grimy concrete as she raced north, past the backs of the buildings of Main Street in a blur. Her heart hammered in her chest, adrenaline fueling her every stride. She didn't stop until she'd reached the end of the row, where the narrow alley spat her out onto Gallagher Street.

Serenity paused, gasping for breath as she took in her surroundings, her eyes darting for any sign of the men who'd pursued her. She was safe for the moment in the bustling streets of Dentonville, Pennsylvania. The city continued to live and breathe around her, oblivious and uncaring.

With the gritty brick facade of Gallagher Title and Escrow firm at her back, she cautiously risked a look around its corner. She breathed a sigh of relief when she saw the coast was clear. She launched herself forward and darted across Gallagher Street, dodging through sparse traffic. Confident she'd shaken her pursuers, Serenity turned south, toward the more run-down part of town, the derelict Gallagher Bank, and the patch of neglected ground nearby that she called home.

At the intersection of Elgin Avenue and Freeport Street, the sounds of city life hummed along with the occasional horn honking or sirens in the distance. Here, Serenity allowed her pace to ease to a slow walk. The knot of tension that had been winding tighter and tighter within her began to uncoil.

Passing by the bakery, the smell of freshly baked bread caused her stomach to growl. She stopped for a moment to glance into the shop's window. The pastries looked like little slices of heaven. She shoved her hand inside her pocket. She'd made two dollars and twenty-five cents before those a-holes ran her off from her most lucrative panhandling spot.

Suddenly, the door to the neighboring flower shop swung open to reveal the face of a little boy. "Finn! Wait for Mommy," a woman's voice admonished from inside.

Finn grinned at Serenity, taking a step onto the sidewalk, followed by a black and tan beagle dog. "Mom says the brioche here's top-notch, but I swear by Mrs. Hughes's pastéis de nata. They've got this wild story—monks, leftover egg yolks, and an old sugar refinery turning it into a bakery hit in the 1800s."

Serenity's mouth dropped open. She couldn't believe such a

young kid could even pronounce pastéis de nata, let alone know who invented them. “How old are you, kid?” Serenity asked.

“I’m six years old. I will be seven on October 13. Grandma Jane is taking me on a tour of the Center for Nanotechnology for my birthday.”

The boy’s dog made a circle around Serenity, sniffing her jeans and sneakers. He stopped in front of her and nudged his nose under her hand. She petted the dog’s head and said, “That sounds interesting.”

Finn nodded.

“So you like science?”

“I’m an inventor, so of course I’m interested in science and technology. I also enjoy music—mostly blues and some classic rock.”

Serenity chuckled at the range of his musical interest.

The kid took two steps forward and thrust out his hand. “I’m Finn, and this is my dog, Gunner.”

Serenity glanced around, expecting the kid’s parents to run up and pull him away from her. Yet Finn just stood there with his hand extended, clearly waiting for her to take it. Serenity shook his hand and took a giant step back—just in case. She didn’t want to be accused of trying to snatch him or something. “I’m Serenity.”

“Are you homeless?” Finn asked in that frank, nonjudgmental way young kids often did.

“Yes.”

“Where do you sleep?”

“In a tent, behind a factory.”

His expression changed from a curious look to one of sadness. The dog moved his head from side to side, staring at the boy, and then he rose and walked back to him.

“My parents got divorced. My mom and I got to keep the house.” The kid’s expression brightened. “My mom owns the flower shop. I come here after school.”

Serenity glanced next door and smiled. “Must be a nice place to do your homework—surrounded by all the pretty flowers.”

“I don’t have homework. I get all my assignments completed at school. I do study here at the shop, though—and read. I love books.

“I’m currently in the second grade, but I’ll advance to the fourth grade in the fall. I read at a fifth-grade level, but Grandma Jane helps me pick out middle-grade books every Saturday.”

A memory fluttered through Serenity’s mind. Her grandmother had bought her a new book every week—until her heart attack. The books were always of a different genre. Gram had wanted to expose Serenity to a wide range of books so she’d know what she enjoyed reading most.

Serenity heard a bell jingle. Gunner bolted inside through the open door as a woman in her early thirties stepped out. “Finn! What have I told you about talking to strangers?”

“She’s not a stranger, Mom. This is Serenity. She lives in a tent.”

“I’m sorry. He likes people.” Finn’s mom grabbed his hand and pulled him back toward the flower shop.

Finn waved goodbye before the door closed behind them. Serenity crossed the street, glanced back at the flower shop one last time, and then turned the corner and entered the alley.

She was safe, for now, and that was all that mattered. As she walked toward her tent, the muted sounds of Dentonville served as a somber soundtrack to the end of her day. The struggles of survival were a constant companion. They were nothing new. She’d been fighting the battle all her life. Today, like many days before, she had won.

Just as she was allowing her thoughts to drift toward the comfort of her tent and the remaining chapters of her worn, secondhand novel, a figure sprang into her path, jolting her back into reality.

~

TWO
Keith Jones

State Correctional Institution (SCI) Green
Waynesburg, Pennsylvania
One Week before Event

A prison cell had become Keith Jones's world. The metal bars, the dull colors, and the constant chatter of other inmates, along with the cold, sterile hallways, served as a daily reminder of his bad choices. The corridor's dim, flickering fluorescent light made Keith's surroundings feel even more oppressive. He had a bad feeling in the pit of his stomach as he walked toward the showers. The cell block echoed with whispers and the shuffling of feet, but one set of footsteps sounded louder, getting closer.

Keith glanced back over his shoulder as he turned into the shower room but saw no one following him. The air in the prison shower room was thick with humidity due to constant use and inadequate ventilation; its grimy white tiles, spotted with mold, and the perpetual stench of decay and cheap disinfectant never failed to turn his stomach.

Steeling himself, Keith stepped onto the wet floor. His footfalls made a muted splash, the sound echoing slightly off the tiled walls. Above him, fluorescent lights buzzed and flickered. Rows of shower heads lined the walls, some dripping water continuously. The sound of the door creaking open again made him tense. Early that day, he'd received a tip from a fellow inmate that an attack on him was imminent. He had enemies inside the prison walls and no way to avoid trouble. Informing the guards would do nothing. Inmates handled issues like that themselves.

Another set of footsteps began to echo through the room, each step deliberate and measured. The sound grew ever louder, reverberating ominously in the closed space. Keith kept his face neutral but heightened his senses, listening intently. Without turning, he positioned himself with his back against the wall to ensure that whoever approached wouldn't catch him off guard. His pulse quickened in anticipation and uncertainty, forming a knot in his stomach.

Juan Rodriguez stepped into view and Keith stiffened. Rodriguez was a known associate to Rafe, Keith's partner in the heist that had landed him behind bars.

"Jones," Rodriguez growled, holding up a sharpened toothbrush honed to a lethal point. "Rafe wants to know where the cash is. He's tired of waiting for his money. Think this might jog your memory?"

Keith's eyes darted to the shank, then back up to Rodriguez. "I don't have it," he said in a steady voice despite the surge of adrenaline. "As I've told you all along—the cops took it."

Rodriguez scowled. "Don't play games with me! The police report says they never recovered the money."

"They did. As they led me away from my house, I saw Officer Brown pick up the duffle and carry it to his patrol car."

"Liar! I'm going to kill you if you don't tell me where you stashed the money!"

Rodriguez lunged at him. The shank made a swift arc through the mist, but Keith's instincts and agility got him out of its way. Barely. Rodriguez's speed caught him off guard, forcing Keith to react with a powerful right hook to the man's cheekbone. The impact reverberated, making Rodriguez's head snap back, his dark eyes momentarily clouded with surprise.

But Keith wasn't about to rest on a single punch. He had to incapacitate his opponent swiftly, so he raised his leg, aiming to deliver a powerful blow to Rodriguez's head. But somehow, Rodriguez jerked to the side and latched on to Keith's foot, causing him to lose balance and crash onto the wet tiles.

Rodriguez towered over him, silhouetted in the shower's

diffused light, ready to plunge the shank into his torso. Summoning all his strength, Keith delivered a swift kick to Rodriguez's knee, bringing him down momentarily. Then Keith sprang up and readied himself to defend or strike as the situation demanded. Now, it was Keith who was standing over his attacker. However, his moment of triumph was cut short by the sound of footfalls from the corridor. It could be prison guards or more inmates ready to join the fight.

In that split second of distraction, Rodriguez aimed the shank straight for Keith's heart. With a burst of adrenaline, Keith caught Rodriguez's wrist, redirected the weapon, and plunged it into Rodriguez's own chest with one swift, brutal motion.

As soon as he took a moment to breathe, a blow landed on Keith's back, knocking him down. Rodriguez's crew had joined the fight. Outnumbered and on slippery ground, Keith fought with the ferocity of a cornered beast and sent one of the attackers reeling with a punch to the throat. But the numbers game was catching up. Just as Keith was on the verge of being overwhelmed, a blaring alarm sounded, and the bright lights of the corridor were joined by the rapid footfalls of approaching guards. The inmates paused, but not for long. The guards might be coming, but Rodriguez wasn't done. From the ground, he shouted for his crew to finish what he'd started. "Get him!"

Keith was nearly at his limit, panting heavily. He managed to land a few more punches in a valiant effort to keep them at bay, while in his peripheral, he watched Rodriguez pulling the shank from his chest with a grimace of pain. Keith tried to shift out of reach, but Rodriguez managed to slice it into Keith's side. Pain seared through Keith, momentarily blinding him.

Then, like the cavalry in a war movie, guards burst into the room with their batons swinging. They quickly subdued the men, but to Keith's shock, he was the one yanked up and cuffed. "Thought you could start a brawl and get away with it, Jones?" one guard sneered, his face inches from Keith's.

Rodriguez, pale and gasping, lay in a puddle of water and blood, his fate uncertain. Keith knew if he didn't make it, he'd be facing another murder charge.

Despite his injuries, Keith was given a cursory check in the infirmary before being thrown into the cold, stark isolation of solitary confinement. And then he was alone, with just the sound of his heavy breathing and the terrifying thought of how much power Rafe had in this jail. Weighed down by guilt and regret, Keith lay in his bunk thinking about his daughter. He had thought about the day that changed their lives countless times, replaying every detail, every choice, and every mistake.

Normally, he only did heists with his own crew, which consisted of long-time friends, including his best friend, Pete, whom Serenity called uncle. However, at the last moment, the driver in Rafe's crew got popped by law enforcement. They should have shut down the job right then. The risk was too great—the guy knew too much—he could talk, and they'd all go to jail. That was Keith's second mistake. The first was agreeing to do a heist with a crew he didn't know all that well and with Rafe Thomas in charge.

That fateful morning had started routinely enough. As Keith had dropped Serenity off at school, her deep blue eyes filled with concern. "Dad, I have a bad feeling about this. Don't do it."

He'd given her a reassuring smile, trying to brush off the unease in his gut. "Everything's going to be fine, baby. Just another job." But deep down, he knew it was a lie. The stakes were higher, the crew was different, and the risk was immeasurable. Keith had always been open with Serenity about the life he led, not in a way that glorified it but in a manner that prepared her for the world he inhabited. She'd grown up knowing his crew, her "uncles" who doted on her while imparting vital survival skills. With his knack for getting into places unnoticed, Carlos taught her the delicate art of picking locks, turning the tumbler just so, feeling the mechanism give.

Pete, ever the mentor, introduced her to the sport of archery.

Keith remembered watching them in the backyard, Pete patiently correcting her stance, guiding her hand to release the string just right. Under his guidance, Serenity had not just learned but excelled. She even joined the school's archery team, and soon, her room was adorned with medals and certificates.

Serenity's words had struck a chord in Keith. She had good instincts. Her unease made Keith feel uneasy, too, since he was having doubts about the job. Pulling away from the school, Keith's thoughts were in turmoil. He dialed Pete, needing the reassurance of his long-time friend.

"Hey, it's me," he began, trying to sound casual, but the strain was evident in his voice. "Look, something came up. Rafe's driver can't make it—he got arrested for outstanding speeding tickets last night. I need you in on this, Pete. I trust you. I need someone I can rely on."

There was a brief pause on the other end. "All right," Pete replied, his voice steady. "But if Rafe's driver got popped, are you sure you want to go through with this? He could be spilling his guts to the cops as we speak."

Keith sighed. "I'm in too deep, Pete. I owe Scarface, and time's running out. But with you there, we can get in and get back out before the cops have time to even talk to the guy."

So the two friends made a plan to meet, not only sealing their fate for the day but setting in motion a series of events that would change their lives forever.

Pete was waiting when Keith got to the meeting point. "Are you sure about this, D?" Pete asked, glancing around nervously. Keith took a deep breath, reminded of his spiraling debts to Scarface. There was no choice, not really. Not when he had to protect Serenity and get out of the ruthless grip of the bookie.

"Let's just get this done," Keith said, trying to hide the dread creeping into his voice.

The plan had been simple on paper: in and out. The guy doing the money laundering for the cartel ran a lax operation. He never thought someone in Dentonville would have the balls to go after a Mexican cartel's money. He had one guard at the door, and the lock on the room where they stored the money waiting to be deposited into a bank account was easy to pick—it was too easy. From the moment they entered the laundromat, Keith felt a nagging sensation that they had underestimated this job. The unease grew ever stronger as they began to move the money.

When they made their way to the exit leading to the alley behind the laundromat and Pete's waiting car, the shrill sound of sirens cut through the morning air. Keith's heart sank. Red and blue lights flashed outside, casting a harsh light onto the unfolding scene. The getaway car was blocked in. Pete was trapped between them. Before Keith could process the situation, Rafe, eyes wild, began shooting.

Unarmed and caught off guard, Pete jumped out of the car to run, but the cops fired, and Pete took a bullet to the chest. Time seemed to slow down. Keith watched in horror as his best friend, his brother in every way but blood, crumbled to the ground. There was no time to mourn; his survival instincts kicked in. Keith and Rafe fled the scene, leaving behind chaos and betrayal.

In the days and months that followed, Keith was arrested, tried, and sentenced to life in prison—with no chance of parole. Serenity was taken away and placed in foster care. The weight of his choices crushed him. His parents moved back from Florida to fight for custody of their granddaughter. They did their best to give Serenity a semblance of normalcy. They bought a home close to the prison and frequently brought her to visit him there. Keith clung to those visits, which were a lifeline in the cold, harsh world of prison.

Keith was haunted by a particularly painful memory that played out with heartbreaking clarity against the backdrop of his mind. He remembered the prison guard approaching, a sealed letter held gingerly in his hand and a somber look painting his features. The weight of the envelope, unassuming as it was, seemed to press down heavily in Keith's trembling hands. Upon breaking the seal, the words blurred as his heart raced. His father, the anchor of his childhood, who had steadied his hand during his first bike ride and taught him how to navigate life's tumultuous seas, had been brutally taken from him. Through clandestine conversations and a few discreet police visits, Keith pieced together the horrifying puzzle.

Rafe and his crew, propelled by their insatiable greed and the misplaced conviction that Keith's father had knowledge of the stolen money's whereabouts, had launched an attack on his residence, killing his father before tossing the house. Guilt ate away at Keith. Rafe hadn't pulled the trigger, but Keith knew he was the one ultimately responsible for what had happened to his dad and his daughter, Serenity. Keith believed the stress of caring for Serenity and having a son in prison had ultimately led to his mother's heart attack. So, in reality, Rafe had killed both his parents.

The weight of his choices pressed down even harder. How had his life led to this?

In the late hours of the night, Keith had spoken to Leo, his cellmate, who was an older man with gray streaks in his hair and a calm disposition. Leo had become a father figure to Keith during their time together, and he often shared wisdom from his own tumultuous past. Leo had spent over half his life behind bars and left behind a family, too. He knew the weight of guilt that was crushing Keith.

"Leo," Keith whispered, voice choked with emotion, "My father is gone. And it's all because of me."

Leo looked up from his book and gestured for Keith to sit beside him. "Life is full of choices, son. Some we're proud of, and others we regret. But it's never too late to change."

Keith looked down, the weight of the world on his shoulders. "I want to, but I don't even know where to begin. I've hurt Serenity so much. She deserves better."

Leo placed a comforting hand on Keith's shoulder. "Begin with her. Reach out, even if it's just a letter. Let her know your regrets, your love, and your hope for her future."

Taking Leo's advice to heart, Keith began to pen letters to Serenity. He wrote of memories of the times he'd been there for her and the times he'd let her down. He shared his remorse and the lessons he had learned. Each word was filled with a father's love and hope for forgiveness. But as weeks turned into months, without any response from his daughter, he had thought she wanted nothing more to do with him. It was as if the ground had been ripped out from beneath him. His daughter, his precious Serenity, was facing the harshest realities, all alone. The thought was unbearable. Every night that followed was sleepless, filled with anguish and guilt.

It's never too late to change, Leo had said.

Keith was determined. He would find a way to turn his life around, to right the wrongs, and most importantly, to find Serenity and get her into the home she deserved—he could think of no better use for the ill-gotten money.

Thank you for reading this sample of *Endure the Dark*, book one in the *Reign of Darkness* series, a *Conquer the Dark* companion series. Click here to order your copy and continue reading Endure the Dark today!

This foundational book lays the groundwork for the epic adventures to come, introducing you to characters whose destinies will intertwine with Ayden and Clara in unforeseen ways.

Don't forget to sign up for my spam-free newsletter today and receive a FREE copy of Last Light: A Reign of Darkness Novella and be the first to know of new releases, giveaways, and special offers.

A REIGN OF DARKNESS NOVELLA
LAST LIGHT
T.L. PAYNE

Also by T L. Payne

Conquer the Dark Series

A Reign of Darkness Companion Series

Collapse

Ruin

Carnage

Desolation (Coming August 27, 2024!)

Resistance (Coming soon!)

Reign of Darkness Series

Endure the Dark

Escape the Destruction

Evade the Ruthless

Engage the Enemy (Pre-order Now!)

Last Light: A Reign of Darkness Novella

(Newsletter signup required)

Days of Want Series

Turbulent

Hunted

Turmoil

Uprising

Upheaval

Mayhem

Defiance

Sudden Chaos: A Post Apocalyptic EMP Survival Story

(Newsletter signup required)

Fall of Houston Series

A Days of Want Companion Series

No Way Out

No Other Choice

No Turning Back

No Surrender

No Man's Land

Gateway to Chaos Series

Seeking Safety

Seeking Refuge

Seeking Justice

Seeking Hope

Survive the Collapse Series

Brink of Darkness

Brink of Chaos

Brink of Panic

Brink of Collapse

Brink of Destruction: A FREE Novelette

Desperate Age Series

Panic in the Rockies

Getting Out of Dodge

Surviving Freedom

Trouble in Tulsa

Defending Camp

This We'll Defend: A Desperate Age Novella

(Newsletter signup required)

Acknowledgments

I'm so thankful for my editors, Joanna Niederer, Three Fates Editing, and Lawrence Editing.

Also, thanks to Kelly Shirer Borgford, Sally Buchholz, Kathleen Lee, Lisa Lockwood, Courtney Santos, Sheri Cawley, Kathy Gurgone, Sue Jackson, Leslie Ingram, Lindsay Smith, Megan Lepley for all your helpful insights, suggestions, and ideas.

About the Author

T. L. Payne is the author of several bestselling post-apocalyptic series. T. L. lives and writes in the Osage Hills region of Oklahoma and enjoys many outdoor activities, including kayaking, rock-hounding, metal detecting, and fishing in the many lakes and rivers of the area.

Don't forget to sign up for T. L.'s VIP Readers Club at www.tlpayne.com to be the first to know of new releases, giveaways, and special offers.

T. L. loves to hear from readers. You may email T. L. at contact@tlpayne.com or join the Facebook reader group at https://www.facebook.com/groups/tlpaynereadergroup

Join TL on Social Media

Facebook Author Page
Facebook Reader Group
Instagram
Follow me on Amazon.com
Website: https://tlpayne.com
Email: contact@tlpayne.com

Made in United States
Orlando, FL
08 November 2024

53605706R00188